A Wartime Christmas

Also by Kitty Danton

Evie's War
Evie's Allies
Evie's Victory

A Wartime Christmas

KITTY DANTON

ORION

First published in Great Britain in 2019
by Orion Books,
an imprint of The Orion Publishing Group Ltd
Carmelite House, 50 Victoria Embankment,
London EC4Y 0DZ

An Hachette UK company

1 3 5 7 9 10 8 6 4 2

A CIP catalogue record for this book
is available from the British Library.

ISBN (Hardback) 978 1 4091 7848 4
ISBN (eBook) 978 1 4091 7850 7

Typeset at The Spartan Press Ltd,
Lymington, Hants

Printed and bound in Great Britain by Clays Ltd,
Elcograf S.p.A.

www.orionbooks.co.uk

For my late mother June, on whom Evie is based,
who sadly never got to read Sukie's adventures.

Chapter One

It should have gone swimmingly.

It was for a good cause – raising money for government war bonds – and Sukie Scott and her colleagues at the Edwardes Hotel in Covent Garden had thought they had covered every eventuality.

They had. Except tedium and boredom. And a worrisome lack of people from outside the hotel attending the fundraiser.

'We still need everybody to do their duty. The war has gone on a long time; we all know that. But it is not over yet, and we have yet to win. Our servicemen and women need us at home to keep fighting too. Everyone is living in times that are frightening and sad, and we are missing our loved ones. All of us realise that every moment could be our last...'

Sukie sighed glumly; it seemed as if speaker after speaker that afternoon had said more or less the same thing, which, bearing in mind it was 1943, and they were in the fourth year of the war, was known by everyone already.

She inspected her nails, and then checked her stockings. It was no good; she was itching for the event to be over.

How dull. Of course everybody wanted to win the war, and their spare funds, if they had any, were donated already, as was time and goodwill, to the war effort.

Sukie looked around the dining room, which had been cleared of tables for the fundraiser, and saw others who looked like they were feeling similarly. From the minute a scratchy record of 'Rule Britannia' was played to kick things off, and the needle of the gramophone had got stuck, with the word 'waves' repeating at least six times, Sukie had realised it was going to be a very long fundraiser.

Her friend Pattie had tucked herself away in a window nook out of sight of the speakers, and she was now staring out of the window, clearly in a world of her own. The bellboy Michael was writing something in a notebook, and the concierge Stephen and maître d' Alan had their heads bent close together as they checked the racing form sheet in that morning's paper.

Sukie could hear Jane, one of the other receptionists at the hotel, checking somebody in to their room from out in the foyer, while Millicent, who made up the trio of receptionists along with Sukie, and who was now sitting at the other end of her row, looked to be writing a letter.

There was a soft snore. It was Chef, who had had an early start that day (as always), being in the kitchen first thing to get the day's bread under way. Mrs Bridge, the hotel's housekeeper, gently elbowed his arm and he sprang awake with a snort, only for his head to drop forward again almost instantaneously.

The room was at best only half-full, and the speakers had obviously noticed that too. In fact, it would have been much emptier but Sukie had felt so awful that hotel manager Mr Bright's best intentions had fallen so flat, that she had run around the six guest floors, and the two staff floors of the hotel, all of which sprawled into the once-posh houses on either side of the main building, determined to rustle up every stray member of staff that she could, telling them to take off their uniforms and look lively about it, as they were needed to swell the numbers downstairs while looking like people who wanted to be at a fundraiser. She had even risked a gentle bullying of some of the nicer guests she ran into, saying she'd be forever in their debt if they helped her out by coming in and sitting down, and if they could look interested, so much the better.

Pattie looked back across the room at Sukie, who was sitting

2

near the exit, and once she knew she had Sukie's attention, Pattie then mimed an extravagant yawn, her hand tapping her mouth, then lowered her hand, fluttering it wildly close to her lap and out of sight of the speakers, clearly referring to the 'waves' of the stuck record earlier.

Sukie forced her lips to remain unsmiling, which made her frown as really she wanted to laugh, and then she turned her head in what she hoped was an alert manner towards the row of speakers at the front of the room. If Pattie were sensible, she would take a leaf out of Sukie's book and, Sukie hoped, look at the speakers in a manner that mirrored Sukie's firm shoulders and alert, rapt face.

Pattie obviously understood the message, but ignored it on purpose. She reached across to borrow Michael's notebook and scribble something down. She tore the page out of the book and soon it was being passed along the row towards Sukie.

'How long do we have to stay for? This is like practising for being dead' was scrawled on the scrap of paper.

Mr Bright was sitting right beside Sukie, and she had to hurriedly crumple the note before he noticed what had been written. She knew he must feel bad enough already. The Edwardes Hotel was no longer *the* place to stay in Covent Garden – guests came erratically, and like all the other genteel-to-well-heeled hotels in London, income was down massively to what it had been prewar, as a lot of the incoming money had always been generated by running functions such as weddings or parties, all of which had dried up since the declaration of hostilities. Mr Bright had told Sukie that maybe if they put on regular fundraisers, he hoped it would drive business to the hotel. His glum face, as he said this, had told her in no uncertain terms that the Edwardes needed income, and quickly.

In theory, running a fundraiser wasn't a bad idea, as there was nearly always a knock-on effect of something benefiting the venue. But in terms of what a fundraiser should be, Sukie and Mr Bright clearly differed wildly in opinion.

This one was dull as ditchwater and tedious in the extreme,

with uninspired speakers and not much else to hold people's attention. Sukie thought she might have to send up some complimentary morning tea the next day to all the guests who had let themselves be persuaded by her to attend; it was the least she could do, after putting them through this.

Sukie looked towards Pattie, and mouthed, 'only an hour to go'. This wasn't the case, as she thought the final speaker was just about to wrap up, but Sukie was trying to tell Pattie off.

Pattie dropped her head forwards, as if she had been knocked unconscious. But she did it such a funny way that Sukie couldn't help smiling.

Sukie looked towards the row of speakers once more, but she saw from the corner of her eye that Mr Bright was now glancing at her in a strange way, as if he was wondering quite what it was that she was grinning to herself about.

Sukie knew Mr Bright was short-sighted, not that he would ever admit it. She doubted he could make out too much of what Pattie was up to.

Sukie tried to force her features into something suitably serious.

It was difficult though, as Pattie was now miming a hangman's noose around her neck, complete with her peepers going crossed-eyed and her tongue poking out to one side.

'Miss Scott, you are not coming down with something, are you?' enquired Mrs Bridge when they were finally able to escape. 'I couldn't help hearing that nasty choking cough you had back there just now.'

Sukie had the grace to look contrite, although not for very long. Pattie had been very funny after all, and Sukie had forgotten quite how good she was at mimicry.

Chapter Two

Several days later Sukie smiled inwardly to herself as she carefully copied out the new supper menu in her best handwriting. She had a spare few moments after the rush of people checking out and before the bustle of weekend clientele arriving to be checked in. It was her favourite time of day.

The heavy quiet of late morning in the hotel's foyer was undisturbed, only broken by the usual sombre tick-tock of the ornate old grandfather clock. Sukie glanced up to check the time, as she had to get the menu to the restaurant before lunch was served, and she finished the final line with a flourish and smiled. It couldn't have been more than a minute or so later that Sukie heard the welcome sound of Pattie approaching along the passage and then turning to make her way through reception, bearing a tray of clean glasses. The smart click of her heels on the old but grand-looking black and white tiles of the foyer sounded distinctly purposeful.

Pattie looked very trim and smart in her dark waitress's uniform, which, despite its advanced age, were kept in excellent condition. What with the rationing that had swept through in the past few years it was getting harder, but the government was keen for women to Make Do and Mend, and so they were all doing their bit.

Unusually, Pattie's hair was held in place by a delicately crocheted black snood signalling that it was nowhere near as clean or shiny as Pattie would have wished. Still, nobody's hair was much to write home about these days, was it?

Nevertheless, they both liked to appear as smart as possible now they were up in London, war or no war.

'Miss Yeo?' Sukie said to Pattie; her voice had the faintest trace of an echo as her words reverberated against the panelled walls and floor tiles of the hotel lobby. 'Could you take this new menu through to the restaurant for me please?'

They had grown up together in the small and picturesque West Country village of Lymbridge, nestled high among the spectacular gorse- and heather-sprigged granite tors on Dartmoor in Devon, Pattie beamed as she headed over to the desk.

While Sukie had always been closer to Pattie's older sister, Evie, as they had been in the same class together at school, she and Pattie had become closer over the months since moving to London.

Their mothers had been childhood friends too, so that when Sukie's parents were killed in a car accident, it left an orphaned Sukie to be brought up by a kindly enough aunt.

After the tragic accident, Evie and Pattie's mother Susan had always ensured that Sukie was made very welcome whenever she'd visited the Yeos' cottage, Bluebells. Sukie loved the hustle and bustle of the lively family all talking at once, or happily bickering with one another, and she had spent many an evening with them.

The homely warmth of the Yeos' kitchen hearthside and the simple but always tasty food Susan would prepare had been a huge draw, too. Although her aunt was well meaning, she was quite mature in years and had very fixed ideas that for a young girl to give in to a hearty appetite wasn't very ladylike and indeed would be 'storing up trouble ahead for the future'. Her aunt also was of the firm opinion that too much heating in midwinter wasn't good for one's health either. After all, what were woollies for, if not to bundle up against the cold, even if Sukie could see puffs of steam in the chill air as she breathed? Sukie had never been able to imagine quite what the trouble ahead would be if she ever had seconds of a meal, or they threw another log on the fire. But her aunt had remained firm in her opinions, and so Sukie's childhood years had verged on the austere.

Although she had done her best to entertain herself at her aunt's house, Sukie had yearned for the warmth of the Yeos' family when she and her aunt had been huddled around an inadequate fire at precisely six o'clock every evening, the crackling of the damp log or two accompanied by the BBC on the ancient wireless.

As children there had naturally been the odd time that Sukie and Evie might not always have been very nice to the younger Pattie. But since moving to London and rooming together at the Eddy, they had become fast friends, so much so that Sukie wondered if Evie was a little bit jealous.

This meant that now, without breaking her stride, Pattie answered politely, 'Of course, Miss Scott,' and gracefully changed direction to pick up the finished menu.

With a quick glance around, Pattie noted that Mr Bright – always eager to keep an eye on the comings, and goings, of the hotel from the little window in his office door – wasn't peering out, and she placed her tray of glasses down on the desk with a smirk.

'So,' she said slyly, 'I heard you switched shifts with Millicent as you're going dancing tonight with Wesley?'

Sukie grinned back. She had caught a glimpse of the headline in that morning's copy of *The Times* and knew Mr Bright would be scouring the paper for news on the British bombing offensive targeting Hamburg and so wouldn't be worrying about the foyer at this time. Winnie – or Winston Churchill as she knew she should call him – had had, as usual, sage comments to make, and Mr Bright would be doing his best to memorise them as he did like to repeat a homily or two to his staff. Sukie allowed herself a quick glance at her left hand, with the slight indentation where her engagement ring would sit when she wasn't on duty.

*

7

As a young girl Sukie never imagined herself falling for somebody like Wesley and, it had to be said, the same was true for him as well. He was always quick to say to anyone that would listen that Sukie was as far out of his league as it was as possible to get, and he was a very, very fortunate bloke that she had even looked at him in the first place. However, what neither of them had been able to deny was that from the very first moment they met at that fateful dance in Lymbridge, it had just felt so incredibly *right* between them.

Even though many people stared at them holding hands in the street, even in London, Sukie had always been able to see past Wesley's stage persona as he stood before them singing in front of the swing band they were dancing to. While some could only see a handsome black man in a dapper suit, she saw a loving heart and a sensitive soul. With her own slight figure and fair complexion, Sukie felt she was the ideal complement to Wesley, and she knew they made a striking couple.

'See you in the staff room later?' Pattie said cheekily, referring to the ancient, lumpy sofa on the staff-only back stairs, as she picked up her tray and the menu and headed for the restaurant. 'I want to hear what you have planned.'

Sukie nodded efficiently and plastered back on her best receptionist smile, mindful of the eagle-eyed Mr Bright, who held strong opinions that the private lives of his staff should be kept strictly to their free time. Not that Sukie or Pattie (or their fellow Eddies, as they liked to call themselves) had much of that these days, what with long hours at the Edwardes Hotel (which they'd dubbed the Eddy, naturally), and their voluntary war work alongside it.

There had been a lull in bomb activity over recent months, especially when compared to the Blitz of 1940, but Sukie had been kept busy enough with her night-time duties as the hotel's fire-watcher. Clambering laboriously through the large skylight above the top-floor corridor and up on to the hotel's roof, clutching the hotel's heavy torch and peering around for signs of fires as she crouched in a flattened nook on the roof tiles. After six straight nights of fire-watching, Sukie was looking forward to the sort of Saturday night that a young, engaged woman of twenty-three might have planned, had war not broken out. However, she told herself that the luxury of both a Saturday and Sunday night where she wasn't expected to sit on the rooftop in her hard hat were well worth it. Wesley, or no Wesley.

'You're needed downstairs.' The concierge's words broke into Sukie's reverie. 'Urgent delivery.'

'Thank you, Stephen,' said Sukie, her eyes sparkling. She knew what this meant.

Pattie sighed deliberately in a put-upon way. She knew who would be holding the fort on reception until Sukie returned, and so deftly turned around and headed back to the reception desk with her tray and menu, whereupon she settled herself in behind it for what might be quite a long wait until she would be relieved.

Chapter Three

'Sukie, my angel, I'm so sorry but I'm not going to be able to see you later, so there'll be no "Crew to Dance and Skylark" for us tonight, I'm afraid,' Wesley told his fiancée as gently as he could almost the moment Sukie stepped out into the alleyway, and as he looked down at her – he was very tall – to see how his disappointing words had gone down, he dabbed away a stray flake of tobacco from his lower lip.

Sukie thought Wesley managed, as always, to make such a mundane movement seem thoroughly captivating.

She hadn't realised quite how much she had been looking forward to their night out though. She felt disappointed, and frustrated – it was so rare for them both to have a whole night off at the same time, that she hated to see the opportunity slip away.

A fat bee ponderously buzzed its way along several flower pots on the windowsill to the scullery in which Chef, a refugee from Italy who was called simply Chef by all the staff at the Eddy, lovingly cultivated a few herbs.

Wesley knew Sukie could be fiery, and so he wisely decided to say nothing in his defence.

Moodily, she crossed her arms in front of her as she concentrated on a smoky spiral slinking gently upwards through a shaft of early-afternoon sunlight from the just-rolled untipped cigarette in Wesley's hand as they stood very close to each other near the metal dustbins, the lids and the bins of which were each amateurishly daubed with a painted 'E' and an 'H' for Edwardes Hotel. There were several other establishments that also backed on to the alley and so each had their dustbins marked with initials of whatever business owned them in order to signify which bin belonged to which back door.

'Oh, Wesley! How annoying. Damn and blast. And dammit again.' Sukie was unable to mask her displeasure when finally she spoke. She even went as far as giving a little stamp of petulance with the heel of her left foot.

'I know.' Wesley did look contrite, but there was an undeniable quiver of excitement about him. 'I was looking forward to spending time with you too.'

Sukie prided herself on always knowing what Wesley was thinking whenever she was at his side, and she could tell he was pleased with himself.

'But there's 'ad to be a change of plan as Will Jones 'as just been nabbed by ENSA to go somewhere or other,' Wesley explained in the soft tones of his Bristolian accent, 'an' so I've bin booked to sing at the late afternoon dance 'e normally does at one of the large 'otels near Piccadilly. It might even lead to a break for me in the business.'

He nudged her gently, and when he saw her mouth soften, he caught hold of the hand that she was lifting unconsciously towards her engagement ring safely nestled on a chain around her neck, currently tucked away from sight under her blouse, and gently he placed it between both of his.

Sukie loved the way his hands felt to her: large and sturdy, and very slightly dry-skinned. Wesley was a very manly man, she often thought, and the way he would grasp her own much daintier mitts always reminded her anew of his manliness, and she would savour this with a delicious tremble of excitement that would race up and down her spine.

All Wesley needed was a little bit of luck; if he could have that, then Sukie was certain his talent would see to the rest of it.

Sukie still felt disappointed, even though she tried to tell herself not to be.

Many, many people were having a perfectly ghastly time, she knew and understood. They could have lost their loved ones, or been badly injured, or had relatives who were being forced to sit the war out in a dismal POW camp; and all of them were obviously in a far worse position than she was. A horrifying number of souls had been made homeless by the bombs, some had had their nearest and dearest evacuated out of London to who knows what fate, while others had seen simply unimaginable suffering and hardships during the Blitz, and Sukie was sure that the shadow of any of those experiences would be very hard to shake off.

Sukie knew she was lucky in many ways. Wesley made it all worthwhile, and she loved him very much. She just wished they could spend more time together.

'I'll make it up to you, my darlin', I promise,' he said, bringing his lips close to her neck.

'Yes, Wesley, you will!' Sukie's gentle tone belied the grumpiness of her words

They stood so near to each other for a moment that even the thinnest of cigarette papers couldn't have been slid between them, before Sukie said reluctantly, 'I must go or else Mr Bright will have my guts for garters. Knock 'em dead, darling.'

With a final squeeze of his hand on hers, Wesley hurried to the end of the alley, and then he paused for a moment and turned back to see Sukie blow him a kiss, which he mimed grabbing and then clutching against his heart, a beam of sunlight shining down on him, as he performed a couple of slick tap-dancing steps in joy, even miming twirling a cane as part of the routine.

Wesley fell serious as he looked straight into Sukie's eyes. He tipped a finger to the rim of his homburg hat and slipped unobtrusively around the corner.

Sukie thought how lucky she was. It felt good to be young and in London, no matter how much Jerry tried to spoil it for everybody.

A cloud passed over the sun and the bright light in the alley-way dimmed. Suddenly it felt very empty.

'Ah, Millicent,' said Sukie a moment later as she opened the door to the hotel and immediately bumped into her co-receptionist in the murkily lit corridor. 'It seems you get your night out dancing after all, as my plans have changed.'

Millicent never did go dancing that Saturday night though, as three hours later a harried young police constable hurried into the Eddy's reception, shattering the calm as he delivered to Sukie the message that she should drop everything and immediately accompany him to the nearest police station.

Chapter Four

Although generally London was experiencing a quiet time in terms of Jerries' attacks on the city, there were still bombs dropping with depressing frequency. The gaping holes of recently destroyed buildings on many streets were a testament to that, as were the craters in the roads, some so big that a double-decker bus could fit inside.

Late that very afternoon, completely unexpectedly, a stray bomb had fallen on the roof of the cinema above the basement ballroom where Wesley was singing his heart out at one of the most popular tea dances in London. Although the cinema took most of the hit, violent shockwaves ricocheted throughout the whole building, with catastrophic consequences for part of the dance hall on the lower floor.

Wesley was the only person killed, although many others were hurt.

At the police station, Sukie was escorted into an untidy side-office where a fatigued-looking policeman, young enough still to have a rash of angry spots near his collar line, explained to her very gently what had happened.

Try as she might to concentrate on what was being said to her in such a serious manner, the young man's words passed over Sukie's head, seeming almost nothing more than a burbling stream. Especially when he placed a familiar watch on the table between them. Wesley's watch. Sukie blinked and tried to swallow; she felt queasy and as if she couldn't breathe properly. In fact she couldn't understand what was happening as only hours before she'd been wishing Wesley luck, dreaming of their wedding day, of their future. Nothing the policeman said hit home. Dear Wesley, he couldn't be gone... Wesley was too full of life not to be here any more.

In an attempt to soften the blow of Wesley's loss, the bobby went on to say that eyewitness accounts reported that he must have died instantly, meaning he wouldn't have known what had happened. Sukie tried to be reassured by the young man, but she was still struggling to take it all in. She was only able to nod slowly, with her eyes unfocused and lace-edged hankie twisting in her hands, unnerving the officer to the point that he had to fetch his superior.

A few minutes later, when the more experienced desk sergeant noticed Sukie's unnaturally pale cheeks, he asked if she could manage a cup of tea. She was unable to reply, and so a telephone receiver was promptly lifted to see if somebody at the Edwardes could come and sit with her.

When they had first arrived in London, Sukie and Pattie couldn't help but be surprised by the obvious Dunkirk spirit most people were demonstrating. In spite of the boarded-up shops, unlit buses when it got dark with conductors who never named the bus stops, and the empty bombed-out spaces that were now merely dark maws of jagged, charred wood and broken bricks, somehow people just accepted it all as they went about their daily lives without fuss and bother.

Even during those heart-sink moments each time the air-raid siren sounded, it was clear for all to see that ordinary people quite often seemed what Sukie could only describe as 'jolly' as they went about their daily routines. She kept being struck by the way that many men would whistle as they walked the lively streets of Covent Garden, while women laughed and gossiped standing in queues for the meagre rationed goods in the shops.

Sukie and Pattie had expected London to be bleaker and more dowdy, but instead they found a city bruised but very much not defeated, with its inhabitants determined to enjoy themselves as much as they could. Sukie claimed at the end of her and Pattie's first week in town that this must be because Britain had been at war since 1939 and now, four years on, many people were simply wearied by the long months of concern, and the endless scrimping and saving. After all, who knew when happiness could be snatched away, and so it seemed criminal not to make the most of every minute.

Following Wesley's death, Sukie thought back to what she had blithely said about happiness being lost so easily and she felt she'd been glib and too innocent, and lacking in imagination. Back then, she had had no idea – no idea at all! – of what the absence of happiness really meant. Surely it was little wonder that life was teaching her otherwise in the wake of the loss of Wesley.

Sukie's grief and upset at the loss of Wesley seemed somehow instantly to permeate the very fabric of the Eddy, as the hotel itself felt somehow nervy and unsettled. For even though living through war meant constant worry and very often believing yourself to be prepared for upsetting news, no one was quite prepared for the worst to happen to them, Sukie realised.

Although he had grown up in Bristol in the West Country, Wesley's funeral had to be held in London, as these days precious fuel and resources simply couldn't be used in moving a body to a different resting place.

Wesley's mother and a favourite aunt of his made the journey up by train for the simple ceremony. Sukie had only met his mother and aunt once before, but it didn't seem to matter, as with Pattie accompanying her to Paddington station to meet them, Sukie soon found solace in their presence, and hoped that they did in hers too.

Wesley's father was abroad somewhere working as a first-aider close to the frontline, and so the funeral had to go ahead without him. Rationing and no spare money meant the service would be as simple and as cheap as they could make it, but Sukie told herself that it didn't mean that Wesley's send-off would be any less heartfelt than if they had all the money in the world to spend on it.

They found a tea shop not far from the station that looked welcoming, and as Pattie went to order some tea, the three women closest to Wesley seemed content to sit quietly together, each lost in their own sorrowful thoughts. It was a wholesome, restorative sort of silence, Sukie discovered, and although she had occasionally wondered previously whether or not Wesley's mother approved of her son's choice of future wife, Sukie couldn't remember having experienced anything quite like the soft and gentle hum of the unspoken words of grief and comfort that swirled in the air around them, or the emotional bolstering that them being together provided.

Once Pattie was sure a pot of tea was on its way, she discreetly positioned herself and her own cup and saucer at the back of the tea shop, as she didn't want to intrude on the grief of Sukie or Wesley's relatives. However, she was pleased to see Sukie's colour brighten a little, even if only to put on a show for Wesley's family. She knew what it cost Sukie to make that special effort, when she was still so shaken after the news of Wesley's death. It was a shock to Pattie too, and she'd written to both her mother and Evie right away to let them know, hoping that their letters – which had arrived soon after – would provide some comfort to Sukie, who was so far away from home.

Evie, and Pattie's other sister Julia, had both written to Sukie, saying how sorry they were about what had happened, how they wished they could be with her, that they were thinking of her, assuring her they weren't expecting a reply as they knew how sad, despondent and exhausted Sukie must be feeling. And Sukie was to make sure she was getting enough rest and not worry at all about not replying. While neither sister mentioned it, Pattie was keeping up a storm of correspondence on Sukie's behalf, so that Evie and Julia were both up to date on the funeral arrangements, though neither could make the journey.

Susan, Evie and Pattie's mother, had written too, and it was this letter that had Sukie returning to it again and again.

There was something about Susan's wise and caring words that had made Sukie tuck that particular letter under her pillow and read it each night before she settled down to try to sleep.

The very first time she read it, Sukie wasn't prepared for the tidal wave of homesickness that swept across her. Suddenly she had an almost overwhelming desire to be back where she grew up. She longed for the quiet of the small village of Lymbridge on Dartmoor, and the clean and fresh West Country air, and to have Evie's arms around her, and Susan making her a cup of tea, and the love of Evie's family to enfold her in a protective embrace.

That first time of reading made Sukie cry for a long while. But then, she felt much better, even though her face was blotchy and her eyes red and sore.

It seemed that the love sent to her from many miles away really had found its way up hill and down dale, and right into the centre of Sukie's heart, fanning gently the flame of her and Wesley's love for each other, before softly helping lay it to rest.

Susan's letter said:

Dearest Sukie,

What absolutely devastating and most tragic news, and my heart goes out to you both, that you and Wesley have each had to experience this. You must feel dreadful, Sukie dear, and very alone right now. I want to say to you that we all know how much Wesley meant to you, and that we all thought very highly of him too. He was a breath of fresh air when he came into our lives as none of us had ever met anyone like him before, and, very quickly, it was clear to all of us how much you and dear Wesley came to mean to each other. In fact, Evie reminded us only last night of the

*time you took him horse riding – he hated it, but he did it
as he loved you so. The horror on his face made Evie laugh
so, she said, and the sight of the two of you jogging away is
one of her fondest memories of the pair of you.*

*Life can be very cruel at times, and it is awful that a
young and gifted man has been cut down so cruelly in his
prime. There are no words that I can say to help you get
through the sense of his passing, other that get through it
you will, I promise, my dear.*

*In your darkest moments, Sukie my love, do please try
to remember though that you are not alone in this, even
though we are not physically together at this awful time.
For everybody at Bluebells, and who lives in Lymbridge and
knows you, loves you very much indeed.*

*I am sure that I am speaking for us all when I say that
we wish this blasted war was over, and we weren't all
having 'to do our duty' as we'd love to have you come
and stay with us at Bluebells for as long as you want. Evie
reminds me that sadly this isn't possible just at the moment,
what with the problems of long-distance travel and getting
time away from the hotel. And although I understand the
reasons why, I do hate this, as we all want you here with
us, sitting in our kitchen and telling us everything that you
loved about dear Wesley. But although we cannot actually
be with you, we are with you in spirit, and we always will
be, and we want you always to remember that.*

*When the war is over – as surely it must be one day –
and we can all travel about at will, and maybe even have
a holiday if we feel like it, the times we are going through
now will seem harsh and cruel, and quite inhumane.*

*You are stronger than you know, Sukie, and your
memories of Wesley will also help you, I promise. I am
hoping very much that there will be a time when you think
of only the nice things about your time with him, and not
how terrible these last few days have been. He was lucky to*

have had you in his life, and you him – and that is the most
important thing for you to hold on to.

Sending you all our love and best wishes, for now and for
ever more,

Mrs Susan Yeo

Sukie thought back to when she had borrowed a couple of
horses for her and Wesley. He really had had a horrible time,
and was saddle-sore afterwards. Sukie was an excellent horse-
woman herself, and she hadn't been very sympathetic. Still, the
afternoon had made them laugh a lot, and it was one of the
most carefree times they had spent together. Sukie was glad that
Evie had seen something special in it too, and she was touched
that Evie had mentioned it to Susan. The Yeos really were very
dear people, and she felt privileged to know them.

Mr Smith, the recent husband of Evie's former headmistress
when she had been teaching at Lymbridge School and who had
helped Sukie and Pattie get their jobs at the Eddy, sent flowers
and a card; he had been a very good friend to Evie over the past
few years, and Sukie was very fond of him too. Mr Smith was
seconded to the West Country doing important War Office work,
Sukie knew, but although his job was crucial to the war effort,
he was the type of man never to forget that simple kind words
counted for an awful lot, and so she appreciated his gesture,
although she couldn't begin to guess how he managed to rustle
up some flowers for her.

Evie's husband Peter was a very proper sort of chap and he
had sent Sukie a note of condolence written on a lavish and
formal black-edged card that must have been produced before
the outbreak of war, the paper being so thick and luxurious,
with a rough feel and what looked like tiny flecks of what might
be cloth or rags mixed into the pulp the card had been pressed
from.

Peter worked in secret offices underneath The Grange, once a
grand home but commandeered by the War Office to be used as

a makeshift hospital for servicemen recuperating from serious injuries. Peter had worked at The Grange at the same time as Sukie had been honing her office skills in the hospital's administration department just a floor above him, and so they knew each other quite well.

She could see that the card was of the very best quality, and was touched that Peter had felt her worthy of something so opulent. Her lips had moved as she read the thick-nibbed words of comfort he had penned in the sepia-coloured ink he always favoured. It felt very grown-up as condolences go (not that Sukie had any experience of them prior to this), but she thought his well-mannered yet heartfelt comments were precisely what she would have expected Peter to send in this situation. Sukie felt a lump in her throat, and she wished Wesley could have known how highly he had been regarded by her friends – she thought it would have meant a lot to him. It certainly did to her.

Pattie, who had sat with Sukie every moment she wasn't working or been on paper-collecting duty, and was treating Sukie with kid gloves despite Sukie's endless entreaties not to, *please*, thought differently. In fact so much so that Pattie couldn't hold back a snort of derision when she saw Peter's card, saying scornfully that he was only a young man yet he always managed to act middle-aged.

Sukie had to tap Pattie's arm and remind her, 'He's very kind, and let's not forget how much Evie loves him and what good care he takes of her.'

Pattie had given a curt nod of agreement, albeit with a scrutinising arch of her brows, before adding, 'Yes.' She inspected her nails. 'But I don't know how Evie puts up with him. Peter would be far too dull for me. I want a man with a bit of life about him, a real spark of energy, if you know what I mean.'

As these words left her mouth, Pattie was instantly mortified and would have done anything to have bitten back her comments. Sukie knew that Evie would have known just what to say, although she found herself groping for words as Pattie's comments had felt a bit like a knife twisting in a wound. But

Pattie was so upset at her tactlessness that Sukie had to comfort her, saying, 'Pattie, you mustn't take on so, do you hear me? I know I'm not at my best right now, but I really hope that all of my friends will find lasting happiness with their Mr Right, whether these Mr Rights are like Peter, or are a bit less fuddy-duddy...' Pattie had looked sceptical, but Sukie hadn't finished. 'And do remember, Pattie, that I'm not made of cut glass. In fact, it would be lovely if you could treat me just as you always do.'

Pattie had tried very hard to so from then on, but it was all very difficult and sometimes ordinary conversations could prove to be an unexpected minefield, or plain awkward and stilted. The two friends had agreed on this the night before Wesley's mother arrived for the funeral as they sat close beside each other on Sukie's narrow bed.

Mr Bright had made a special effort and allowed Wesley's mother and aunt to stay in one of the cheaper rooms at the Eddy. This was after Pattie begged him to allow this the day before their arrival, asking him to take double the price of the room from her wages. There had been a dicey moment when Mr Bright weighed up a bit too obviously whether the dark hue of their skin would offend other guests. But Pattie hastily suggested giving them a room with private bath, and saying that they would eat their meals in their room, which she would per-sonally take charge of, to avoid any unwelcome or unexpected encounters in the corridors of the hotel.

Mr Bright had nodded agreement.

And when Wesley's mother and aunt entered the Eddy for the first time, Mr Bright had bustled out of his office to greet them. Glancing briefly at their scrupulously clean and pressed but undeniably down-at-heel clothes, and their well-worn shoes that were obviously their 'best', he stepped forward to shake their hands. His smile of welcome was the biggest smile he had ever been seen to make, a gesture Sukie appreciated even through the deep fog of her grief, as it was much more than she had expected.

And so the potentially sticky moment of their arrival at the

Eddy was glossed over in a perfectly satisfactory manner, and it wasn't long before Wesley's mother and his aunt were making themselves at home in their room.

Pattie took Mr Bright a cup of tea as a thank you.

He cleared his throat, and then he looked as if he was going to say something important. But he seemed to lose heart, instead only pointing out that Pattie had a mere five minutes before she needed to be in the dining room ready for the early diners and she'd better look sharp. To which Pattie said meekly in an efficient-sounding voice, 'I'm on my way, Mr Bright.'

The small and simple funeral passed uneventfully the next morning, although when Wesley's mother and aunt returned to the hotel afterwards there was a knock at their bedroom door, and it turned out that Mr Bright had asked Millicent to run upstairs with two tots of brandy that were each in a crystal balloon glass and placed on a silver tray.

Neither woman ordinarily drank alcohol, and they sipped the beverages tentatively, grimacing to one another at the sharp taste. But that night they slept better than they had expected, and so they were grateful for the hotel manager's gesture.

Chapter Five

Very early in the morning, the day after the funeral, Sukie and Pattie headed over to Trafalgar Square where they caught the number 12 bus to make their way to the depths of south-east London to where Wesley had lodged.

They found it an eye-opener of a journey, the red bus inching slowly through the shocking destruction of much of Elephant and Castle, an area that had been so heavily bombed that it seemed to be more or less annihilated, and then down the Walworth Road. They got off and headed to a back street that wasn't far from Camberwell Green.

It was the first time Sukie had ventured to where Wesley had been staying, and she and Pattie walked nervously up the depressed-looking staircase that reeked of other lodgers' cigarette smoke. They were following in the wake of the tired-looking landlady who herself was wheezily puffing on a small cigar held in one hand, the other hand being used to check her pin-curls under a wrap of holey scarf that looked a little too tightly tied above her brow to be comfy.

The landlady unlocked Wesley's door, and then turned to go downstairs with a muttered, 'I trust you'll see yerselves out when yer's finished. Don't make too much noise, or take anything that wasn't 'is.'

Sukie and Pattie looked at each other askance after she had gone.

'What a foul woman,' Pattie whispered with a shake of her head. 'Come on, Sukie dear, let's get this over as quickly as we can. Let's hope the landlady has been honest and left Wesley's room alone, as I don't know what we'll do if she's gone through everything.'

Sukie nodded in sad agreement, and followed Pattie further in, only to stop in her tracks when she reached the middle of Wesley's bedroom.

She was shocked to the core at just how rundown his dank and unheated room was.

There was no carpet on the grimy-looking floorboards, the wallpaper was peeling and there was an ominous ochre-coloured water stain on the ceiling. Only a see-through, raggedy curtain flapped in front of the breeze coming in through the ill-fitting window frame, dangling on a piece of wire, the unravelling hem not even long enough to cover the whole pane. In the far corner was a single bed with a meagre blanket and thin lumpy pillow that looked most uncomfortable. Her gaze then fell on the narrow windowsill where Wesley's comb and toothbrush stood forlornly in a chipped mug, along with his razor. The room was tidy – Wesley had always been very fastidious – but that was about all.

What made the grim sight of the room even more poignant to Sukie and Pattie was that it must have been the best he'd been able to do for himself.

Sukie knew Wesley had found it almost impossible to find a landlady who would rent him a room when he moved to London about a month after she did. And although they never actually said it out loud to each other, they knew that this was because of the colour of his skin, as many landladies wouldn't take in black people, or dogs or the Irish.

Wesley had never uttered a word of complaint to Sukie, and nor had he hinted in any way as to how horrible his dank lodgings were.

As she stood in his bedroom for the first and last time, she loved him all the more for him not wanting to upset her, as he knew she would have been cross.

She reached out and touched his blanket and breathed in the scent of him one last time.

The watch that the police officer had already given to her was in her purse and while she'd found the weight of carrying it around a real comfort, she knew she needed to part with it soon, so she found a cardboard suitcase on top of his cupboard and began to pack. And there was the thinnest of silver linings in this particular cloud. For the cigar-loving landlady proved herself honest; everything of Wesley's was there, as far as Sukie could tell at least, and it was all apparently quite untouched.

'I feel mean now,' said a contrite Pattie as she helped gather his clothes and fetched his comb and toothbrush from the ledge.

'So do I,' agreed Sukie quietly, and she sat on the bed and put her face in her hands until she could compose herself.

Pitifully, Wesley's paltry collection of possessions fitted into the single, sad cardboard suitcase with plenty of room to spare, although Sukie kept his favourite hanky, spotlessly washed and carefully ironed, which she slipped into her pocket.

Sukie knew that his clothes would be passed on to his younger brothers and she spent quite a lot of time carefully folding everything, feeling as if this was one of the last things that she could do for Wesley.

His Bible was well thumbed and Sukie felt her heart take a heavy beat when she picked it up. She held it to her cheek for a moment, as she hoped he had been comforted by it. She wasn't particularly religious herself – her parents being snatched so cruelly away when she was a child having put paid to any notions of that – but Wesley had always gone to church each Sunday. He'd told her too without any trace of embarrassment that he'd prayed each night before going to sleep, and so she wondered if that had made a difference to him on his passing.

Although the police insisted he'd died peacefully there was a worm of doubt that had burrowed deep into her chest that claims of Wesley's instant death was more a means of consoling her and his family, than it was likely to be true. Still, if Wesley had known anything about what was happening to him, Sukie wanted him to have found comfort in his religious beliefs.

Wesley's savings, hidden under a floorboard, were more substantial than Sukie had expected. Refusing to mull on the fact that Wesley had intended them to provide for their wedding, Sukie carefully placed the cash in the bottom of her handbag in a second clean hanky, knotted at the corners, so that it would be ready to give to his mother later that morning. She knew how tight money was for the family and it was right for them to have it.

In fact, his mother could take back to Bristol everything Wesley had owned, including the Bible, his watch and the engagement ring, Sukie decided. She was happy with only his favourite hanky and her memories.

As Pattie checked around Wesley's bedroom one last time to make sure that nothing had been forgotten, Sukie sat down once more on the bed, and stared unhappily at the suitcase.

It didn't seem much at all to mark his loss.

Pattie guessed what Sukie was thinking, and leaned over to hug her, saying, 'Sukie, Wesley was larger than life and he wanted for nothing. He knew he'd won the greatest prize of all, which was you.'

Sukie thought Pattie was just trying to be comforting, but Pattie meant every word.

The last that Sukie saw of the suitcase was later that afternoon, when a porter at Paddington train station hoisted it up and onto the Bristol-bound train, with Wesley's mother anxiously moving her handbag from one hand to another as she hovered right behind the porter, watching him intently all the while.

His mother had been very grateful when Sukie had pressed on her Wesley's savings, not mentioning of course that this was their wedding fund, as Sukie really did want Wesley's carefully saved money to do good within his family. Wesley was the eldest child from a large brood, and there wasn't a penny to spare,

Sukie knew. Indeed, his mother hadn't been able to say anything in response to Sukie's gesture, she had been so touched, although the warm goodbye hug between her and her son's intended spoke volumes.

Wesley's mother had refused, however, to accept the engagement ring when Sukie urged her to take it. And now Sukie was grateful for this as she wasn't ready to part with it, she realised.

The stationmaster blew his whistle to announce the train was almost ready to leave, as Wesley's mother turned sorrowfully to give Sukie a sad wave of farewell.

Looking as if she were bearing the weight of the whole world on her bowed shoulders, she then turned back towards the carriage door. With a loud click to both knees she grabbed the inside of the open door and with an effort pulled herself up into the carriage after Wesley's suitcase, with the aunt following close behind.

Sukie held her head high, defiantly, her engagement ring on a delicate gold chain around her neck seeming to tap on the skin directly above her heart.

She had loved Wesley with all her might and she had been honoured to be seen on his arm, and so Sukie was determined to act as bravely as she could in this last show of obvious support on his behalf, even though inside she felt she was, quite literally, crumbling to nothing.

The steam hissed out from the underbelly of the train and then the slow turn of its wheels started, and Sukie momentarily felt her heart move in rhythm with the growing momentum of the giant iron being.

She let out her breath slowly as there was a piercing whistle, and then Wesley's mother and Wesley's suitcase were rolled forlornly away.

'So that's that,' Sukie whispered in a way that Pattie couldn't quite interpret. And then Sukie repeated even more faintly, as if talking to herself, 'That is that.'

Pattie slid her arm through Sukie's, noting how thin her friend felt and how angular her elbow. 'Come on, Sukie, let's nip back to the Eddy.'

There was a silence and then Sukie replied by placing her spare hand on Pattie's arm, and giving a small squeeze.

It was better than nothing, Pattie supposed.

Mr Bright never did dock any wages from Pattie for the cost of the room, complete with bath.

Chapter Six

Mr Bright was of the opinion that a pretty, happy face on reception did a lot for business, and so during the weeks immediately after the funeral, the clearly unhappy and swollen-faced Sukie was dispatched to work in a poky office at basement level. She was put to work quietly but diligently trawling through all the various ledgers and accounts books checking for errors, in order that that they be ready for any sort of Ministry inspection the authorities might make. Meanwhile, Pattie stood in for Sukie at the front desk.

This could have been a lonely experience for Sukie, but she found the silence and the absence of the hubbub of being on reception very soothing, and it wasn't long before she began to look forward to when her fellow Eddies stopped by her small room with a cup of tea and a kind word, which happened much more frequently than Mr Bright knew.

Generally, Sukie *was* very appreciative of her friends rallying around her, although she felt herself to be quite incapable of showing this to them, not least because she doubted they could have any inkling at all of quite how empty and removed from everyday life she felt.

She spent her days constantly trying to make some sort of sense of what had happened, but it was as if she were underwater and in a bad dream. It felt like it was all happening to someone else standing right beside her and not herself. But each morning she woke up to find the nightmare had actually happened, and for a few seconds she experienced afresh the pain of losing Wesley all over again.

When sleep eluded her after her fire-watching duty Sukie would read Susan's letter, and then she would wish that for all the world she was holed up back in her home village, and that she and Wesley had never come to London. After all, Lymbridge was where she and Wesley had met, and where they had enjoyed some of their most memorable times.

Not only that, but Sukie missed Evie greatly, as her dear friend was the sort of person who always seemed to know exactly how Sukie was feeling, and what she should say.

Sukie longed to be in the Yeos' warm kitchen at Bluebells, with a cup of tea and Susan shooing everyone out, in order that Evie and Sukie could nestle close to each other on the window seat to have a private chat. They might have run out of make-up years ago, and never had stockings without a plethora of darns, or enough soap and shampoo – and they were always hungry as the rations didn't ever quite fill their tummies up – but Sukie and Evie has always felt as rich as Croesus when they were together. Just the thought of Evie's warm expression, and the way she loved to put an arm around Sukie, helped Sukie get through some very sombre hours.

Almost as if she could feel Sukie's pain, Evie posted her some photographs from the first night Sukie and Wesley had met. It had been a night to remember as Sukie had accidentally booked Wesley's then band for a New Year's dance at Lymbridge's draughty and distinctly insalubrious village hall, under the misapprehension that she was booking a band with white musicians and singer. The frisson when Wesley and his fellow band members, all black, had arrived had sent an electric shock throughout the village that Sukie had found both hilarious and exhilarating.

One of the pictures had caught Wesley smiling at Sukie from his place at the front of the band as they stood on the small stage, and Sukie grinning back in a way that suggested that she was thrilled beyond all measure that her best-laid plans had backfired in quite such an intoxicating manner.

They looked so happy, and unutterably connected, that every time she looked at it (which she did almost every night), Sukie couldn't help but swallow back the tears that threatened. However, she found that the clench in the back of her throat felt a little more cleansed each time she stared at that particular picture, leaving her feeling better than she had for quite some time.

Once she was sated by gazing at that precious moment, Sukie would carefully slip the photograph into her hanky case for safety, knowing that she would cherish it for years to come. Then she would promise herself that she would write Evie a long letter, just as soon as she could summon enough energy.

Even Mr Bright did what he could to help Sukie feel better, saying (only slightly pompously, for which Pattie was grateful as she was very worried about how low her friend was feeling, and was anxious nothing would further vex Sukie) that each morning at eleven o'clock Sukie would be allowed a small cup of precious real coffee.

This was a grand gesture on Mr Bright's part, seeing as the hotel's scant supply of real coffee was already stretched out as far as it would go. Normally, the freshly ground beans were wholly reserved for the guests, and Chef would brew a hot beverage that, although weak, was still far superior to the familiar but acquired-taste of Camp chicory coffee that the staff were allowed a small cup of each day. Even Mr Bright restricted himself to Camp coffee and so Sukie knew that he was offering her something of the very highest order.

However, Sukie discovered that she had got maybe a bit too used to Camp coffee syrup and its distinctive tang as on the very first morning she sipped a demitasse of the real thing, she felt quite dizzy afterwards. Still, she thought it best not to let Mr Bright know.

As Sukie confided to Pattie several weeks later, Wesley's passing and his funeral had all seemed to happen too quickly. Even though she knew this was a consequence of everybody having to pull together and just get on with things, it seemed increasingly strange to her that someone as large as life as Wesley could be there one minute, and the next – *pouf!* – well, the next it was almost as if the poor dear man had never existed at all.

Sukie knew that, in part, this feeling of befuddlement was because it was wartime and everything was skewed towards the odd and peculiar anyway. But it was also an unexpected indication of her grief, combined as it was with trying to come to terms with the physical symptoms – the headaches, the continual sense of feeling chilled, and a nagging ache in her jaw – caused by the sheer shock of what had happened.

Whatever way she thought about it, Wesley's loss made little or no sense, no matter what was going on elsewhere in the wider world.

Naturally she tried her level best not to make an undue fuss, all too aware that plenty of other people all over Great Britain and its allies were experiencing very similar thoughts and emotions. When she did allow herself the luxury of a few tears, which happened less and less as the days passed, sometimes she thought her sobs were as much for all these other people and hurts, as for herself and Wesley.

When one's heart is broken, Sukie decided, it's as if a layer of skin has been removed, making all the sadness in the world a salty sting. She couldn't imagine a time ever again when she would be happy, although she knew too that she had leaked so many tears that the well of sorrow within her must dry up at some point.

Chapter Seven

As the weeks passed and the summer days seemed endless, Sukie knew that she couldn't hide herself away for ever. Like everywhere, they were short staffed at the Eddy, and it was time for her to return to reception and face the world.

Millicent had had to return home to Scunthorpe indefinitely as her mother had been taken poorly. There had once been hopes for the newest member of staff at the hotel, Beatrice, who was, like Pattie, a chambermaid-cum-waitress-cum-general-dogsbody, would turn out to be good. But she had been given her marching orders by Mr Bright when she was found to be in the family way, unwed and – although fortunately Mr Bright didn't know this as poor Beatrice would have been berated in no uncertain terms – unsure of who the father of her forthcoming baby actually was.

After Beatrice had been showing off a pair of stockings she'd been given just before she left, Pattie was pretty certain the father was one of the American GIs that were flooding London currently, with whom Beatrice had been very taken, although quite where the baby would have been conceived could hardly bear thinking about.

Mrs Bridge had tried to hold on to her for as long as possible but there came a time when the coming baby could be hidden no longer. Pattie had been filling Sukie in on the comings-and-goings she had missed while working in the basement office, and she whispered to Sukie late one night that when Mr Bright twigged what was happening under his very nose, it was a case of 'light the blue touchpaper and stand well back'.

Sukie could only imagine, as while she hadn't been able to make out the specific words, she had heard Mr Bright's yelps of displeasure as he tore a strip off Beatrice in the scullery. His anger had been so forceful, it had travelled all the way across the downstairs level of the Eddy right through to where she was beavering away in her diminutive office at the front of the hotel. Poor Beatrice.

Grateful as she had been for the few weeks of routine administration, there was something about Mr Bright's cross voice that reminded Sukie that many people felt tense and under pressure, as Mr Bright clearly was. She knew how difficult it was to staff the Eddy so that everything ran smoothly, and so Sukie took this as a sign it was time for her to pick up the reins to her life, or, as the government's Ministry of Information posters instructed everyone, to make all efforts to 'Keep Calm and Carry On'.

So, she attempted to lock away her memories of Wesley in a secret compartment deep within her heart, and turn a calm albeit more subdued face to the world.

She couldn't hide for ever and, as she'd come to realise, Wesley wouldn't have wanted her to either.

Life was for living, he always said, and now she had to live for the both of them.

When she'd gone to Mr Bright's office to leave him a note saying she felt ready to resume her duties on the hotel's reception desk, she felt her spirits lift a little, imagining Wesley's pride in this small act of defiance in the face of her sorrow.

An hour or so later Pattie had to put on a brave face after being ousted by Mr Bright from her spot behind the reception desk. She had been sharing receptionist responsibilities with Jane, and had hoped she'd be kept on, as it wasn't so long ago that the Eddy had had three receptionists, when Millicent was there. But Mr Bright explained a little tersely that economies were having to be made across the board, and so from now on there would be two receptionists only, Jane and Sukie, and as far as Pattie was concerned, with Beatrice gone, she was badly needed doing what she used to do.

Pattie sighed and risked a frown, both of which Mr Bright ignored. She had rather come to enjoy being the first representative of the Eddy that a prospective guest would talk to, especially as it was a much less physically taxing job than waiting on tables in the hotel's restaurant or changing bed linen and cleaning bedrooms.

Still, she would have cut her own tongue out rather than let Sukie know she felt miffed. As Sukie sat in Mr Bright's office while he went through all of her duties as a receptionist in excruciating detail (as if she would have forgotten!), Pattie contented herself during her last hour at the front desk by writing Sukie little notes along the lines of 'chin up' and 'best foot forward' and 'a day – or an hour – at a time'. She then tucked these notes into the petty cash book and behind the first envelope in the stack of hotel stationery behind the built-up bit around the reception desk that shielded any untidiness from those standing on the other side, and so on. If Sukie was feeling shaky and unsure, Pattie hoped she'd find these notes and would know that Pattie was thinking of her.

As Sukie made her way down to the kitchen for a late and hasty breakfast after speaking with Mr Bright, and before she went to stand in her old spot, she couldn't stop a small sigh escaping. After all of her wallowing it seemed she was edging towards acceptance of the ups and downs of life, and, she realised, that she was looking forward to the distraction of the guests.

As she turned a welcoming smile towards the first guest to approach her on reception, it was five whole minutes before her mind flicked back to think of Wesley once again.

Chapter Eight

'Sukie Scott! As I'm livin' and breathin', it's Sukie blimmin' Scott. What a sight for sore eyes.'

Sukie's head flipped up. It was several months later and the void in her heart wasn't as all-consuming as it had been, although sometimes still she found herself lost in thought about Wesley.

It took her a second or two to recognise the voice, and, to her surprise, and pleasure, it was John Williams.

The last time she had seen him, he was standing behind the bar at the Haywain, the sole public house in Lymbridge, sliding a rare (in fact, so rare as to be almost unheard of) on-the-house port and lemon across the counter in Sukie's direction as a goodbye send-off the day before she and Pattie left for London.

Sukie's face broke into a broad smile, one of the first natural smiles since Wesley's passing and, forgetting herself, she rounded the desk to greet him properly.

'John – hello! What a surprise. What on earth are you doing here? However's the Haywain going to manage without you? Does Pattie know you're in London?'

John and Pattie had walked out together for a few months the previous year, when John had been staying with his cousin, the landlord of the Haywain. But since Pattie had jumped at the chance to come to London, Sukie assumed it hadn't been particularly serious on either side.

John had originally been a merchant seaman, and was only in

the Lymbridge area after his ship was torpedoed in the North Sea. He'd been fortunate enough to have been rescued and was recovering from a shoulder injury, working in the pub, making it clear to anyone that asked that it was only temporary, as he hoped to be returning to his old job soon, although Sukie had noticed the way he would wince in pain when moving a barrel if he thought nobody was looking, and so she had always doubted he could go back to sea again as his shoulder was definitely giving him gyp.

Having arrived in the village at a time when young men were few and far between, other than those in reserved occupations, John had sent more than a few hearts aflutter. He'd proved a diversion from the gripes and groans about shortages, and queuing, and no meat being in sausages any longer, and all the other moans of the womenfolk of Lymbridge. The consequence was that John had been showered with female attention and compliments, and, although Sukie had no idea whether there had been any peccadilloes despite there being something a little flirty in his eyes, it was to his credit that he was always talked about in appreciative tones by the local lasses.

Meanwhile Pattie had lived in Lymbridge her whole life and had been drawn to the worldly new arrival, as he'd seemed much more grown-up than the boys who were still around. However, Sukie hadn't heard that Pattie had been in touch with John since they'd left Lymbridge, although now she felt a bit guilty about this, as she realised she had been so caught up in her own grief she hadn't even asked Pattie about John, and whether she was missing him.

'No, Pattie's not got an inkling I'm in town. I thought I'd surprise her,' John said, reaching out to shake Sukie's hand in greeting, flashing the bright eyes that had had so many Lymbridge women sighing.

'Not half! You certainly will,' agreed Sukie. 'Pattie's just nipped out to buy some tea towels as our supplier has let us down, but she shouldn't be too long. Would you like a cup of tea while you wait?'

But before Sukie could indicate to John where the sitting room was, there was the click of Mr Bright's office door opening and she raced back behind her desk. Of course, Mr Bright was unable to resist butting in, alerted even through his closed door by the unusual familiarity in Sukie's voice.

Looking for all the world like a slightly ruffled pigeon, with his light-grey suit waistcoat stretched dangerously across his chest under his darker grey jacket, he beetled quickly over to John, the angle of his jutting chin only adding to the impression.

Sukie was surprised she'd never noticed this about Mr Bright before, but now that she had, she wondered whether she would always connect the hotel manager and pigeons whenever she thought of him.

Sukie quickly explained to Mr Bright that she and Pattie had had the acquaintance of John for some time. She couldn't miss the amused look on John's face as she spoke, although John was very careful to make sure that only Sukie could see it.

He'd obviously got the measure of Mr Bright very quickly, as exactly the sort of unnecessarily officious person that he was.

'Ah, yes, I see,' said Mr Bright, in a way that suggested clearly that he didn't see at all.

John hadn't spent months working behind a bar not to be smart on the uptake, so he stood up straight and looked squarely at Mr Bright.

'I'm in London to trial as crew on a river ambulance,' John said proudly, before clarifying, 'I was in the Merchant Navy but had to spend some time in Lymbridge after my cargo ship *Brynmill* was lost in the North Sea, as my shoulder was done in. I'm recovered now, although not yet to Merchant Navy standards, and I want to get back in the thick of it, so it seems I might make a crewman on the Thames. The river ambulances are proving very successful, but they are finding it hard to find people who can both crew, if needed, and who have a knowledge of medical procedures, and I have a decent knowledge of these.'

'John helped his cousin behind the bar of the Haywain, the public house in Lymbridge, where Pattie and I grew up,' Sukie chipped in when Mr Bright didn't immediately say anything back to John, 'and he's a very good friend of Pattie's.'

Mr Bright's social skills left a lot to be desired, but his memory of the staff rosters was second to none and he looked a lot happier when he was able to contribute something useful to the conversation.

'Miss Yeo finishes her morning shift at three o'clock today,' Mr Bright said in a firm voice, 'and then she will start her evening shift at five-thirty sharp.'

John took the hint and announced that he'd come back to the hotel at five minutes past three, adding that hopefully Pattie would fancy spending an hour or two with him, and if she did, then they could catch up on old times.

Presumably she did, as Pattie disappeared for the rest of the day, with Sukie having to cover for her when Pattie's beds needed turning down in the early evening. Sukie thought it probably had been worth the risk of Mr Bright being peeved that Pattie didn't do her shift.

This was because for days afterwards Pattie could be heard humming happily 'Me and My Girl' or 'That Old Black Magic', sometimes giving the odd dance step or a little wiggle to her hips as she pushed her cleaning trolley from one guest's room to another on one of the upper floors, or walked across the foyer in front of Sukie.

And when John found out he got the position of river ambulance man and confirmed he was indeed moving to London, she had a happy grin permanently glued to her face, although sometimes this was a little tested when John disappeared for days at a time, citing lots of evening work, or once when Pattie came across him whispering something in Jane's ear that was making Sukie's co-receptionist blush quite prettily. Sukie had also seen a man who looked a bit like John walking with a woman who wasn't Pattie one day in Trafalgar Square, although Pattie said later that she and he had been to the flicks that afternoon, and so Sukie decided she must have been mistaken.

Chapter Nine

Although Sukie was no longer mourning Wesley with the intensity she had right after she died, Pattie's happiness at spending time with John did sometimes prove an unwelcome contrast.

One morning Sukie woke feeling blue, and wasn't able to talk herself out of feeling miserable. She'd had to clench her teeth not to be snappy as Pattie hummed while she pottered around in their room as she got ready to go downstairs. And once Sukie was up she spent a long time stirring a cup of tea in the kitchen, unable to think about eating anything.

Normally at this time of the day the kitchen was a hive of activity as the tail end of the breakfast clear-up would under way. At the same time a kitchen porter would usually be almost hidden behind a sizeable mound of potatoes and greens, as he began the veg prep for lunch.

Today, however, Chef had spirited everyone away with him to the Covent Garden vegetable market, which took place a couple of streets away, towards the tube station. There was going to be a rumoured delivery mid-morning of a whole variety of vegetables coming down from Lincolnshire, and Chef wanted help with the buying and the carrying as there was sure to be a scramble among other establishment chefs, and some greengrocers too, if the rumours were true. This was because everybody would be looking for something different, now that much of the summer produce was close to the end of its season. Chef had let everyone understand that he was particularly excited about whether there'd be some early Brussels sprouts.

'I lost my Brian, you know.' These sad words interrupted Sukie's reverie.

Sukie jumped, and a little of her tea sloshed into her saucer. She hadn't been aware there was anyone in the kitchen with her.

It was Mrs Bridge. Not long after their arrival, Sukie and Pattie had once joked that Mrs Bridge looked exactly like one would expect a housekeeper to look, being homely and yet very capable. Mrs Bridge had the knack of never losing her temper, but always managing to get her way without, as far as Sukie could tell, ever needing to raise her voice even a notch.

This was no mean feat as quite often the junior staff could verge on the temperamental, especially at the end of the day when they had been on their feet for hours. Sometimes guests' requests would come in late at night and the staff would be sent back up to the very top of the hotel, after only just making their way to the kitchen and the prospect of a nice cup of tea. Added to Mr Bright's rule that no staff were allowed to use the small lift, Sukie and Pattie had been very surprised that Mrs Bridge was able to hold her temper and her nerve so well in the face of some very sullen expressions flung her way.

The only concession to Mr Bright's firm rule, that only guests were allowed to use the small lift, was Michael, the bellboy (or concierge attendant as Michael tried with only varying degrees of success to get everyone to call him, not helped by Stephen, who was the concierge, always reminding the Eddies that *he* was the concierge, and he didn't have, or need, an attendant). This was because Michael was kept very busy dealing with the luggage after guests checked in, or when they were leaving the hotel, and it took too long if he had to carry heavy cases up to the top floor. Mr Bright had a lot of other rules too, such as the staff weren't to fraternise with the guests, or to run out-of-hotel errands for them, although Stephen quite often openly flouted Mr Bright's instructions on this. But if Mr Bright didn't see what was going on, the Eddies would reason that they were

44

only bending the rules a tiny bit, as opposed to breaking them outright, and so Sukie, who was naturally very law-abiding, would do her best to look the other way at these times.

Fortunately Mr Bright, while eagle-eyed when walking about, didn't seem to have much of an imagination, and so if everything *looked* as it should, then he rarely questioned it. Sukie sometimes wondered if this was genuine, or if he just pretended not to see what was really going on beneath the surface.

Mrs Bridge and Chef were much more sanguine about hotel rules though, taking the view that as long as nobody was getting hurt, and the reputation of the Eddy remained squeaky-clean, plus Mr Bright didn't find out, then they would turn a blind eye too.

'I'm sorry, Mrs Bridge,' Sukie said now, once she had refocused her eyes to look attentively at the older woman. 'I was off with the fairies. I missed what you were saying.'

'I lost my Brian, Miss Scott. I'm saying,' said Mrs Bridge with warmth and understanding in her eyes, 'that I know how you are feeling, as I have been through it myself. But I am also pointing out that you are a young woman, and that it's time for you to put your hanky away and to start looking around you. And you need to take better care of yourself. You know what I mean, I'm sure.' Mrs Bridge's even tone was deliberately pitched so as not to be offensive, but with an unflinching stare at Sukie's shrunken waistline that couldn't be missed.

Sukie realised that she did know what Mrs Bridge was talking about. The housekeeper was saying that Sukie needed to concentrate on looking forwards, and not backwards. And she was saying too that she thought Sukie should eat more.

'I . . . er, I . . .' Sukie couldn't quite find the words to explain to Mrs Bridge, in a polite but firm manner, that although clearly well intentioned, the older woman should be minding her own business as far as Sukie was concerned.

'You think I'm going too far to say anything like this to you when you want to be left alone,' said Mrs Bridge. She spoke in a way that declared Sukie's hesitation as a statement of fact.

'Well, I wasn't expecting you to be quite so forthright, I suppose,' Sukie admitted a bit hesitatingly. 'It was a surprise first thing.'

'That, my dear, is precisely the point,' Mrs Bridge bulldozed on. Then she carefully positioned her comfortable behind on a wooden chair. She pulled it close to the large prep table as if she was settling in for quite some chat. She nodded at Sukie to indicate that she should sit down too. 'It's time for some straight-talking, and so here we are.'

Sukie swallowed audibly as she didn't much like this idea.

Mrs Bridge ignored Sukie's obvious reluctance to have this conversation and ploughed on. 'Whatever you do from now on is not going to bring your fiancé back, and it never will. His loss *is* tragic – nobody would deny that – but it has happened. You can't alter that, I'm afraid, but what you can affect is how you live your life from now on. Perhaps the question to ask yourself is whether he... Weston, was it?'

'Wesley,' Sukie said weakly, surrendering herself as she pulled out a chair to sit on. While she was desperate to leave the kitchen with whatever else Mrs Bridge had to say to her left unsaid, Sukie felt that for her to do so would be unforgivably rude. She couldn't just go upstairs to her reception desk; if Mrs Bridge was determined to have this conversation, it would only be putting off the inevitable. She looked at the housekeeper and, yes, it was plain to see that Mrs Bridge was unwilling to give up.

With a sigh of submission, Sukie held up her cup, silently asking if Mrs Bridge would like a cuppa. There was a firm nod and Sukie neatly poured the housekeeper some tea from the large metal teapot resting on the range, placed the cup and saucer, along with the milk jug, in front of the housekeeper, and then she sat down.

'Wesley. Well, would Wesley want you to keep moping around?' Mrs Bridge asked, obviously pleased that she now had Sukie's full attention.

'No, he wouldn't,' Sukie admitted quietly. 'I do understand that, Mrs Bridge, really I do. But everything feels wrong and uncomfortable, and I don't think it's ever going to feel right again.'

With a 'there, there', Mrs Bridge touched Sukie briefly on her arm. And then Mrs Bridge said, 'Gasper?' and pushed an open cigarette packet across the table to offer her a cigarette, which Sukie shook her head at as she only smoked very occasionally on a night out.

The match made a scritchy noise as it was drawn across the box, and Mrs Bridge inhaled deeply with a suck of satisfaction, before blowing out a long puff of smoke.

'I know. It is a very bad time for you, Miss Scott. We can all see that. And the truth of it is this: it may feel a bit worse before it gets better. But you will get through it, I promise. You need to try and remember Wesley at his best, and remind yourself again and again of how lucky you were to have known him. If you can concentrate on the good times you two shared together and how he would want you to be happy, then you will begin to feel almost back to normal much more quickly, I'm sure.'

Sukie stared dejectedly at her cooling tea. The housekeeper's words reverberated around her mind. They were incredibly sensible, and very similar to Susan's letter, which she still read most nights.

Sukie felt tired all the way down to her very bones, she realised, as if right at that moment there was nothing she wanted more than put her forehead on the table and close her eyes. 'Back to normal' seemed an impossible concept.

'Call me Sukie, please,' she said in a weary voice.

'In that case, you can call me Muriel, although we'll still be Mrs Bridge and Miss Scott to each other when the Eddies are around.'

'I think you'll always be Mrs Bridge to me.'

The housekeeper barked a quick Ha! of amusement, but then went on to say in an immediately serious voice, 'Sukie, there are a lot of young women these days pining for something or someone whom they can no longer have, and who are throwing their lives away. You owe it to yourself not to be one of them.

You have a lot to give, and you deserve to fall in love with somebody else in time, and to allow yourself to be happy. But this won't happen if you go on as you are.'

Sukie could feel one of her lids twitching with tiny punches from a vein close to her eye socket as she looked at Mrs Bridge, and her neck stiffened. 'Any man I meet in the future could never be like Wesley, or make me feel as he did,' she said.

With a sympathetic expression Mrs Bridge nodded in agreement, and then sipped her tea, content to let Sukie mull over her words.

There was a short silence, and then in an attempt to move the conversation away from herself, Sukie said, 'Why don't you tell me about your Brian?'

Mrs Bridge sighed, her smile slipping as her voice softened. Sukie wondered what was to come as she had never seen the housekeeper looking wistful.

'We were to be married, but he was sent to the front in the Great War after he signed up when the government first put out the call. He was gassed, came home and spent time in hospital. He went back to the front, and just a couple of weeks later he lost part of his jaw during the Arras Offensive, and he was returned to Britain and put in hospital. I couldn't recognise him at first as he was so badly hurt and was literally screaming in pain—' Sukie winced '—but he was one of the lucky ones as nearly all of those he went with off with originally died. After a merry-go-round of London hospitals, Brian ended up at the Queen's Hospital in Sidcup in Kent, and I would travel down to see him on my afternoons off. But he died under the anaesthetic in 1920, during his fourth operation for maxillofacial surgery. And just like you, Sukie dear, I felt for many months as if I would never recover from his death.'

Sukie's thoughts flickered to Prime Minister Winston Churchill's famous saying of 'the darkest hour' that he had uttered earlier in the war. Then, he'd been alluding to the very real feeling of an imminent threat of invasion during the evacuation of British troops from the beaches of Dunkirk in France, when on a single night in May over two years earlier more than 1,500 ordinary folk had died in London alone, killed by the dropping of myriad Luftwaffe bombs.

That had been a very bleak time for the country and Sukie could remember well the shockwaves that shot across the land, feelings made worse with each traumatising announcement on the wireless or bleak newspaper headlines.

But war was made up of private losses and hurts, as well as collective ones, Sukie had decided over the past few months, and so for her, trapped in her own private war, this was her darkest hour. But although it was tough, it was her personal battle she was going through, she knew.

However, for the first time Sukie began to appreciate how awful being at war again must be for the older generation, having been through it all before, a mere twenty or so years previously.

Sukie looked at Mrs Bridge with different, wiser, more sympathetic and less self-obsessed eyes.

'I'll let you into a secret,' Mrs Bridge went on, leaning close to Sukie and dropping her voice to a whisper as if she didn't want to be overheard in what she was about to say, even though they were quite alone in the kitchen. 'My Brian had left me in the family way when he returned to the front in 1917. Our daughter is Mavis, and she was three when Brian died. She is the spitting image of her papa.'

Sukie took a sharp intake of breath. She hadn't expected this. 'How sad. Poor Brian, and poor you and Mavis. I take it you mean Mavis, who helps serve in the bar on Fridays and Saturdays, and who works in the War Office?'

'That's right. I know that while she's alive, then Brian will never be totally gone.'

'I had no idea! Neither of you give any indication.'

'Well, of course not, as we don't want everyone knowing our business. It is only because of what you've been through that I am telling you. Mr Bright knows, of course, and Chef, but other than that, we don't really talk about it.'

Sukie assured Mrs Bridge of her discretion, and said she wouldn't mention anything to the very glamorous Mavis – whom Sukie was slightly in awe of – to indicate that she knew about her illegitimacy, and nor would she breathe a word about any of this to Pattie either. Sukie commiserated that it must have been very hard bringing up a child outside of marriage.

'It was,' Mrs Bridge agreed, although she didn't look in the least sorry about it. 'But I wasn't the only one, and there'll be many in the same position following *this* war too, and I wouldn't criticise any of those women, not a single one of them. As every time I look at Mavis, I know that all the hurt and pain and worry when she was small was quite, quite worthwhile.'

Sukie immediately remembered the chambermaid Beatrice whom Mr Bright had so unceremoniously packed off home when she couldn't hide her growing stomach any longer, and she thought Mrs Bridge probably did too (and it made more sense now to Sukie as to how hard the housekeeper had fought to keep Beatrice employed for as long as possible).

Mrs Bridge continued a trifle more sombrely as her memories surfaced, 'I was heartbroken and scared when I saw Brian for the first time in hospital. And then I told myself that even without half his jaw, I loved him very much, and I think we would have been happy together. But then a few years after my Brian died, I did go on to marry a very nice man called Vince, who worked for the electricity plant at Holborn Viaduct, although – dear man – he died of a heart attack when Mavis was only twelve.

'It was at that point I moved to the Eddy, along with Mavis, and after that I told myself not to bother with a man again. Mr Bright is my cousin, and he has looked out for me ever since.'

'Cousin!' exclaimed Sukie. 'I can't imagine Mr Bright having a family. You must have known him as a child, which I can't imagine either. In my mind's eye he seems to have been always a grown man wearing a grey suit.'

And so, Sukie thought, Mr Bright had looked out for his cousin as presumably Mrs Bridge hadn't been eligible for Brian's pension. She remembered the way he had shaken the hands of

Wesley's mother and his aunt, and decided that perhaps their hotel manager wasn't such a bad old stick, after all.

'He wasn't too different to look at back then, truth to tell,' said Mrs Bridge. 'And he was known in the family for his very strong opinions. He's a kind man underneath the bluster, not that he wants the Eddies to know.'

The women smiled at each other in a conspiratorial manner, and Sukie imagined an officious-sounding little boy with a sticky-out bony chest bossing other small boys around in the school playground.

There was a clumping sound on the outside steps leading to the kitchen, and Sukie could see Chef and the others returning from the market through the basement windows. Mrs Bridge stubbed out her cigarette and stood up, as the peaceful atmosphere they'd enjoyed was about to be broken.

'Thank you for being so kind,' said Sukie quickly, as she smoothed the curls of her hair.

'It's not a kindness, but just something for you to think about. You won't ever forget Wesley, I know that, and you do too. Remember him all you want, but make sure that you think on it too that he is gone and you can't bring him back; he certainly wouldn't want you to become an old maid because of what happened to him. And the fact Wesley made you so happy means that you know how it feels, which is more than many do, and so if you meet someone who might make you feel a bit like this again, it would be a real shame if you let your loss get in the way,' Mrs Bright said, and Sukie nodded.

Chapter Ten

'Wake up, Sukie, wake up.'

With a sigh, Sukie forced her eyes open at Pattie's instruction, but immediately shut them again. She'd been having an afternoon nap, as she'd been on the roof until dawn had broken, peering all around her for any fires – there had been some bombers flying over and incendiaries dropped, and so she'd had to concentrate for hours, although none had fallen in the streets she was responsible for. On her morning shift, Sukie had felt overcome with tiredness for her last hour on reception; it was a weariness that was still as bone-deep now as it had been forty-five minutes earlier, when Sukie had pulled her and Pattie's thin curtains, removed her skirt and blouse, and crept under the bed covers.

'Sukie! Wake up.'

That doesn't sound quite right, thought Sukie, as she fell asleep again.

'Sukie, dammit. I've something to show you,' urged Pattie, sounding much more normal this time, as she shook Sukie's shoulder.

'Dammit!' said a male voice. 'Hook, line and sinker! Bugger off!! Something to show you. Just a small one then.'

Pattie's laughter pealed across the room and burrowed into Sukie's consciousness.

Sukie shot awake immediately, and sat up.

How very, very rude. What on earth was Pattie thinking, allowing a man into their room while she was resting? And especially one that sounded tipsy at best, and roaring drunk at worst.

But what she saw before her was beyond her wildest imaginings.

There was no man in their bedroom. Instead Pattie was perched on the edge of Sukie's bed and on her extended index finger sat a grey parrot, with an expression on its face that Sukie could only think made it look immensely pleased with itself.

It lifted a claw as if in a small wave at Sukie, and announced in a sing-song voice, 'Well, who's a pretty boy then?' quickly followed by a much more masculine, 'Roll the bandage the other way. You twerp. Where's the rum?'

Pattie tried to stifle another laugh, and the parrot looked up at her and made a blowing-a-kiss noise.

This only made Pattie giggle harder, and so the claw that had been lifted in Sukie's direction was now hoicked up further in order to reach its bent-down head for a scratch, making it look for all the world as if it was rubbing its head in puzzlement at the sight of Pattie, who certainly was being regarded by the bird with a look on its face as if as far as it was concerned, she really wasn't coming up to the standard expected of her.

'This is...' began Pattie.

'Don't tell me. Polly.'

'It *is*!' said Pattie, deliberately ignoring the slightly sarcastic tinge to Sukie's voice. 'Everyone thinks it's a he, but he was already called Polly by the time it was decided he was definitely a he, and then it seemed too late to change it as it's what he answers to.'

Sukie looked at the parrot again to find that he was staring back at her intently as he organised his wings and legs after his scratch. He gave a final little shake to smooth any stray ruffled feathers, and Sukie thought it was as if he was raising his shoulders in a '*Of course I think Polly very infra dig as a name. But what can you do? One just can't get the staff these days'* manner.

The little beady eyes staring at Sukie seemed to indicate that the parrot thought he was cleverer than the average psittaciform. Then Sukie reminded herself she had never met a parrot before, so how on earth would she know?

The parrot shrugged again, in disappointment at Sukie this time, it seemed to her.

He raised some feathers above one eye as if cocking an eyebrow in a silent appeal that she re-evaluate his intelligence.

'Oh, my lord!' said Sukie, a little aghast as she wasn't particularly fond of birds, although on occasion she had in the old days been exceptionally partial to a little roast chicken on a Sunday. 'What on earth have you got there, Pattie?'

'Lord Pattie,' said the parrot. He'd manage to replicate exactly the exclamation of Sukie's tone in the Lord, and the old-friend's familiarity that had oozed out of Sukie's words by the time she came to the 'Pattie' bit.

All right, the parrot was quite amusing, Sukie conceded.

She lifted her eyebrows and mouthed 'Lord Pattie' at her friend, followed by (out loud), 'Seriously?'

'Yup! OK, I'll pop him in his cage. He's very tame and if I put the cover over the cage, I'm told he goes straight to sleep,' said Pattie.

'Lucky him,' said Sukie. 'I might have to borrow that blanket.'

'Sleep. Go to sleep...' said the parrot in a silly voice, which was presumably mirroring the manner in which some former owner had spoken to him, followed by a final cheeky, 'Lord Pattie'.

Sukie saw that on the floor behind the door was positioned quite a large cage that hadn't been there when Sukie had gone to bed. The cage had a wooden stick stretching across its middle. She couldn't believe she had dozed while it was being positioned in their room.

As Pattie stuck her hand in through the open door with the parrot aboard, the parrot dipped his head to take a better look, and then very primly stepped from Pattie's finger across and on to the stick, and then he shuffled himself along its length so that he pressed himself against the bars of the cage in order to look up at Sukie.

'A wee dram, guvnor' were his last words, smothered by Pattie putting a tartan car blanket over the whole cage.

'He's an African Grey, and probably quite valuable. John says they live for many years.'

'Give me strength,' said Sukie.

'John says Polly is notorious down at the docks. He was on several merchant navy ships, and was then at a pub down in Bermondsey, and then a pub in Borough. But both of the pubs got bombed out, and so since then he's been in the mess room of the river ambulances crew. Then somebody complained about him as he does on occasion have a potty mouth, and so they tried to find a home, but couldn't... This morning John was told to wring his neck, and I hated the idea of that, and so now here he is.' Pattie allowed Sukie to think about this for a moment, and then she declared, 'John and myself think that Polly will cheer you up.'

'Oh my lord,' said Sukie, with less of an exclamation to her tone this time. 'What on earth were you thinking, Pattie? I am perfectly cheerful, thank you.'

Pattie's expression told Sukie otherwise.

Sukie acknowledged to herself that Pattie's opinion of her psychological state might have a smidgen of truth to it.

An equally flat-sounding 'Lord' echoed back at them from somewhere under the blanket.

Pattie and Sukie looked at each other until there was another, fainter but nonetheless slightly more insistent 'Lord Pattie' thrown their way by the blanket.

'John has got a lot to answer for,' said Sukie.

Pattie grinned.

Sukie refused to be drawn. 'What on earth will Mr Bright say? And what are you going to feed him on? Polly, I mean, not Mr Bright.'

'Polly likes seeds and nuts, I'm told. And my plan is that Mr Bright never finds out. I thought Polly could stay in our room, well out of his way, and he can make you laugh, and teach you to swear like a trooper. I told John that I thought Polly would really jolly you up.'

'That John has got a lot to answer for,' said Sukie a second time, deliberately making her voice more downbeat than she actually felt. 'And I already know how to swear like a trooper, thank you. Where on earth are you going to find "nuts and seeds"? Mr Bright will find out, as sure as eggs are eggs. And then he is going to throw a fit, you mark my words, Pattie. I remember somebody saying once that caged birds need lots of fresh air but no draughts, so if you thought our room was chilly before that's going to be nothing to what it is with fresh air blowing through.'

There was a silence as Sukie made heavy weather of making good on her words, laboriously getting out of bed to ensure the top of their window was open half an inch. She climbed back into bed with a dramatic sigh.

Pattie's smile didn't budge for an instant; she knew Sukie was exaggerating.

A deadened but nonetheless insistent 'Where's the rum, Mr Bright?' rang out from beneath the blanket.

It was quite some minutes later before Sukie and Pattie could stop laughing, as every time one of them began to grow serious the other would pipe up with another 'And where's the rum, Mr Bright?', which would set them off again. It wouldn't have been so funny if Mr Bright wasn't so pompous, or if either of them had ever seen him with an alcoholic drink in his hands. But he was, and they hadn't, and so Polly's off-the-feathered-cuff comment really tickled their funny bones.

Although she didn't approve – not at all – of what Pattie had done, as Sukie slipped back into her blouse and skirt again to go downstairs a little while later, she realised that having shared such a good belly laugh had improved her spirits no end.

Perhaps having Polly around would prove to be something of a tonic, after all.

There was a snorting sound from under the blanket, recognisable if one concentrated, as some sort of familiar sounding guffaw.

But Pattie hadn't snorted at all when she laughed.

Sukie realised then that rather than sounding like a lady, with a tinkling cascade of humour, as she had always hoped she herself did, in reality she had to accept that, as Polly had just pointed out, she sounded like nothing more and nothing less than a happy piglet rooting in mud for acorns when she laughed heartily.

Oh lord, what a thought.

Chapter Eleven

As the days passed, Sukie noticed a real change in Pattie, who previously would grumble as she got up for her chambermaid duties; now she seemed to have a perpetual spring in her step, and to be very agreeable to whatever she was asked to do, whether she had been on her feet all day or not, and even if it was the hundredth time she had had to run up to the top guest floor.

Sukie found she was pleased that John had arrived in London as his presence meant that Pattie was spending more time out of the Eddy and having a life away from work, just like any twenty-year-old woman should.

As far as Sukie could tell, it seemed that Pattie and John had picked up more or less where they left off the previous year, and they managed to spend a fair amount of time together. They would go dancing or to the flicks when they could snatch a few hours together between Pattie's shifts. Her war work outside the Eddy comprised of helping organise collections of paper and metal, which, she discovered, could be bolstered by spending a bit of time down with the river ambulances, as she came by quite a bit of flotsam and jetsam fished out of the river or found on its banks.

Sukie filled Evie in on this recent development in Pattie's social life in her weekly letters, thrilled to once again have something to impart to her dear friend that didn't rely on humorous stories gleaned from her hours in the Eddy's foyer, which usually comprised some jiggery pokery between Stephen and Michael, or Michael and Alan good-naturedly arguing the toss over some racehorse or other.

John was becoming, apparently, rather a good river ambulance man, although Pattie said she was too squeamish for some of the things he wanted to tell her about. Sukie didn't fully trust Pattie's interpretation of how well John was doing, as in Pattie's eyes he had now clearly risen to hero status, and was therefore a man who could conquer anything, and do no wrong.

But John had an air about him of a confident man-about-town, and so Sukie thought he probably was doing quite well, now that he was in London, and she always insisted that Pattie go out with him if Pattie ever looked at her a bit guiltily for spending so much time with John.

Sukie didn't often think of John, but if she did she would remember that Lymbridge had always seemed to be a rather small place for him to be. He was better suited to somewhere more lively, as was Pattie, Sukie was sure, although she couldn't quite quell the occasional niggle that John was something of a dark horse, not that she ever shared this with Pattie.

Sukie was honest enough to realise that part of the reason that she encouraged Pattie seeing John as much as possible was because it meant that most of Pattie's free hours were accounted for elsewhere, and the fact of this felt like a weight had been lifted from Sukie's shoulders.

She hadn't realised that unconsciously she had been feeling incredibly responsible for Pattie's happiness. And now, while Sukie couldn't imagine anything she less wanted to do herself than go dancing or to the pictures, she suspected that her own sad mood had weighed down Pattie for too long.

Pattie was young and should be having as much fun as possible, Sukie firmly believed. No lipstick and having to wear a snood over grubby hair was depressing if there wasn't something, or someone to cheer up a girl like Pattie at the same time.

If walking out with John made Pattie happy, then Sukie was delighted, as her friend deserved all the happiness in the world after caring for her so carefully during her darkest time.

The leaves began to fall from the trees, the nights shorten and the crisp cold air at night now tickled the back of Sukie's nose when she was up on the roof watching for fires. She could, quite literally, smell autumn all around her.

This meant that winter was only just around the corner, and Sukie couldn't be more pleased as it was her favourite season. She wondered what Christmas in London would be like.

Very different, she suspected, to when she and Pattie had been back on Dartmoor, surrounded by their loved ones. Sitting on the cold roof, bundled up as well as she could, her torch at the ready and hard hat making her skull feel all the colder, she felt a burst of sudden happiness at the mere thought of the Yeos' warm kitchen and Evie starting to think about Christmas. They'd all always had fun during the festive season at the Haywain, and at Bluebells, with everybody determined to forget the war. They'd sung carols and had made paper chains, and had gathered fir cones, and ivy, and – of course – mistletoe.

Wesley had been in Lymbridge for the previous Christmas, and he had led a wonderful sing-song at the Haywain, and then he and Sukie had kept accidentally on purpose bumping into each other under the mistletoe... What lovely memories!

Sukie knew that meanwhile the Eddy had more or less put Christmas on hold since 1938. What a pity, she thought, as it was a shame that both the guests and the Eddies hadn't built a bank of happy Yuletide recollections to look back on.

1943 was coming to an end, and Sukie wondered if they would all still be at war this time the following year. And she wondered if it was time for a change.

The very next day the weather turned from cold to damp and continued to worsen. Rain came in short squally bursts that would splatter hard against the windows and drench a person unlucky enough to be caught in it. Sukie found that the big standard lamps in the Eddy's foyer had to be turned on earlier and earlier, so that the first impression new guests had – once they'd negotiated the thick blackout drapes hanging inside the doors – wasn't one of gloominess. Sukie hoped to keep the Eddy as inviting as possible, despite the fact that no replacement staff had been hired and they were all running particularly ragged. Alan looked very tired these days after his evenings showing diners to their tables in the restaurant, and Stephen was perpetually grumpy, and so Sukie thought that anything she could do to lighten the atmosphere might be deemed a good thing.

During a particularly rainy late October afternoon, when they had a lot of checkings-in and checkings-out, the doorman had had to pop inside constantly to quickly mop the floor tiles in the hotel foyer to remove footmarks and drips from umbrellas, as Sukie was worried about somebody slipping and hurting themselves on the marble tiles.

Of course, she'd never been one to think herself above her station, but a trifle bored at answering the same questions from the new guests again and again (could they order newspapers; what time was breakfast; and where was the dining room), watching this ridiculous scene play out over the afternoon, Sukie found herself increasingly riveted by the doorman trotting inside again and again to wield a mop.

She decided to say something to Mrs Bridge. She realised she was still a little afraid of her – all the other Eddies found her to be terribly officious if she was caught at a bad moment – and so Sukie steeled herself before she went to speak with her. They had had their chat in the kitchen though, Sukie reminded herself, and she had often thought back to the housekeeper's wise words of comfort, and so she took heart.

Mrs Bridge looked at Sukie with a warm expression, and thus encouraged, Sukie suggested that a larger door mat could perhaps be rustled up for inside the foyer doors. She added that if the umbrella stand was moved closer to the reception desk, or better still, they place an umbrella stand just inside the front door, and another beside the reception desk, it might help cut down on the watery marks being left on the floor from the dripping brollies.

Thrillingly Mrs Bridge loved her ideas, implementing them right away, and Sukie even earned a smile from Mr Bright for her resourcefulness.

She felt that if given the opportunity she could have lots of ideas about small improvements that could be made to how the Eddy operated. While she recognised her role as receptionist didn't really offer this leeway, she knew too that Mr Bright had lost his under-manager to conscription not long before she'd started at the Eddy earlier in the year, and several other experienced administration staff had also left over the previous years.

So, she reasoned, it couldn't hurt her promotion prospects to have Mr Bright impressed by her work, and it even made her wonder if she could perhaps move into an office at some point if she continued to show her efficiency. She knew that she'd certainly done quite well with the paperwork during those weeks in the basement office, and she wondered if maybe the time was coming when she could show Mr Bright how capable she really was. It wasn't that she didn't like being the Eddy's main daytime receptionist – she did enjoy it, very much – but it was more the case that she thought she had more to offer the Eddy than was currently being asked of her.

Buoyed by this exciting thought, Sukie found herself looking around the hotel with fresh eyes, wondering all the while what little improvements she might be able to bring. It felt nice to be useful and to have a little private project on the go, although she told herself to tread carefully as she didn't want Mr Bright or Mrs Bridge to think she was becoming bumptious.

Still, one evening she made Mrs Bridge some cocoa, and asked her to describe the best Christmases of the 1930s at the Eddy.

Mrs Bridge's eyes shone as she remembered. 'Well, we'd get guests from all over the British Isles and the rest of the Commonwealth staying. We would have a huge Christmas tree in reception, with real candles in little metal holders on it that would be lit in the evening. We'd imported the holders from

Germany, and there was a lot of debate about that at the time as many people didn't want to support German trade after the Great War, but Mr Bright wasn't able to find what he wanted from English suppliers, and so he ordered them from Germany anyway. The tree looked so pretty when the candles were lit, that I think everyone soon pretended to forget where the holders had come from. We'd wrap boxes in coloured paper so there would be a stack of pretend presents underneath, and on Christmas morning Mr Bright would dress up as Santa Claus to give small gifts of toys to all the children that would be staying. Us Eddies would rehearse carols, and we would line up the first flight of stairs up from reception on Christmas Eve, and the guests would gather in the foyer drinking mulled wine while we sang to them, with Mr Bright playing the piano, which we would move into reception. There'd be song sheets, and so the guests could sing with us.

'And on Christmas Day there'd be smoked salmon on brown bread, served with champagne and sherry in the morning, and at two o'clock a huge Christmas lunch with all the trimmings for the guests. By the time we were ready for the figgy pudding it would be dark outside, and we'd turn off the lights and Mr Bright would douse it in brandy and then wheel it across the restaurant. Everyone would clap, it was so pretty. There'd be crackers and paper hats, and everybody would be very cheerful.

'The guests would be sent to the bar and the foyer, which we'd use as a sitting room, and we would get entertainers in to keep them happy. Meanwhile, Eddies would have their lunch in the dining room right afterwards, served by me and Chef and Mr Bright, to thank everyone for their hard work over the year, and there would be an hour of party games and charades afterwards just for the staff. Mr Bright and I would make sure each and every Eddie had a Christmas present, usually stockings for the ladies and some Pond's cold cream, and some Trumper's shaving soap for the men. And at eight o'clock in the evening there'd be game pie and a huge ham and pickles served in the bar, and mince pies and brandy cream, and both the Eddies and the guests could mingle and talk to each other.'

'That sounds really fun,' said Sukie. She'd breathed in as she remembered the distinctive fragrance of Pond's cold cream. Her mother had used it every night and so this took her straight back to the happy years of her early childhood. Sukie then realised that she hadn't smelt Pond's for years. Face creams were a thing of the past, what with the shortages. 'What a shame those days are gone.'

'It was fun, it really was!' said Mrs Bridge, who was getting into her stride now. 'Once, in thirty-six I think it was, everyone began playing Sardines at about ten o'clock at night, and Mr Bright allowed all the public areas of the hotel to be used, and we turned off most of the lights and we all ran around with torches. I don't think that game stopped until the small hours, and although there may have been the odd kiss exchanged, I do remember how carefree everyone was, and very well behaved, although Stephen kept hanging up little sprigs of mistletoe in new doorways. I also remember that Alan hid in a laundry cupboard on the fifth floor, and was found fast asleep! And it was Michael's first Christmas with us, and Mavis had to be very curt with him when he chased her into the scullery with some mistletoe!'

The housekeeper clearly enjoyed describing the 'good old days' of plenty and profligacy. And so Sukie, who was becoming rather fond of Mrs Bridge, encouraged her further, and listened with a careful concentration when the housekeeper described how during the rest of the year a fortune was spent on having extravagant displays of blooms delivered every single day to the hotel, and there had even been a specialist cleaner who would come in at two o'clock in the morning on one day a month, before breakfast service, to clean the delicate hanging crystal prisms on the grand chandeliers in the dining room. There had also been a piano tuner who would come in once a fortnight. All the bed linen and towels – even those the Eddies used – would be sent out to a laundry that would return everything smelling of lavender and neatly tied up with satin bows, while a single handmade chocolate lovingly made by a master chocolatier in a small shop near Long Acre would be left in a little gold paper cup on each guest's pillow by the chambermaids when the beds were turned down.

Sukie and Mrs Bridge shook their heads sadly, as those days of endless luxury were well and truly over. In fact, there had even been the occasional day when they were so short-staffed at the Eddy that Michael, to his chagrin, had had to help with the turning down of the beds in the early evening and Mr Bright had to stand in on reception if Sukie was on fire-watching duty and Jane was having to help serve the diners in the restaurant. The guests' bed linen, guest towels, table cloths and napkins were still laundered out of the hotel, but long gone were the days of satin bows being tied around bundles of clean linen and lavender water used in abandonment.

Nevertheless a seed had been planted in Sukie's mind. The slippery slope into destitution that the Eddy seemed stuck on was now about to be halted, at least if Miss Sukie Scott had anything to do with it.

As winter set in properly, Sukie and Pattie's bedroom now felt very chill in the mornings, as none of the staff rooms had heating.

Encouraged by her successful plan in the foyer, Sukie talked to Pattie about perhaps leaving their door open all the time in order that any residual warmth from the corridors and guest bedrooms downstairs could waft upwards via the staff stairs.

Any valuables belonging to the Eddy were already stored in the gigantic hotel safe in Mr Bright's office (although Sukie still wore her engagement ring on its chain around her neck, rather than placing it out of harm's way in the safe), and the guests' stairway and lift only rose as high as the floor below, so Sukie felt quite confident, as it was impossible to think of anyone who worked at the Eddy doing any harm. They were all friends now, rather than colleagues, Sukie felt, and she didn't think there was a bad egg among them.

Leaving the bedroom door open was a system that worked better than Sukie had expected as the circulating slightly warm air did take the edge off a cold morning, and soon everyone on their landing was doing likewise.

As Sukie lay awake deep into the early hours of the morning, trying to will some warmth back into her icy fingers and toes after her fire-watching duty, she thought that a very small change like this did, in fact, make quite a lot of difference. Then she would try to lull herself into sleep by working out who each of the various snores emanated from, and she discovered this was a very successful tactic at sending her straight to sleep.

Chapter Twelve

Sukie found her mind was buzzing with ideas concerning how the Eddy could be run slightly differently. But she was wary, as she didn't want to scupper her chances seeing these through as she knew Mr Bright could be tricky to deal with and could take offence at the smallest thing if he were in the mood; he would hate it if he thought Sukie was behaving in a manner above her station. Still, she didn't mind too much keeping her powder dry for a bit longer, telling herself she just had to be smart and carefully pick her moments when she made suggestions to him.

She felt she was thinking of Mr Bright with a kinder heart. Sure, he could be difficult and tiresomely nosy, but then Sukie would remember that he had been very kind to Mrs Bridge in her hour of need when he knew she needed a place to live and bring up Mavis. And he had been exceptionally good to Wesley's mother and aunt. Sukie knew that many people would not have behaved so sympathetically or treated these two poor black women so respectfully or so graciously. He'd been less nice in the case of Beatrice, of course, but Sukie told herself that he had been juggling problems with staffing and not quite enough income through the books, which would be enough to try the temper of anyone.

She began to examine how she was feeling these days in other areas of her life. She recognised she had felt numb for what had felt like ages and that she'd got used to this; it was almost as if she had been whacked very hard on the head and had been suffering a severe concussion. Now, Sukie discovered, she didn't feel quite this way now. There was a world around her she was starting to notice.

And when she thought about Wesley, Sukie realised she was sorry that she and Wesley had never embarked on sexual relations. It had seemed so very important just a few short months ago that she hadn't risked any chance of a pregnancy out of wedlock, as she'd felt that people would judge her and Wesley very harshly if they'd made so bold, indeed much more so than if she had been engaged to a white man. However, now there was a sliver of Sukie's heart that was sad she wasn't right now carrying Wesley's child. She doubted she could have been so brave about it as Mrs Bridge must have been when left as an unwed mother with Mavis, but Sukie felt regretful that all the wonderful things about Wesley had died with him. She was sure that any child of his would have been extraordinary, just like he was.

Sukie suspected that times were changing across a whole gamut of things – would women who were enjoying their jobs be content to go back to keeping house once their menfolk came home, for instance? – and that perhaps an unplanned pregnancy for a young unmarried mother might not now be frowned upon in *quite* the way it must have been in 1917 or 1918, although had such a thing occurred she couldn't deny that it would still harm anybody's marriage prospects.

What she should do, she told herself firmly, was to learn from this. So what if she and Wesley had spent a night – or many nights – together? For, in the big scheme of things, who on earth really cared what Sukie Scott had got up to, as long as nobody else got hurt? She was sorry that she and Wesley hadn't spent at least one night together; that was the truth of it now.

The world didn't end with Sukie realising that she had regrets over something that once she would have thought impossible, she decided. Encouraged, she began paying a bit more attention as to what was going on around her.

And the first thing she noticed was that although she couldn't quite put her finger on precisely why, she couldn't help but notice that Pattie seemed to have an energy about her that Sukie couldn't quite recognise.

Pattie and John were certainly spending a lot of time together and Pattie seemed so cheery that Sukie assumed that was the reason for Pattie's high spirits. Still, Pattie's eyes had taken on a new sheen, and she was so jolly, that Sukie was suspicious.

Mr Bright called Sukie into his office one day when she was on an early shift, and asked if she would go right away to the post office to buy some stamps, while Pattie covered for her on reception.

Sukie felt her brow tuck into a small frown between her eyebrows as she nodded towards Mr Bright to indicate that she would go.

Normally Pattie or one of the other underlings would be sent on this sort of errand. And so privately Sukie didn't see why she was being asked to go and Pattie wasn't, not that she would dream of saying this out loud to Mr Bright as she knew how much he hated any of his orders to be questioned. She certainly wouldn't say anything to Pattie either, as Pattie had gone beyond the call of duty to be kind to her over the past months and Sukie felt in debt to her.

But what was especially strange about the matter was the fact that Sukie knew that there were two hundred first-class stamps in the top drawer of Mr Bright's oak desk, in three perforated sheets. She herself had put them in his stamp folder only the previous afternoon, and there was nothing waiting in the To Post cubbyhole on the reception desk that the doorman would whisk to the post box later, which meant that Sukie knew that Mr Bright hadn't been up and busy writing letters throughout the night. She was pretty certain too that he knew the stamps were there, and so it was all very curious.

Pattie was no help either, as there'd been a flurry of people checking out or who wanted to change their order for the morning newspapers that Stephen would deliver first thing the next day to their rooms. And now she was busy with a couple of gents who were letting her know a bit too obviously that they were both members of Parliament, and had two nights booked as they needed to attend a Very Important Discussion in the House of Commons, and then they needed to *hurry* back to their constituencies as they were badly needed there.

Outside, it was a crisp and sunny winter's day, and, once Sukie had realised how uplifting the weather was, she slowed her pace from brisk to amble and found herself grateful to be out in the fresh air.

She angled her face towards the sun, luxuriating in its weak warmth. She rarely spent time in natural daylight these days, and she was sure that this was contributing in part to her pallor.

She had some clothing coupons saved and on the way back to the Eddy after collecting the stamps, and promising herself she would work a bit later to make up the time at the end of her shift, Sukie dawdled even more as she enjoyed a little window shopping, eventually treating herself to another pair of badly needed stockings.

In a newsagent that still had some sweets behind the counter in large glass jars, she spied some liquorice Pontefract cakes, and so using her sugar ration two ounces of shiny black coins were carefully weighed on a large silver scale and then tipped into a small brown paper bag that Sukie placed in her handbag to share with Pattie later.

Sukie felt frivolous as she couldn't remember the last time she had bought anything for herself or eaten a sweet, and just for a moment she felt grateful she was able to make such choices.

'Here are your stamps, Mr Bright,' Sukie said cheerfully, once she was back at the Eddy. Before she went into his office, she slid the stockings and liquorice on to the familiar empty shelf under the reception desk. She tried to be as unobtrusive as possible because Pattie was checking in a new guest, and so she quietly removed her coat and hung it in the hidden staff cupboard that masqueraded as one of the wooden panels lining the walls of the foyer.

Mr Bright was busy peering through the window of his office into reception as she stole past him and opened the desk drawer to take out the stamp folder. He jumped, and then made a half-hearted attempt to stop her, but it was too late.

Neither said a word as they both gazed down at the three pristine sheets of stamps that were already there that revealed George IV's face staring accusingly up at Mr Bright out of each of the many blue 2½d stamps Sukie had carefully closeted there only the day before.

Silently she placed the new stamps on top of the others, and slipped the folder back into the drawer.

'Um, Miss Scott, thank you,' said an unusually flustered Mr Bright, whose cheeks had gone pink. 'I wonder if now you can fetch the list of the latest tariffs from the bar for me, please?'

Again, how strange, thought Sukie, as normally Mr Bright would go and get something like that himself if he wanted it, mostly (Sukie was convinced) as he liked to be seen out and about in the hotel as much as possible, believing it kept his staff on their toes.

Sukie tried to catch Pattie's eye on reception as she went by, in case Pattie could shed any light on Mr Bright's odd behaviour. But irritatingly Pattie was now holding the telephone receiver to her ear as she took down a message.

There was no Eddie standing behind the bar, which wasn't unusual during the day. If a guest wanted a drink and the barman wasn't on duty, there was a silver black-handled bell left on the bar to summon Pattie, or even Sukie at a pinch, to serve.

Collecting the list of tariffs, Sukie stood for a moment as she checked carefully that she hadn't typed up any mistakes that Mr Bright could take umbrage with. But she couldn't see anything wrong or that shouldn't be there.

Indeed, below the price list there was the new addition of a line that read 'NO MEAL IN THE RESTAURANT MORE THAN 5/-', followed as the final line by: 'Impressively tasty meal at the Edwardes Hotel,' *Daily Telegraph and Courier (London)*.

She smiled as she read these lines. It had been her idea that Mr

Bright should ask newspapers in London whether they would like to send a member of staff and a guest for an evening meal on the house in the Eddy's restaurant, with the purpose of a staff writer then providing a published review of the dining facilities at the hotel.

It had been a successful strategy in terms of publicity coverage, with several papers sending a journalist over to eat, and Chef's cooking going down well with the press.

Now, when she typed out the bar tariffs, Sukie made sure she added admiring comments from the press at strategic points on the typed drinks price lists, and on the bottom of the daily menus, which she would write with her ink pen as she had a good italic hand. A copy of both would be placed in the brass holder on the outside wall beside the entrance doorway that was there especially for this purpose, as a gentle reminder to guests and visitors, or people walking past the front of the hotel in the street, that the Eddy boasted a restaurant, and a rather good one at that.

It seemed a policy that was driving business as Mr Bright had remarked only that morning to Sukie that there had been a welcome upturn in the guests' spending while they were on hotel premises.

Pattie had told Sukie she liked the way that across all of these price lists Sukie had made a virtue of the fact that, as the government had decreed to all of the London hotels, from the most lowly and right up to very poshest, there was a 5/- limit on how much could be charged for a meal, with no meal being more than three courses.

Sukie had also suggested to Mr Bright it might be a good idea to put up another brass holder in the bar so that the daily restaurant menu could be clearly on display there, in case anyone from outside the hotel who was visiting just for drinks and who was standing at the bar fancied seeing what the lunchtime or evening meal choices were.

About a third of the bar had recently been designated – again on Sukie's suggestion – as a no smoking area, with a couple of windows cranked open a little to encourage the fresh air in. She hadn't seen this done anywhere, but although very occasionally she did enjoy a cigarette in her own time, she had always opted to sit in the least smoky part of the Ladies Bar that she could at the Haywain in Lymbridge. Likewise, these no smoking seats were proving popular of an evening, and so Sukie noticed at least one more table that could easily be incorporated into the area without compromising the more usual workings of the hotel bar.

Sukie suspected that these ideas of hers were nothing special, as they all seemed very obvious to her, which meant that other people elsewhere would have had them too. But her ideas had worked in terms of driving trade to *their* restaurant, as to her it looked as if more and more diners were starting to come to the Eddy just for an evening meal.

Covent Garden was a busy area in the evening now that the theatres and dance halls were back in use again, and Sukie suspected that while the Eddy had always been popular for a pre-dinner drink, it was slowly growing a reputation as a reliable and discreet place to eat of an evening.

Now, as she inspected the sheet of tariffs, out of the blue the hairs on her arm lifted, and Sukie realised suddenly that the atmosphere in the room felt peculiar in a way that she couldn't quite fathom. Carefully, she put the card back down and turned around.

'Thank goodness, Sukes!' rang out in dearly familiar tones across the empty table and chairs to the bar. 'I thought you'd gone blind as well as daft. I wasn't going to be able to hold my breath or keep still as a mouse for much longer! I've a cold and I was dying to sneeze!'

Sukie felt a thrill of excitement engulf her.

'Evie!' she cried.

Evie's eyes sparkled playfully as she looked back at her friend and she trilled an excited answering, 'Sukes!'

'Evie!' Sukie cried for the second time and then she almost flew across the room as she hurried towards her best friend who had a broad grin on her face as she was prising herself to a standing position from a gilt chair that had been hidden behind the open door to the bar.

It was obvious that Pattie, with Mr Bright's help, had decided to give Sukie a surprise – and what a wonderful surprise it was.

Sukie sobbed as she hugged Evie as hard as she could. It was a wonderful feeling to stand there with Evie's arms around her. But although she was awash with emotion, Sukie couldn't help but be slightly flummoxed by why something seemed to be in the way.

Then the penny dropped with a clang, and Sukie sprang backwards so that she could inspect carefully Evie's protruding stomach. This was why Evie had stood up so slowly.

'You're having a baby!!' Sukie almost screamed.

And then the pair of them were half laughing and half crying as they held on to each other, swaying from side to side, with Evie replying just as excitedly, 'I am. And you're going to be a godmother, we hope?'

Pattie popped her head around the door to announce in a mock-serious voice that Mr Bright had said as they were being so noisy then Sukie could have a break to be with her friend, and that she could also knock off a bit early later on.

As Sukie stood beaming at Evie, Pattie couldn't resist adding it had been the devil's own job to manoeuvre Sukie out of the hotel for long enough to spirit Evie inside and get her hidden, and that Evie had had to stand for far too long in the alley at the hotel's rear until the coast was clear, and so Sukie had better take Evie somewhere nice to make up for her slack attitude and poor behaviour.

There was a quick clench to Sukie's heart as she remembered that where Evie had probably been standing in the alleyway would have been precisely where Sukie stood the very last time she had glimpsed Wesley.

Then, with only a small effort, Sukie reminded herself of Mrs Bridge's wise counsel about not dwelling negatively on what she couldn't change, and she smiled warmly at Evie. Her dearest friend was here and that was all that mattered at this minute. If losing Wesley had taught her anything, it was that she should hold on to the good moments for all they were worth, and the precious people in life, as you never know how long they will be there for.

Chapter Thirteen

Mr Bright allowed Sukie to have two hours off to spend with Evie.

As they buttoned their coats while standing on the steps to the Eddy, it was still just as sunny as it had been when Sukie had gone out earlier to get the stamps.

Sukie found herself quite unable to wipe the happy expression from her face as the doorman waved them off, and she linked her arm through the crook of Evie's elbow as they walked from the hotel.

With the ease of someone now used to living in a city, Sukie guided Evie through the hustle and bustle of Covent Garden towards an old coffee house in the Aldwych she'd been longing to try.

To Sukie's exasperation, the coffee house turned out to be closed. A hasty notice had been daubed with what Sukie guessed was pink Windolene on the window that said 'Open when water back on', while a workman was sweeping what looked like broken slates from the roof into a pile. Well, he had been sweeping, but right at that moment he and several other men in grubby overalls were standing chatting and putting the world to rights as they drank steaming mugs of tea from white metal mugs with a rim of royal blue that had been dispensed from the hatch of a mobile canteen, which had pulled up beside the workers.

'Oh, bother,' said Sukie. 'This sort of thing happens all the time. But look at how those chaps are loving the mobile canteen – they are really popular.'

'Well, I'm not surprised,' said Evie. 'It must be a filthy job doing all this clearing up, and I know I'd love a cup of tea if I'd been working hard. And actually, that makes me gasp for one too right now – this baby seems to demand I get filled up constantly.'

'I know where we'll go,' said Sukie, and led Evie back towards Trafalgar Square and the trusty Lyons Corner House. 'I guess an incendiary has taken the water main out, although it didn't happen on my watch as this is one of my streets – it happens all the time. There's not been anything like that in Lymbridge, I hope?'

Evie said that aside from rationing and making do and mending becoming ever more constricting, Lymbridge was, so far, unscathed from having had a physical pasting and was pretty much as it had been when Sukie and Pattie had left. It wasn't the same at their nearest large town, Plymouth, as this south coast port had been very heavily bombed.

Sukie nodded, although she knew this already because a lot of the damage there had happened before she had left Devon. It was because of Plymouth's strategic position close to where Britain pointed its toe towards the Atlantic, but also because of the large naval docks that formed a vital part of the lively fabric of the town.

'Of course, we read the newspapers and listen to the wireless, but it is shocking actually to see what it's like in London,' said Evie. 'It's my first time here and I just wasn't expecting it to be quite as grim as this.'

'I know,' Sukie agreed. 'I felt exactly the same when Pattie and I first arrived, as the bomb damage was mind-blowing, and the queues of women waiting outside the shops for their family's rations staggeringly long, but now all of this merely feels a part of everyday life, and actually I notice more the way people laugh and chat. I can't decide whether that is a good thing or a bad thing. It is horrible sometimes, and especially if children are hurt. And when I'm fire-watching, I always hope that when an incendiary drops I'm not watching people lose their lives.'

'I think you are marvellous,' said Evie. 'It's so brave of you to be up on the roof night after night with no protection and getting rained on. I take my hat off to you, really I do.'

Sukie shook her head and said she didn't deserve any praise. There were many much braver people than her, and all she had to do was sit on her bottom for a few hours.

'And you saying that, Sukie Scott, reminds me why I love you so much,' said Evie, leaning over to give her friend a peck on the check.

At the Lyons Corner House they were quickly shown to a table at the back and served almost immediately with Camp coffee and toasted fruit tea cakes.

When the tea cakes came, Evie's had just three currants and Sukie's two, and this made them laugh.

'What lovely surprises, Evie Rose, both seeing you, and to find out that there's going to be a little Evie and Peter soon.' Sukie looked at Evie after they had sat in a moment or two of silence. 'I almost feel like it's old times again.'

'I wish I could take the credit for it, but actually it was Mr Smith's idea – although not the baby bit, of course! – as he was coming up to London anyway, and so he suggested that Peter and I could have a ride up in his car and that way I could spend a little time with you. I thought I should do it while I can, as once this baby arrives I'm going to be tied to the house for a while.'

'Dear Mr Smith,' said Sukie. 'He had a bunch of flowers delivered to the Eddy when Wesley died, saying I would be very sad but if I looked closely at them I could see that the world offers great beauty as well as great tragedy. I've no idea how he managed to do this, but they were lovely.'

'Yes, he is a sweetie, just like always. And I suppose he has friends in high places that can arrange things like flowers even now. But we had to leave at two o'clock this morning, can you believe? We drove in near pitch-black almost all the way to London. Once I'd told Pattie I wanted to surprise you and she thought it a good idea as you were so down, then Mr Smith telephoned the Edwardes and had to use a funny voice apparently when he asked to be put through to Mr Bright, just in case it was you who answered.'

Sukie nodded, as she knew how persuasive Mr Smith could be. For an older gent, he really was an exceptionally nice person. He had been instrumental in so many things that had gone on in Lymbridge, and of course in getting Pattie and Sukie their jobs at the Eddy.

'Peter is here in town too, but you won't see him unfortunately as he is doing something hush-hush over in Whitehall, and you won't see Mr Smith either, as right after dropping me off he left for Dover, as he's got to run some checks on something there,' Evie went on, 'although I think he'll be back at his flat later. He is putting Peter and me up at the flat tonight, which is nice of him, and Peter and I shall get the train back tomorrow.'

Sukie smiled. Evie was obviously proud of what it had taken to bring the two dear friends together, and Sukie was humbled that such an effort had been made on her behalf, although it was *so* good to see Evie. But what a long way to come, just for a few hours; Sukie considered herself very lucky.

Peter had also moved to Lymbridge early in the war, around the time that Mr Smith had, and was involved in top-secret scientific work that had him squirrelled away in hidden offices underneath the auxiliary hospital. Sukie had never quite known precisely what area Peter was such an expert in, even back when she had worked on the floor directly above his, although Evie had said once that it was something to do with him developing a visual system to help British pilots fly at night.

Sukie looked across the table at Evie. Her friend looked contented, and very well. Married life was clearly suiting her immensely.

For a second Sukie felt envious of Evie's obvious joy, but then she reminded herself to be happy for Evie. She moved a salt cellar to one side and then leaned across the table and reached for Evie's hand. Evie clasped Sukie's back.

'What does Peter think about the baby?' Sukie said.

Evie flushed a little. 'Well, was he surprised! He was so flustered when I told him that he said, "How did that happen?" and when I offered to draw him a diagram, he looked very shocked, and I had to explain I was joking... He's very pleased though and said he'd be *extremely* happy if we have a girl, and *exceptionally* delighted if it's a boy, so I think all bases are covered. And we think Keith is expecting kittens too, so come Christmas we're going to have a full household.'

'Bless him, and bless Keith too.' Sukie smiled. Despite the name 'Keith', the little tabby cat with a rambunctious purr that seemed out of all proportion to her small size was most definitely a female, and Sukie knew how fond Evie was of her. 'I dare say Keith will be jealous when you have your own baby to look after, and will be cross that you won't be pandering to her every whim as I expect you still do. And if you have a little girl I'm sure she will be just like you, and a boy exactly like Peter. Well, fingers crossed it's that way around!'

They laughed at the thought of a girl looking like Peter and a boy like Evie.

Then Evie turned serious.

'Pattie has been very, very worried about you, you know, and so I have I,' Evie said gently, and the happy look faded from Sukie's face. 'She telephoned me several times to say how concerned she has been and written me, and Mother, countless letters about this. I've not known what to do or say for the best – it was a dreadful thing that you have been through – but I didn't want my letters to seem as if they were putting you on the spot. I know how much Wesley meant to you. Did you know that Julia and I went to church, and the vicar said a special prayer for Wesley?

'And the very next week after Pattie told us what had happened I found out for definite I was probably nearly four months pregnant, although I had wondered for a while as I was getting so plump and suddenly craved herrings, which I'd always found repulsive before. And then I felt that I couldn't tell you just then about the baby, as it seemed wrong that I felt so happy just as you were feeling very sad and dreadful. For a long while it seemed to me that if I did say anything to you, it would be as if I was rubbing salt into your wounds. It meant too I couldn't tell Pattie either as she is such a blabbermouth, and I knew she wouldn't be able to keep it secret.'

Sukie knew that like herself, Evie was only at best an irregular churchgoer, and so she thought her friend had made a heartfelt gesture by requesting a prayer be said for Wesley.

She wanted to insist to Evie that she would have loved to hear about the coming baby, but actually that would have been a lie, at least shortly after Wesley had died. Sukie was candid enough to acknowledge privately that she would have felt at least a tiny bit bitter over Evie's happy news coming at the same time as she was feeling so desperate.

Sukie didn't want to spoil the still-lovely feeling between them though by admitting to this openly, and so instead she said, 'Evie, I can't tell you how wonderful it is to see you. I've missed you so much.'

Evie promptly burst into tears. She insisted they were tears of pleasure at the nice thing Sukie had said, but Sukie wasn't sure. And then Evie said that being pregnant might also be to blame – everything seemed to make her cry these days, even watching Mr Smith check the pressure in his car tyres that morning before they set off from Devon.

Sukie admitted that likewise she was still feeling a bit bruised and soft-hearted, and that she had found herself welling up only the previous morning when she saw a pigeon on the nearby roof that had only one leg, and this was in spite of the pigeon seeming perfectly happy with its current situation.

They each made a silly face over their soppiness, and then agreed they were an utter pair of nincompoops.

Chapter Fourteen

Unfortunately Evie and Peter had to head back to Devon first thing the following morning as Peter was needed urgently back in his office. Sukie had noticed Evie looked a bit swollen-ankled and in need of some time with her feet up. She was sorry to see them go, and very touched that Evie had made the effort to come all the way to London just to spend a little time with her, as clearly it had been exhausting for her.

Mr Bright allowed Sukie to go and wave them off from Paddington Station, Pattie once again covering her shift.

Peter seemed older and a bit careworn, Sukie thought as she looked at him in the grey light of a dour November day as they huddled outside the station in the icy blustery wind that whipped at her and Evie's skirts. It was hard to believe how balmy the bright weather of the previous day had been.

She wondered if the exceptionally long hours Peter had been putting in on secretly developing work for night-time aircraft systems were starting to catch up with him. The arrival of a new baby wouldn't do much to make sure he was getting good quality sleep in the few hours he did have to spend at home, Sukie was sure, but she doubted that either he or Evie would give their lack of sleep a second thought once their baby had arrived. She hoped that would be the case, anyway.

Peter shook Sukie's hand very warmly as they said goodbye to each other, and then he stood politely to one side, as Sukie and Evie then extravagantly hugged each other farewell. Peter was always polite, Sukie thought; if she ever had to sum him up in one word, 'polite' would be the word that she would choose. Evie's descriptive word would be 'irrepressible', Sukie decided as she savoured a final sniff of Evie's hair, which smelled, as it always did, of the heather and gorse and the fresh moorland air of the Dartmoor tors, making Sukie feel terribly homesick for a moment.

Sukie was pleased to note the loving way Peter helped Evie onto the train, and then how fondly he fussed around his wife, making sure she was comfy in her seat and that their overnight bag was safely stowed out of harm's way on the rack above their seats. He had to open the window to hand Sukie a jar of home-made mincemeat for a Christmas treat of mince pies, Evie must have been carrying it around in her bag all the time and nearly forgotten to give it to her.

The train's whistle blew, and for a moment Sukie was struck by how radiant Evie looked as she waved her lace-edged hankie at Sukie; marriage and pregnancy really suited her, that much was plain to see.

With only the minutest sliver of jealousy somewhere just behind her heart, Sukie waved them off with a mouthed goodbye of 'You're nearly a mummy!' as she grinned at Evie as she trotted along the station platform, keeping pace with their window as the train began to chug slowly West Country-bound.

Evie guessed more or less what Sukie meant and with both of her white-gloved hands she blew Sukie a kiss, and then mimed rocking a baby in her arms. The last that Sukie saw of Evie was Evie holding an imaginary bit of mistletoe above her head and blowing Sukie a kiss. The smiles on Evie and Sukie's faces perfectly matched each other's.

What a wonderful few hours, Sukie thought, as her pace fell to a walk. Evie was always such a tonic, and Sukie felt all the better for seeing her, although she had a pang of disappointment that, for the first time ever, they wouldn't be seeing each other on Christmas Day.

Sukie told herself she must remember to thank Mr Bright very much for letting her spend a little time with Evie; it was beyond what he had to do, and Sukie very much appreciated his gesture. She wondered if she could take him a small gift back as a thank you.

Once the train was completely out of view Sukie felt her grin fade slowly as she turned to head back towards the concourse, her attention caught by the colourful posters that adorned the station's outer flank as she walked.

'Be Like Dad – Keep Mum!' exhorted one poster, while another had a blue-boiler-suited, muscular-armed and very determined-looking Rosie the Riveter insisting from beneath the jaunty red headscarf keeping her hair in place, 'We Can Do It!', with Rosie vying for attention with a green poster pasted next to hers that said 'Food is a Weapon – Don't Waste It! Buy Wisely – Cook Carefully – Eat It all'.

Sukie liked the attitude of Rosie the Riveter; she looked saucy, and strong. Sukie wanted to be like that. She smiled to herself as she imagined what Mr Bright would say if she dared to wear a boiler suit and roll up her sleeves to show a muscular forearm.

Sukie thought the posters did a good job of reminding people that it was the small things that counted for a lot on the home front. It might not sound much if somebody bit back a snippet of gossip, but the truth of it could be that if something sensitive was said near somebody who shouldn't hear it, then it could end a life. And food wastage was not to be condoned in any circumstance, even though that sentiment was sometimes hard to swallow if the food were burned and yet you were being told to eat up as 'it has an egg in it'. Sukie realised that she had got used to Chef's good cooking, and the availability of food at the Eddy. While the guests weren't rationed, the staff were, but Chef was very clever at preparing delicious food for the Eddies that gave no hint of parsimony and scrimping.

87

Sukie saw that near the end of the wall there was a poster of something to do with American servicemen, but she couldn't read what the slogan said because someone has used what looked to be some charcoal to scribble in angry letters on the poster's surface 'Yanks – Hands Off Our Wives!', the writer being so impassioned that the charcoal letters had been gone over again and again. Sukie was a bit surprised that nobody in the concourse at Paddington Station had stopped whoever it was who had written these furious words, but then she thought that everyone had better things to do these days than get excited by some comments daubed on a poster.

As if by black magic, she suddenly heard a cheerily happy sound, a loud laugh that caused her to turn to see who had made that jubilant noise. She was surprised to see that it came from a small group of American GIs who were waiting for their train.

Despite the pent-up emotion lying behind the graffiti on the last poster – feelings she could understand as some women, starved of their menfolk away fighting, were having their heads turned by handsome Americans now flooding the country – Sukie found herself grinning.

'Good luck,' she called to the GIs as she passed, who raised their fingers to their caps in salute of her acknowledgement.

Determinedly not looking their way again, and before they could try and engage her attention further, Sukie headed swiftly towards the sign to the underground station where she made for the Bakerloo line that would take her down to Trafalgar Square tube station.

The GIs had all looked strong and healthy, and as if they were nice and well-brought-up young men, Sukie thought. They seemed a beacon of light and hopefulness in a pretty bleak world. She very much hoped that they would all make it unscathed through their time in Europe.

She wondered if the GIs understood that Sukie, and most of the British public, were very grateful for their presence (the person who'd made their feelings clear on the poster aside, of course). She hoped they did.

As she had left the tube station Sukie spied a Romany woman, who looked very dejected and down at heel, selling small plants of violets in tiny clay pots. 'Dearie, cross my hand with silver for good luck,' she said, when Sukie stopped to look.

Sukie dug out sixpence from her purse and purchased two small pots. She had no idea whether Mr Bright or Mrs Bridge liked violets, but she hoped they would each appreciate the gesture. She wanted them to know she was grateful for the kindness they had shown and, after all, who didn't need a little bit of good luck these days?

Back at the Eddy, Sukie was just relieving Jane of the reception desk when Mr Bright stuck his head around his office door with a 'I trust your friends got off safely'.

Sukie smiled and thrust one of the small pots into his hands, saying, 'Yes, thank you, they did, Mr Bright. I very much appreciate you letting me see them off, and allowing me to spend a little time with my friend yesterday. I hope you don't mind such a small gift, but I'm told this will bring you luck.'

Mr Bright opened and shut his mouth; it was the first time Sukie had seen him lost for words. Then, with a curt nod in her direction, he hurriedly withdrew into his office.

Two weeks and a day later, on 19th November, Sukie and Pattie received a joint telegram from Peter that announced the arrival of a little girl who was to be called Petronella Sukie Pipe, or Nellie for short. She had been 6 lb 1 oz, and mother and Nellie were doing famously.

Sukie and Pattie had an unexpected couple of hours off that afternoon, as the hotel was being inspected to make sure it was meeting the latest fire regulations and so Mr Bright was overseeing this personally, and had told a proportion of the staff to go to their rooms in case the inspectors thought them a hazard, at which the Eddies couldn't help but chortle.

But up in their bedroom, what began as 'Let's knit something for Nellie' quickly descended into chaos.

'I can't do a purl, let alone a plain and then a purl,' moaned Sukie, once she had spent nearly an hour on just the toe of a bootee, after spending an inordinate amount of time unpicking and then rolling a ball of two-ply from a cardie she had never particularly liked and had rarely worn, and which she thought would make both the sets of bootees that Pattie and she would make.

And Pattie's tension was so loose that her first bootee looked as if it would fit most five-year-olds.

'You twerp,' cried Polly. Pattie threw her bootee gently at him. He grabbed hold and then wouldn't let it go, holding it aloft in a claw as he shouted, 'Rum.'

'Yes, very rum,' said Sukie, trying to distract Polly with a peanut. Polly held on to the bootee, while swiftly snaffling the peanut with his other foot.

It was all downhill from there, and it wasn't long before Sukie and Pattie had to admit defeat on the knitting front. They decided to club together to pay one of the Eddies to knit a layette very quickly from the wool that was in the rest of the cardie (luckily there was an arm and the back that hadn't been purloined for the first attempt), and a couple of days later they posted the small and now beautifully worked garments off to Evie.

As Pattie said to Sukie on the way back from the post office, 'We won't be fooling Evie, as she'll know we haven't made these ourselves. In fact, she'll be thankful we haven't, as these are much nicer that what we could have done, and so she and Nellie will be thrilled.'

Back in their bedroom, Sukie looked again at the two bootees she had completed after far too many hours, and she had to agree. It was hard to imagine the mother who would have been delighted to receive two such monstrosities, or the baby that could have been born with such wildly differing-sized feet that he or she could actually have worn the bootees.

Polly meanwhile was delighted with his plaything, and for days afterwards was usually to be found with the increasingly ramshackle bootee in his claw, waving it at Pattie as if it were a small trophy, and one that he was very proud of, and so it wasn't long before Sukie was writing to Evie.

Dearest Evie,

I wish you were here with us to see what has happened to Pattie's woeful bootee. Polly believes it a prize of the highest order. I am thinking, however, that Polly might need some specs...

While Sukie was sorry she didn't have more skills at knitting, she wasn't going to let this get in the way of having a small joke at Pattie's expense. Pattie must have felt similarly, although Sukie never discovered quite what Pattie had said to her sister.

For Sukie received a letter from Evie a few days later, and on the back of the envelope for anyone to see, Evie had drawn a cartoon of Polly wearing bootees and sucking on a dummy. Evie had wreathed her sketch with decorative sprigs of festive holly and a small double frond of mistletoe dangled above Polly's head.

Sukie chuckled when she noticed this last touch as Christmas wasn't very far away, and Evie knew how much she loved it.

Evie was an inventive and very skilled caricaturist, in spite of never having seen Polly, and Sukie thought the drawing so fine that she tacked it to the wall of the lavatory on the staff floor.

What tickled her especially was that the design of each bootee comprised a word: one read 'Pattie', and the other – of course – 'Sukie'.

It started a craze of the other Eddies drawing two bootees that they would pin up, putting a word on one bootee, leaving another Eddie to match it. 'Christmas' and 'Carol' was followed by 'Frankincense' and 'Myrrh', and then 'Egg' and 'Nog', and so on. It was after 'Brandy' and 'Butter' that Pattie couldn't resist adding 'Rum' to the bootee of a new pair she'd drawn, and Sukie then had to add 'M.B.', as she knew Pattie would remember Polly's 'Where's the rum, Mr Bright?' Although Sukie didn't dare actually put 'Mr Bright' on the other bootee in case he were ever to see it and had only risked initials.

Chapter Fifteen

'Excuse me, Miss, er, *Miss Scott*.'

There was something vaguely off-kilter about the owner of the voice as it leaned down to look at the badge on Sukie's left lapel where she had written her name. It had been Sukie's idea that all the staff wore name badges, and she had spent a whole afternoon writing the names with a flourish of her italic pen, although after the first couple she had to forgo including Christian names as it was taking too long to pencil them into the space on the badges so that the words looked well spaced and not unduly squashed.

Although her ears were ordinarily pretty sharp at detecting all sorts of things about a speaker, this time Sukie couldn't tell if she was being addressed by a man or a woman. She hadn't heard anyone sneak up to the reception desk, which was quite a feat too on the hard shininess of the black and white floor tiles. Sukie's interest was piqued.

Trying not to be anything less than completely professional, she stopped her musings on Christmas tree availability and Christmas party games, and looked up from filling her pen with ink, and smiled.

Hmmmn. Sukie felt no wiser now that she could see the person before her.

The garb was distinctly male – the elephant-grey pinstripe suit and shiny conker-brown brogues definitely looked expensive and spankingly unworn in a pre-war embracing of luxury manner that one rarely came across nowadays – and there was a sharp shirt and tie under the suit's jacket; however, the androgynous face before her was smooth-skinned, as if never shaved. Despite the brevity of her glimpse, Sukie was able to spy eyebrows so exact they must have been shaped with tweezers, and short dark hair that had been expertly pomaded so that in the shine of the lamp on reception she was reminded of how the light of the moon would glint at night-time on what would look like the oily slick on the velvety undulations of the River Thames. When Sukie had first arrived in London, she had loved going down to the nearby river to look across its broad expanse at the moonlight shimmering across its tidal ebbs and flows. Lately she had been wishing there could be fireworks like back in the old days to celebrate Guy Fawkes and then the festive season, and later to see in the New Year, as she would have loved to see the sparkles and rockets reflected romantically in the water.

'Good afternoon. How may I assist you?' Sukie asked.

She realised there was something exciting about the way this person looked. The first time Sukie had experienced a similar thrill was when she and Wesley had gone to the flicks to see *Morocco*. It was an old film but Sukie had never seen a woman wear men's clothes in quite the way that Marlene Dietrich did, and she had found it an eye-opener.

'I wonder if you might have a vacancy, for tonight and to-morrow, possibly continuing for several more days after that, and maybe even longer?'

'Let me check.' Sukie knew very well that the Eddy had several room vacancies as they weren't at full occupation, despite the general shortage of hotel rooms in London, as there had been a couple of most unwelcome cancellations just the day before.

But she wanted the excuse of pulling the bookings chart before her as that way she might be able to risk a look at the enquirer's hands as she turned her eyes downwards, as neither the voice nor its owner were hinting quite clearly enough yet as to the sex of the speaker.

'Double or single, and with a bath, or without?' Sukie enquired.

The hands were larger certainly than most women's, Sukie noticed in the briefest of brief glances that she dared cast that way, and if she wasn't mistaken, they had been manicured as that soft sheen of the nails looked as if buffed. But they were elegant hands that seemed slightly at odds with their size. The owner sported a mannish gold signet ring on a little finger, and Sukie couldn't prevent her eyelids fractionally widening apart when she spied, thrillingly, a tiny coiled snake that looked to be tattooed between the two finger joints on the front of the middle finger that was right before her. Sukie had never seen anything like this before, and it seemed impressively daring, and very, very slightly challenging.

'A double, ideally, and with bath.'

'Let me see what I can do,' Sukie said.

The guest sniffed gently as if imagining something unbearably naughty that Sukie might be able to do for him or her.

How forward. But, Sukie thought, how strange that it didn't feel in the slightest offensive, or at least not in the skin-crawling way that some of the Eddy's male guests occasionally made her feel during her interactions with them.

She'd come to be on her guard when an obviously drunk older man would lurch across the hotel foyer in her direction, as some of their 'personal' requests could be thoroughly outrageous, not that she'd ever said as much to Mr Bright. She felt that if she did so, he'd be in a quandary, both wanting to protect her honour, but wanting also not to upset any well-heeled guest, and she didn't want to put him in that position.

Sukie had discovered that if she totally ignored the inappropriate requests and comments, then after a while most people gave in gracefully. Stephen was good at keeping an eye on things too, and so he would come and stand by the reception desk, and ask very clearly if he could be of any assistance, while Michael and Alan would hover in the background for backup, if needed.

So far, these techniques had been enough, and Sukie hoped very much that she was never going to be tested further.

Just in case though, she had brought an old school bell from a junk shop on Fleet Street. She'd tested the bell in the shop to make sure it was loud – it certainly was! – and that it didn't sound in any way like the air-raid siren. And then she placed it within easy reach of anyone working behind reception, on a lower shelf near the floor. Sukie told everyone that anyone on reception or at the door of the Eddy could clang the bell in an emergency. Jane and Pattie had both said they felt safer for knowing it was there, and they all agreed that somebody would have to be both *very* forward and *very* drunk to persist if the school bell was alerting the Eddies that there was trouble in reception.

'Ah yes, we have the River Suite – it's a trifle pricier as it has a small sitting room as part of the room price, but it is a king-size double, with its own bath. Or, if you prefer, we have a single on the third floor, with no bath, and naturally that rate would be much more economical,' Sukie explained to the owner of the snake tattoo.

Mr Bright encouraged Sukie always to offer the more expensive room first, and then to draw attention to the 'economy' of the cheaper room. As often as not, guests liked to show they didn't need to compromise on the best they could afford.

And naturally Sukie was very aware that in terms of income coming in to a hotel like the Eddy, it was much better if the expensive rooms were filled first, as those rooms made much more profit. Just like every other establishment in London, the Eddy had cut as many staff from its roster as was feasible and watched every penny as profit had been cut to the bone compared to what it had been pre-war, and so Mr Bright was always saying to the Eddies that they needed to encourage people to spend as much as possible while on the premises.

Now, as it nearly always did, the technique of drawing attention to the merits of the more expensive room worked as, squirrelling out a sizeable fold of money from a trouser pocket, the speaker said, 'In that case, the River Suite it is. I'd like to pay in advance. I'll leave some money on account to cover *extras*.'

There was a perk of challenge about the lilt of the word 'extras'. Sukie didn't dare dwell on what the speaker might have in mind.

More than a couple of large denomination notes were removed from the fold and passed across the reception desk to Sukie.

She said thank you and slid the register and a pen towards the guest, who signed with a flourish as Tracy Benn, with the address column on the large page other guests had filled in above as simply: Whitehall. That was less than a mile away, but perhaps there had been bomb damage, and in any case it wasn't unusual for the well heeled in London to spend a lot of time living in hotels because this meant they could avoid food rationing.

Damn and blast. Sukie had dealt with female *and* males guests with the Christian name Tracy, and now she didn't know whether to say Mr Benn, or Mrs Benn or even Miss Benn. There was no sign of a wedding ring but of course not everyone wore a wedding ring even if they were wed, and especially if they were moneyed.

Sukie turned around to get the room key from the rack on the wall behind her, and as she did so she beckoned the bellboy over, with a 'The River Suite please, Michael'.

Michael picked up a barely worn, sturdy brown leather suitcase standing next to reception, and surreptitiously caught Sukie's eye. He was wondering about Tracy Benn too, it seemed. It was a large suitcase, and was evidently heavy to judge by Michael's stifled grunt of effort. Michael wasn't an especially short person even though he'd had polio as a child and had an affected leg that meant a built-up shoe on one foot, but this guest towered over him in height.

Sukie ignored Michael, and stared straight into the guest's eyes as she said, 'I very much hope you enjoy your stay with us at the Edwardes. Do let me know if there's anything I can do to assist you.'

'Thank you. And I like to be known as Tracy, by the way,' the guest replied with an intense and unblinking look.

Sukie couldn't quite bring herself to let Tracy Benn disappear just yet. She found there to be something most alluring about the self-assurance of this new guest; it was fascinating. 'We start serving supper at seven, if you plan to eat in the restaurant.'

'And would you recommend eating here?' came the almost drawling reply.

'Chef is very experienced, and we are lucky to have him.' Sukie had a spare menu on reception just for this purpose, and she passed it across the desk.

There was a moment when they looked into each other's eyes again.

Michael escorted Tracy Benn into the lift, the bellboy looking diminutive beside the tall guest as they squeezed into the small space, either side of the leather suitcase. Sukie felt her eyes had been opened. She didn't know to what, or to whom, but nonetheless she felt she had just experienced a clarion call to confidence and individuality.

For while the men's suit had been beautifully tailored, Sukie was almost sure that Tracy Benn was wearing mascara, and had liberally doused temples and wrists with Houbigant Chantilly ladies' perfume. Well, Sukie was one hundred per cent sure about the scent, truth be told.

She recognised the smell of the distinctive scent as she had once heard one of their posher guests asking a mink-clad woman when they ran into each other in the foyer what the *divine* fragrance was that she was wearing – the same as this – and Chantilly had been the answer.

Not long afterwards Sukie had been sent out illicitly by Stephen one day in her lunchtime to buy another patron some cologne for his wife, and she had seen Chantilly for sale as she stood by one of the perfume counters in Selfridges, near Marble Arch. Asking the price, she was shocked to discover that a small bottle cost far more than she earned in a whole week.

And – the sight of this had been tantalisingly brief but Sukie knew what she had observed – there had been a small indentation above Tracy Benn's left eyebrow that told Sukie a piercing had been inserted there until very recently.

Deep in thought, Sukie began to doodle a picture of a coiled snake in the margin of a memo she was drafting to Mr Bridge about whether if once or twice a week they got in a pianist who could also sing. Then the Eddy could provide a soft background atmosphere that might encourage diners to linger longer over supper and maybe enjoy some after-dinner drinks. The benefit to the Eddy being that they possibly might be able to charge a small additional cover charge, Sukie felt.

Mr Bright stepped out of the lift several minutes later.

'Might you have a moment, Mr Bright?' said Sukie. She was a trifle hesitant as she hadn't expected to see him just then but she spoke before she had quite meant to.

Mr Bright looked at her in his tight-lipped way that Sukie had always thought was designed to put off Eddies coming to him with their problems.

She pictured the tattoo and imagined the Chantilly scent – would Tracy Benn be put off by a mere look? Sukie wondered.

She doubted it, and so she took heart.

'Would you like a cup of tea?' Sukie enquired in a stronger voice. 'I was thinking you might have five minutes to listen to how we might be able to add a slightly larger cover charge one or two nights a week in the restaurant.'

Mr Bright looked at Sukie appraisingly. 'I think Chef has just baked some ginger biscuits when you go downstairs. And do bring a cup up for yourself, after you've made sure there is cover on reception,' he said.

Sukie spied Alan, who was talking to Michael at the other side of the foyer.

She went over to him with her very best smile on her face, and said, 'It will only be for a minute, and so I wonder if you can hold the fort on reception while I have a word with Mr Bright. Anything difficult and I'll only be in the office behind reception.'

Alan turned a bit pink, and he stuck a finger at the front of his shirt collar and gave a pull as if to loosen it. Sukie's best smile often had that effect.

'Delighted, I'm sure.'

'You are wonderful. And if Chef has made some ginger biscuits, as Mr Bright claims, I'll make sure to bring you one,' Sukie said to him, still smiling. 'I might even give you a shilling for a bet the next time you are in the bookies, as long as I can choose the runner and rider!'

Alan's cheeks turned quite ruby.

Chapter Sixteen

Dearest Evie,

Thank you for the scarf – it is toasty warm, and I can say that most definitely as I am wearing it <u>right now</u>, in my eyrie on the roof. What a thoughtful present, from the most thoughtful of thoughtful friends! Take a bow, Evie Pipe!

I don't have much news otherwise, other than life goes on pretty much as when you visited. Mr Bright is still Mr Bright, and Pattie is Pattie. She and John seem tight, which is keeping her cheerful. I'm throwing myself into life at the Eddy – do you remember that New Year's party that you started to organise, when Wesley turned up to sing? Every time I plan something new here – and I'm starting to think 'Christmas!' – I think back to that night, and it still makes me laugh every time. What a lovely party that was, especially coming so soon after you had had such a miserable Christmas with the influenza, and so I think it really perked you up.

Meanwhile, how are you, and Nellie, and Peter? All well, I

That was as far as Sukie had got before she lost interest in her letter, which she was scribbling in the vivid moonlight that made the night seem almost as brightly lit as day. Luckily, Jerry seemed to have other things to do, and she hadn't heard the engine throb of a single aeroplane during this evening stint on the roof.

But although this evening was perishing cold, Sukie thought it was one of the most tranquil times she had been on fire-watching duty, so quiet while up on high she was certain she could have heard a pin drop far down in the street. Her breath caught in her throat as it was all very beautiful, as the sky looked velvety black, and the rooftops around her somehow even darker, with a moon that shone out a gossamer silver light. It was breathtaking, no matter which way Sukie stared around her.

She heard a noise behind her, and she turned around to see Pattie wobbling up through the skylight, carrying a Thermos.

'Oh, Pattie! Thank you,' said Sukie. 'What a treat.'

She shuffled along the wooden plank to make room for Pattie, who pulled out from her pocket a folded napkin that turned out to contain a slice of still-warm toast folded over, with a sardine inside, which she pushed Sukie's way.

'Housekeeping says you need feeding up,' said Pattie. 'And so Chef's put a whole teaspoon of sugar in your cocoa.'

'Bless,' said Sukie.

For the first time in ages she felt peckish, and she made short work of the toast. She told Pattie to share the cocoa with her, as a thank you for climbing all the way up on to the roof with these treats.

'Slow night tonight?'

'Nothing happening,' said Sukie. 'So far nothing to report.'

In her time as a fire-watcher, she had been very diligent in her duties, and her team leader had been full of praise, insisting she had saved many lives. Privately, however, Sukie didn't feel that an ability to stay awake, or a knack for studying a floppy-paged *Geographers' A-Z Street Atlas* in the dim light of a torch so that she could pass on an accurate location for the fire-fighters, or her efficient way of scooting back down the fold-out ladder to the corridor below to make a call to HQ, really counted as 'saving lives'. That accolade should be reserved for those who dash fearlessly into a burning building to bring out the injured, or who would check smoking ruins for survivors with barely a thought as to how unsafe the badly damaged building above might be, Sukie was convinced.

'A bit like downstairs then tonight,' said Pattie.

Evidently it felt as slow down in the depths of the Eddy, as it did from up here, Sukie thought. Sometimes the Eddy did feel very lifeless indeed, with time hanging heavily on everybody's hands. At other times it felt abuzz with people and activity. It was very hard to predict. It was almost as if the hotel had a personality all of its own, and Sukie rather liked that about the Eddy.

They talked about what London would look like if there were no blackout. Christmas wasn't far away, and many people would have had trees in their windows, with small candles burning brightly.

'What a fire risk' Sukie was just starting to say when there was a faint squawking sound from the floor below. Sukie and Pattie laughed; they knew who *that* was.

Although she didn't want to admit outright to Pattie that Polly had livened up their bedroom no end, as he always seemed to have something to say, Sukie did find him quite diverting. He was, most definitely, a parrot of immense character, even if this character was 'mostly bad' (Sukie, jokingly) or 'funny and quick-witted' (Pattie, seriously, seemingly unaware that Polly didn't understand what he was saying).

'Evie says I am to find out how you are,' said Pattie.

'Well, you can tell Evie that I think her visit was the turning point – I've felt much, much better since then. It was *so* lovely to see her, and I'm thrilled for her and Peter that Nellie seems to be thriving. In fact I was just writing to her when you came up.'

'It looked more like staring over the rooftops to me, rather than writing. Actually I think Evie is wondering more how you are feeling now about what happened with Wesley?' Pattie said gently. This was the first time since Wesley's death that Pattie had been quite so forthright, having contented herself previously in skirting around the issue much more vaguely.

'I'm not sure, to be honest. There are good days, and not-so-good days. Today has been quite a good day,' said Sukie, realising that she didn't much feel like talking about it, at least not right now, and for some reason not with Pattie, which was probably to do with the fact that right after Wesley had died, Sukie had probably talked about him too much with her room-mate.

But she didn't want Pattie to feel that she was avoiding the question, and so to distract Pattie, Sukie paused and then asked something she had been wondering about, 'What about you? How are you and John getting on?'

Sukie hadn't realised that she'd voiced quite such a leading question.

But Pattie launched into a glowing description of their relationship, which actually had far too much information. It seemed that John was *wonderful*, that he knew *everything* and that he could kiss *like a dream*. And so on.

'You think he's happy working on the river?' said Sukie. 'It must seem tame after sailing with the Merchant Navy.'

'His shoulder still isn't great, and isn't ever likely to be, not for a ship at sea. Not that there are many cargo ships now, what with the U-boats. And so I think John likes the river ambulance well enough. He told me though that it's London where he really wants to be,' Pattie whispered, almost as if John was in danger of overhearing their conversation.

'So, do you think you two will make this official in some way?' Sukie asked. 'If you don't have any doubts, that is.'

'Well, I'd like to, now, I think,' replied Pattie. 'But if I ever say anything that might suggest that we plan for something in the future, he always points out that I'm young and that it's best not to rush things, and so I think we're waiting.'

'Best not to rush things for whom?' said Sukie, before she could stop herself. 'You, or him?'

'I hadn't thought about it like that.'

Pattie's formerly happy tone now sounded subdued and doubtful, and Sukie felt a bit mean. She was incredibly fond of Pattie and the last thing she wanted to do was rain on her parade if she and John really were perfect for each other, and were destined to spend the rest of their lives together. And Sukie was incredibly pleased that John had made Pattie so cheerful over the past months, of course she was.

It was just that John did seem a bit worldly-wise. And, in Sukie's eyes at least, he appeared to have a bit too much influence over Pattie, who was indeed, as he had pointed out, still very young.

But Sukie thought it wiser not to say any of this. Either the relationship would fizzle, or Pattie and John would become closer. She certainly didn't want to create any trouble, as John had always been very pleasant to her, and it was very possible that she was a trifle cautious about him simply because of the painful emotions she had herself experienced over the past few months and he had just been around during this very testing time.

And so Sukie put her arm around Pattie's shoulders and pulled her close. 'Is there any of that cocoa left?' she said, and Pattie said she thought there might be, but if there wasn't she would pop down to the kitchen and make some more.

Chapter Seventeen

Late at night a day or two later – or was it the early hours of the following morning? – Sukie climbed wearily down from her latest fire-watching stretch. She could see it had been a busy night south of the river, but the local fire-watchers there would have dealt with that. It had been a quiet time for her. But while the effects of the aerial activity hadn't been too bad around Covent Garden, the drone of planes and the erratic flashes had made her jumpy and tense.

She stood stock-still in surprise, just inside her and Pattie's open bedroom door, when she discovered Pattie wearing her crocheted bed jacket and sitting up in the narrow single bed on her side of the room. Pattie's knees were crooked upwards towards the ceiling and her hands wrapped around a mug of weak cocoa.

Polly was under the blanket, but she could hear him softly mimicking the snores emanating from the corridor.

The subdued light from the bedside lamp cast a warm glow over Pattie, and Sukie thought the way her chum was sitting in the puddle of light would make a lovely painting. The shadows she was casting around her looked very dramatic and almost fairytale-like, but while Pattie herself looked the picture of innocence it was in perfect contrast to the murk and gloom of the rest of the bedroom.

'Can't you sleep?' Sukie whispered as she didn't want to wake any of the other Eddies on their floor, as she tried to rub some warmth into her frozen fingers by wringing her hands together. She undid the buttons of her own coat, which she'd named Old Faithful as it had done such sterling service for her up on the roof over this winter and then the buttons on the tweed coat that a guest had left behind many moons ago.

Sukie knew that she appeared much larger than normal in her fire-watching outfit, as she also had pulled on rubber galoshes over her shoes, a blackberry-coloured felt cloche hat and an ancient but very lovely William Morris-patterned Liberty silk scarf around her neck. The look was completed by a giant and hideous knitted blanket knotted over the whole lot that Mrs Bridge had made from odds and ends of wool she'd been able to scavenge. Sukie and Pattie had lovingly nicknamed it 'Thing' after Mrs Bridge presented it to Sukie to wear on the roof as the weather turned wintry. In addition Sukie had had on not one, but two pairs of woollen gloves. And, as she hadn't planned on being seen by any of the guests, she had tucked the skirt of her dress into the roomy twill waistband of her only pair of trousers. It was an extremely chilly night, and despite wrapping up so thoroughly, Sukie felt chilled right down to her very marrow.

Pattie was normally sound asleep the second her head touched the pillow, an ability Sukie was deeply envious of, but tonight she appeared alert and wide awake.

Something must have happened, and it wasn't a good something, Sukie guessed, as Pattie's face was serious.

Sukie knew that she must present a comical sight as she stood there, but Pattie wasn't laughing, instead she seemed to be deep in thought.

'I don't feel tired,' Pattie whispered back to Sukie suddenly, as she lifted her paint-chipped alarm clock to get a better look in the lamplight. 'Although I know I'll be sorry in the morning, as I'll have to be shaking a leg in less than four hours from now. But it was just *too* much tonight.

'Did you hear that Alan had a funny turn almost the moment he went down to the kitchen to get the latest gen for the dinner service, right while he was talking to Housekeeping in the kitchen as he was about to change into his dinner jacket? He's been taken very poorly and is in hospital.'

'Oh no!' said Sukie as she shook her head.

She'd been in their bedroom right after she'd finished on reception at six, taking advantage of a nap for a quarter of an hour despite all of Polly's best intentions at keeping her awake with judicious 'Lord Pattie's bandied about just as Sukie dropped off. And then she had headed straight up to her by now too-familiar eyrie high up on the Eddy's roof, with only a vacuum Thermos flask of some thin carrot and potato soup for company, and the hotel's binoculars to see if there were any blazes she should be alerting the authorities to.

As regards Alan, Sukie had been completely unaware of any shenanigans taking place below stairs at the Eddy. She had been far too distracted over the previous few hours by imagining that if she ever met Dr Carrot or Potato Pete face to face she would have a fair bit of grumbling to do in their direction as Chef seemed to have forgotten about any other vegetables for the Eddies' staff soup just at the moment.

Now, guiltily, Sukie remembered how Alan was always very partial to Chef's soup, and especially if it were carrot, and that he would probably have given anything to be sipping on some right now. He'd joked with her only a couple of days ago that the carrots helped him nip backwards and forwards in the dining room as he escorted people to their tables, and summoned the sommelier, and later gave the diners their bills.

'Luckily,' Pattie elaborated, 'it was just before service began in the dining room – well, not luckily for Alan, obviously – but lucky in that we don't think any of the guests or the diners knew what happened. They might have heard a bit of a crash though, as Alan did knock that large silver soup tureen off the table and on to the floor. He went down like a ninepin, and now the tureen's got a dent you've got to see to believe as it did hit the floor with a big crash, and the lid spun around and around on the flags, making a right racket. Honestly, one moment Alan was talking quite happily, and then he just keeled over without warning. John and I were having a cup of tea in the kitchen, and we'd never seen anything like it. Thank goodness Chef was running a bit late, and so he'd not yet taken the beef consommé off the heat, and this meant the tureen was empty.'

Sukie's mouth watered quickly. Chef often served the guests beef consommé as he'd adapted an old recipe to make something tasty, clear and glossy-looking but that didn't require much actual meat, relying as it did for most of its flavour on some trusty Oxo cubes, some beef bones the butcher would send over for stock, and a secret infusion of herbs that Chef would cut from his beloved flower pots (which were now wintering happily enough along the back of the large wooden draining board in the scullery).

'Anyway,' Pattie said, 'Alan had to be carted unceremoniously off to hospital as John felt for his pulse in his wrist, and said he thought it was dicky. And so Housekeeping told me that I had to go out and hail a taxi on the quiet as the doorman was dealing with a flurry of new guests arriving, which turned out to be easier said than done, and I virtually had to throw myself in front of one who had just done a drop-off here. And – you'll have seen this too – when I got outside I could see there was a lot of ack-ack activity south of the river and so we – John and I, that is – didn't think we'd have been able to get an ambulance to come over to us anyway as it looked as if the ack-acks might have brought down something, as the skies were so lit up it looked like a heavy attack. So John and Michael bundled Alan back into his coat again and then heaved him up the alley to the side street where I was waiting with the taxi that must have been one of the very last ones working, as they wouldn't dare go south of the river if they thought our ack-acks were going to bring down a bomber or two on top of them.'

'Oh my goodness!' exclaimed Sukie, who hadn't wanted to interrupt Pattie. 'Poor Alan! I had no idea.'

'Well, poor Alan must be about a hundred years old—'

'Pattie!' Sukie said. It was a gross exaggeration. The maître d' was no spring chicken certainly, but Sukie knew that he probably wasn't yet fifty years of age. It was at moments like this that Pattie showed just how young she was in her attitude, Sukie thought.

'Pattie!' echoed the blanket in equal admonishment.

Pattie smiled a vague acknowledgement at Sukie's interjection, but she wasn't contrite in the slightest and continued to exaggerate. 'Poor Alan is near enough that old, I'm sure, as he's very grey and his eyes are all crinkly.' Sukie rolled her own eyes at this, with a muttered 'give over', which Pattie might or might not have heard as Sukie was having a bit of a wrestle just then separating the tweed coat from Thing's clutches and so it was possible that her voice had been stifled by a copious amount of irregular knitted wool.

Pattie was undeterred. 'And so when I got back to the kitchen I heard Housekeeping speak to Mr Bright on the telephone in her cubby hole – I don't know where *he* was, but it can't have been in the hotel, as we had to send Alan to St Thomas's in the taxi with only Michael for company as Chef had to go back to getting the dinners ready, although Alan made it clear that he only wanted Michael with him. Michael were right worried, as they've been pals a long time. And Mr Bright never showed his face the whole time, and you know how he loves to get in everyone's way if there's any sort of fun and games going on.'

'Pattie!' Sukie exclaimed a second time, her eyes flicking briefly towards the door.

Although Mr Bright's bedroom was in an almost hidden annexe on the same floor as reception, it would be a poor show if for some reason he was in the corridor outside their room – as would be perfectly within his rights as Mr Bright often threatened a night patrol if he thought there was the slightest whiff of improper behaviour or bedroom hopping between any of the Eddies. ('You are not alley cats,' Sukie having heard him say when Michael had been caught merely pecking the long-departed Beatrice on the cheek as a happy birthday, and that was in the middle of the kitchen with everyone else standing around, and so it was hard to think of a less salacious scenario.)

But if Mr Bright heard by mistake the flippant way with which Pattie was speaking about him, it really wouldn't be very proper at all, and would go down very badly. Indeed the very thought of it made Sukie feel most awkward.

'Anyway, then Housekeeping suggested that John wear Alan's dinner jacket and tie that he always keeps here, and John could step in as maître d' for the evening, and she said that he could be paid for the shift,' Pattie went on. 'And so John worked in the restaurant all night, and did very well from what I've heard.'

'Good for John,' said Sukie levelly, even though she thought Pattie sounded a mite too impressed over John's maître d' abilities. 'I'm sure he's a quick learner. He'd have some experience of the drinks side at least, and as the menu is limited to just three choices for mains today, I can see that he wouldn't have too much trouble in talking the guests through the meals. I wonder if Mr Bright will offer him a regular stint, until Alan gets better?'

'I thought about that too,' said Pattie. 'And to see how bad Alan was in the face as I shut the taxi door on him and gave Michael some money Housekeeping had given me for the fare, I suspect it might be more *if* Alan gets better, rather than *when.*'

Sukie opened her mouth to say 'Pattie!' again, but then gave it up as a bad job and of course it could be that Pattie was right as to Alan's prognosis.

Polly filled the gap with a random 'Lord Pattie'.

Ignoring the parrot, Pattie paused for a moment more, and then she added, 'John enjoyed the service, although he says we've got a pansy staying.'

'Pansy?' Sukie had no idea what Pattie meant.

'You know, a *musical . . .*'

'I'm sorry?'

'Goodness me, how can you be so naïve, Sukie Scott? As I live and breathe! There's a tall, dapper gent staying in River—'

'Oh, you mean Tracy Benn.' Sukie at least knew whom they

were talking about now, even if she was uncertain as to precisely what Pattie was actually alluding to.

'That's him! Your Tracy Benn is a man who likes the attention of other men, or giving said attention, according to John, in an *intimate* way, which, as we all know, is strictly *illegal*. John says he can always tell a lavender.'

Pattie sounded heady at the thought of the Eddies having the chance to rub shoulders, no matter how briefly, with somebody who might be happy to indulge in illicit behaviour well on the other side of the law.

Sukie was more circumspect, although she wondered if what two men would get up to under the cover of darkness, or in a park or squeezed into a stall in some public conveniences, might be much less of an exciting thought for Pattie, if she cared to consider it a bit more deeply.

In fact Sukie had occasionally wondered if the real illicit behaviour of these wartime years – those that dealt in spying and then slipping secrets to the enemy, say, or the spivs who were happily trading black market goods – wouldn't in fact be taking place right under the noses of them all at the Eddy, with neither Mr Bright nor the Eddies being any the wiser. For surely the most successful spies or greasy spivs would look just like any ordinary person, their sheer ordinariness being what would make them good at their illegal goings-on. And the staid respectability of the Eddy would provide a perfect cover as it looked the last place in London where one could imagine illegal plans being made. In comparison, whatever two men got up to late at night in private didn't seem to Sukie to be nearly as reprehensible, as long as they were both willing partners.

'Unless you are very rich and have a huge amount of influence, John says, when the police might just turn a blind eye to what is going on – he calls it cottaging, by the way – and especially if there is a softening backhander for the police. Although, sometimes not even then, as sometimes they need to make an example, John says,' Pattie concluded.

John seemed to have too many views on the matter, Sukie

decided. She didn't care to think too carefully about where Pattie, or John for that matter too, had learned so much about the ways of the world to do with bribes or illegal sexual behaviour. However, it was undeniable that Pattie seemed to know more than Sukie about these things, at any rate.

Sukie thought back to when Tracy Benn had registered at the Eddy.

'No! I don't believe it. There's what I think might be a tattoo on one finger that I wanted to gawp at a bit more than I could, but I still don't think John is correct about that guest.' Sukie's murmured opinion was nevertheless staunch in her defence of Tracy Benn despite the low volume at which she spoke, while the sharpness in Pattie's answering but wryly amused expression told Sukie that Pattie wasn't convinced.

'Gawp' went the blanket.

Although Sukie had had the sort of upbringing where her aunt had tried hard to protect her from any seedy aspects of the way people behaved, which meant she had no personal experience of any of the things that Pattie was alluding to, she was perfectly aware that some men preferred men, finding the thought of being with a women in the bedroom sense quite repulsive.

But she couldn't agree with the comments that Pattie was so gleefully sharing, and that undoubtedly would be gossip fodder for the Eddies tomorrow, as Sukie hadn't been left the impression that he – or was it she? – was only interested in men.

'You mark my words,' Pattie prattled on as she placed her empty cocoa mug on the wooden bedside table, seemingly unaware of Sukie's unusual hesitation in voicing her own opinion. 'I trust John's judgement, and when Mr Bright gets wind we have a lavender in one of the best suites, there'll be hell to pay as he won't want the Eddy to be tarnished by this sort of thing.'

'I do hate terms like pansy, musical and lavender – they seem so demeaning. But you might be right about Mr Bright,' admitted Sukie somewhat reluctantly, 'and it was me who booked Tracy Benn in, and so I might be for the high jump too.'

Pattie's answering 'Ah!' was eloquent, despite its brevity.

There didn't seem anything else for either of them to say on the matter, and even Polly didn't have a final 'gawp' to throw into the mix, and so after checking the window was sufficiently open for Polly, Sukie quickly wriggled into her flannelette nightie and turned off the light.

She got into her own bed, and the two pals each pulled their eiderdowns a little more snugly up to their necks as they wished each other good night.

But right before Sukie drifted off to sleep, she fancied for the merest instant she could smell once more the tiniest whiff of Chantilly.

Chapter Eighteen

Sukie didn't sleep at all well after her and Pattie's discussion, which was very annoying.

She had trouble warming up enough to go to sleep, and so she had to heave herself up and out of bed in order to put some bed socks on and, twenty minutes later, a woolly. And then, when she still couldn't drift off, she decided she was thirsty even though she had already drunk the glass of water Pattie had left for her on the bedside table. The only solution was that she had to pad all the way down to the kitchen to make herself a mug of Ovaltine. As she tottered down what felt like too many flights of staff stairs while trying to be as quiet as possible, she felt more than a bit shaky and there seemed to be an uncomfortable lump high in her throat, close to her tonsils, that bobbed about when she swallowed.

What was especially irksome was that somehow a gently snoring Pattie had managed to flip her legs over Sukie's well-worn dressing gown. This, for a reason Sukie couldn't fathom (usually she kept all her clothes in their tiny cupboard, and so Pattie must have borrowed it when she went for her weekly bath), was heaped in a untidy scrunch on the matelassé bedspread – a coverlet so old that it was worn thin by years of washing and, in parts, threadbare – that stretched over Pattie's bed.

Rather than risk waking Pattie by pulling out the dressing gown from under her, Sukie had had to nip downstairs to make her warm drink under the tented confines of Thing, hoping all the while that she didn't run into any of the Eddies, as she wasn't at all in the mood to be teased for looking a fright.

Her brow felt unnaturally hot and a bit damp, and she thought she maybe ought to take an aspirin, but Sukie couldn't remember where Mrs Bridge had told her they were kept. This wasn't like her at all as normally her memory was very good, while she always liked to pride herself on her robust constitution and her ability to swerve dextrously any colds or sniffles that were going about. Sukie decided she'd just have to grin and bear it, as she couldn't possibly wake Mrs Bridge over such a minor thing, especially right in the middle of the night.

The next morning the ringing alarm and the subsequent sounds of Pattie moving about in their still pitch-dark room as her chambermaid's duties meant that she had to get up an hour before Sukie needed to, seemed to take place about a second – but was in fact close to two hours – after Sukie had finally fallen fitfully asleep.

Worse, these getting-up sounds were incorporated into a disturbing dream of evil-faced half-moons and dangerously crumbling chimneys, a drama played out with a clock continuously striking midnight as anti-aircraft beams were pointed upwards into the sky as they slashed this way and that. It was a dream that had Sukie running about in panic on high-up roof tiles that threatened to plunge her into the River Thames as she failed miserably to find the binoculars to see where the fires were; and then the binoculars turned out to be pregnant, giving birth to a multitude of minuscule wriggling creatures that were arguing among themselves whether they were worms or snakes... Ugh.

Before she left their bedroom Pattie had re-set the alarm clock for Sukie, and when it went off for the second time that morning Sukie woke up properly with it still being dark outside, but feeling inexplicably anxious and bone-weary, and with the dry catch of the inside of her mouth that made her wonder if she had been snoring with her mouth open. Unpleasantly, the gutter of her spine felt saltily sweaty. Despite all of this she was relieved not to be asleep any longer as a strange mood in the aftermath of the dream was lingering, and she had trouble trying to shake it off.

The roof tiles opposite their window had a sprinkle of frost, the glint of which Sukie could just make out in the faint illumination across the alleyway that was coming now from the windows of the other Eddies' bedrooms, as by now practically everyone would have their lamps on as they were getting up for work.

Disconcertingly, a bedraggled pigeon roosting on the windowsill stared intently at Sukie, its head cocked to one side, as she sat on the edge of her bed with her face in her hands, while she massaged her temples. Sukie thought that though its feathers were less than pristine, the poor pigeon was looking distinctly chirpier than she was feeling.

What was it with birds? she wondered. The pigeon and Polly both had knowing ball-bearings for eyes that seemed at once to be hideously knowledgeable and accusing. Sukie felt they were able to intuit much more about her than she was about them. She decided she really didn't like anything with feathers very much, and she wondered how she could get Polly removed from their bedroom without upsetting Pattie. Then she watched Polly grooming himself with his beak and thought she would miss it if he wasn't there.

Goodness, what was going on? It really wasn't like her to be so contrary, Sukie knew. But unable to shake the peculiar feeling that the insinuating dream had left her with, or to push away a heavy, unmoving stone of foreboding from deep within her, Sukie shivered as she headed down to the kitchen to have her breakfast.

Once there she was immediately greeted by Michael bounding down the outside stairs, and throwing the door open with a bang he announced to Mrs Bridge without preamble that he'd been at the hospital all night as Alan had indeed had a stroke.

Suddenly Sukie felt hot and cold at the same time, and she realised that she didn't feel hungry in the slightest.

Michael wasn't paying attention to her however. He said that it had been very busy at St Thomas's Hospital down in Lambeth when he and Alan had got there in the taxi. This was because there had been a serious collision during the ten o'clock chucking-out time from all the public houses at the bottom of

Fleet Street when, at a junction on Ludgate Hill, two buses in the blackout had both swerved to miss a group of exiled Norwegian ensigns. It seemed the ensigns had been drowning their sorrows in a public house and as one they had walked right out of the hostelry's door after drinking far too much, and stumbled straight out into the road without looking for traffic. Unfortunately the swerve that each driver had to take to miss them brought their own bus directly into the path of the other's, causing quite a head-on bump and a lot of screamingly dented metal. Worse, many of the passengers sustained cuts, nicks and bruises from the buses' glass windows that sheered into small and sharp pieces that shot across everyone.

There had been an interminably long wait on hard wooden chairs in a draughty corridor before Alan had been admitted to a men's ward of closely packed beds, and Michael had been allowed to stand beside him until he was settled.

'I could 'ardly make out wot our Alan was sayin', 'is mouth were so stiff on one side an' that eye were shut. But 'e managed ter git over 'e didn't 'ave no next o' kin,' Michael said. "E were quieter though than many t'others on t'ward, as they were makin' a racket so I thought they must be in agonies. 'E won't be gittin' much sleep, that's fer certain. I didn't want to leave 'im, but it were time fer work and so I 'ad to go.'

How depressing, Sukie thought. Suddenly she felt swamped with sympathy. While she didn't know Alan particularly well, he had always seemed a nice person, and when she and Pattie had arrived at the Eddy he had taken great pains to explain to them the workings of the restaurant, and what it was a maître d' actually did (she and Pattie had never even heard of one before). He was a sweet-natured man and Sukie was sure he didn't deserve what he was now going through.

In fact she felt distinctly blue all around.

Sukie realised that this was in no small part because she didn't have any next of kin either, aside from the aunt who had brought her up. But the aunt had moved to Canada about a year after the war had began, when an old school friend emigrated there and asked her aunt to go with her as her companion. This meant that Sukie wasn't sure her aunt really counted any longer as she doubted that she would ever move back to Britain again, and if Sukie were to die, she thought at best her aunt would feel regretful but not quite heartbroken.

It was an unsettling notion, Sukie thought morbidly, that if she were to die that very day, there wouldn't be a single family member in the country related to her by blood who would properly mourn her. Sukie knew her friends in Lymbridge, Evie and Susan especially, would be upset if she passed before her time, but she didn't feel that was quite the same as if she had had a sister or a brother, or her parents hadn't died in the car crash all those years ago. And as for the yawning pain of the loss of poor dear Wesley...

She tried to tell herself that she did have her own family as she was an honorary Yeo, but this felt at that particular moment like too little, too late, when she was in such a morbid mood.

It was all too much, and, as Mrs Bridge began to tell Michael about the night that St Thomas's had been bombed at the start of the Blitz, when Mrs Bridge had gone to help search the rubble for buried nurses, as the nurses' home adjacent to the hospital had taken the bulk of the hit, Sukie felt her lips and the muscles in the lower part of her face tremble uncontrollably.

The room around her began to shrink, and then magnify, almost as if it were breathing, and she had to nip adroitly to the staff toilets as tears were threatening.

The morning didn't get much better as Sukie found she had the beginnings of a debilitating headache and that she felt increasingly queasy and dry-throated. Her appetite had returned in recent weeks but that morning she found she couldn't countenance the thought of food or drink passing her lips.

About an hour or so before the restaurant opened for lunch service, Sukie was feeling even more under par, to the point she was seriously considering asking Mr Bright if Pattie could cover for her while she went back to bed for an hour. Or at the very least if she could pop up to her room to put on something a bit warmer, as she couldn't seem to stop shivering and her fingers felt were so stiff with cold she was finding it quite difficult to hold her pen. She realised with a jolt that she had spent the last four nights consecutively fire-watching from the roof, after long hours behind the reception desk, and so she thought Mr Bright might agree to give her a bit of a break.

Just as she was about to knock at the hotel manager's office door, without warning a very drunk, but exceptionally well-dressed, middle-aged gentleman lurched through the doorway. He must have sneaked past the doorman and now stood swaying inside the foyer with feet planted wide apart swinging his head slowly from side to side to stare with seemingly unfocused eyes.

There was no sign of Stephen or Michael, and Sukie wondered if she should reach for the school bell under the desk to raise the alarm, not that she had ever dared to do so for any reason previously.

Her hesitation was enough. For the drunk man stumbled forward with surprising speed, unleashing in an extremely loud voice a string of swear words that could have taught most navvies a ripe expression or two. Without pausing for breath, he began swinging punches loosely in the direction of two American army officers, even though he was standing too far back from them to make any physical contact.

American officers had recently started to book rooms at the Eddy, as the hotel attracted a lot of custom from the mid- to top brass from the British military when in town, and this seemed to be mirrored increasingly by their US counterparts.

These two officers had been happily minding their own business as they'd talked together in subdued voices, sharing a small pot of coffee on one of the ornate brocade sofas at the side of the lobby. They glanced at the drunk but didn't seem to feel he was any real threat to judge by their lack of action.

Of course Mr Bright chose that very moment to bustle out of his office to see what all the commotion was about, and said in an officious tone, 'Stop that!'

The drunk man turned a bleary eye towards him and there was something belligerent about him that made Sukie felt weak-kneed.

'Now, now, let's have none of that. Haven't you got a home to go to?' Mr Bright hurried forward and put out his hands as if to chivvy the drunk back towards the door, looking like a farmer might if he was herding a couple of geese on their way.

The drunk was having none of it and gave a loud 'Harumph!' And he ducked and dived, throwing an unexpected, but obviously het-up sucker-punch vaguely in the direction of Mr Bright.

Against the odds, it was perfectly timed.

The drunk's right-handed cross caught the hotel manager straight under the jaw just as Mr Bright leaned forward in an effort to make his chivvying more successful. When Mr Bright's teeth cracked together on impact, there was such an audible clap that it made Sukie jump.

The blow caused Mr Bright's steel-rimmed spectacles to fly off and skitter right to the other side of the foyer across the tiled floor, such was the force of the clout.

Mr Bright seemed to stand stock-still for the merest second, and the American servicemen sprang to their feet and the hotel manager let out a mild 'Ooof!' before crumpling gracefully to the floor with a gentle sigh.

Sukie looked around desperately; she couldn't see the uniformed doorman who'd usually be on the other side of the entrance doors and there was still no sign of Stephen or Michael either. She didn't dare shout for them, or ring the school bell, as this might draw the guests' attention to the drama unfurling in the foyer.

Unable to come up with a better alternative, she spoke urgently down the telephone receiver to downstairs for Chef to come and help.

And then with a breathy cry of 'DOORMAN!' in case he could hear, Sukie ran over to Mr Bright's prone body on the floor to discover that he had been knocked out cold.

Sukie found herself totally frozen as she stood beside him, with absolutely no idea as to what she should do. Thankfully the American officers were much more on top of the unfolding situation. They'd each grabbed an arm of Mr Bright's assailant, who was now slowly slumping to the floor, where he lay in an untidy heap making very peculiar noises as he muttered to himself incoherently.

By the time Chef ran up and into the lobby, and Stephen and Michael shot over as they stepped out of the lift, there were two lifeless bodies prone on the floor, and Sukie standing nearby trembling violently from shock. She had never been party to anything like this before.

Luckily one of the officers had had some professional medical training, and he took care of the drunk, and soon he and Michael were dragging him off to the left luggage room, the toes of his expensive shoes scuffing as they were dragged over the foyer's black and white tiles. The left luggage room was really little more than a lockable nook just under the guest stairway upstairs, but it was a secure place to dump the drunk man. Then the US officer suggested that Stephen should run to fetch a metal pail, just in case, and as he did this the officer got down to piling the small amount of left luggage out of the way so that they had a bit of room.

Mrs Bridge had dug out the smelling salts in her wooden first-aid box that she had hidden away in the pantry for an emergency – Sukie would never have thought of looking in the pantry for an aspirin – and as she pounded across the tiles and unscrewed the cap and held the small glass bottle under Mr Bright's nose, first his moustache twitched dramatically, and then he sat upright very rapidly. It was only a short reprieve as immediately he flopped backwards again on to the unforgiving hard surface just as quickly as he had sat up, his head making a small whump as it connected once again with the floor tiles. Although no longer totally unconscious, he seemed more than a bit dazed, and his eyes watered furiously from the chemicals in the smelling salts, and then he closed them once more.

Sukie rallied at last. She hurried back to the reception desk, where she picked up the telephone receiver, although she could hardly keep hold of the handset while she did so as her hand

and arm felt as floppy as jelly, and she couldn't seem to catch her breath properly.

With a huge force of effort she stutteringly asked the Covent Garden switchboard operator to put her through quickly please to the nearest police station as it was an emergency. It seemed an age before a series of clicks indicated the operator was moving the requisite connecting wires about. Then when Sukie did finally get through, it was only to be informed that currently there was an emergency on the river to do with a ferry and a barge, and as nobody seemed badly hurt at the Eddy it might be a while before they could send anyone over as they were stretched thin that day as a lot of officers had been working through the night... and so on.

Silently Sukie replaced the handset while the duty officer was still talking, and she tried by force of will, and then by insisting to herself she'd not got anything inside her, to keep down the surge of vomit that threatened.

Picking the handset back up, she telephoned the hotel's doctor, and his secretary said she'd send him right over. Sukie knew he wouldn't take long to get there as his practice was only a couple of streets away.

Now Chef was helping a clearly groggy Mr Bright to his feet, but he still didn't seem quite with it and Chef slung one of the hotel manager's arms across his own neck, and with a supporting arm around the waist, half-walked and half-dragged Mr Bright to the privacy of his office.

Sukie went across the lobby for Mr Bright's spectacles and saw a delicate spray of blood droplets on the wall, presumably from when Mr Bright had been hit. She shook her head, and cast her eyes around as staring at the geometrical shape of the black and white floor tiles was began to make her feel dizzy.

The second American officer handed her the spectacles, and when she saw them Sukie knew Mr Bright would be furious as the lens on one side had a vertical crack right through it, while the frames themselves looked buckled.

She composed herself for second, and when she took the specs through to the hotel manager's office a minute later, she thought it kinder not to point out what had happened to the lens of the spectacles. Mr Bright was sitting in the chair behind his desk, his hands holding tightly on to the wooden arms of his chair to judge by how white his knuckles looked, but he didn't look up towards Sukie or acknowledge the arrival of his glasses.

Sukie closed Mr Bright's office door after she came out, although as she did so, and completely without warning, suddenly the floor seemed to be tipping this way and that in an incredibly disorientating way. She had to reach out a hand behind her to remind herself as to where the wall was.

Sukie felt the quick throb of her heart beating wildly in her ribcage, and a strange rushing sound in her ears that seemed to be drowning out everything else. The foyer and her reception desk seemed suddenly to be a very long way away, as if she was looking at them through the wrong end of a telescope.

Panicked at the peculiar sensations, she wondered what on earth was going on and whether the Eddy had been hit by a bomb. She thought she might be about to faint, and she shut her eyes in an effort to make the floor stabilise once more.

'Whoa there, my lovely, whoa I say,' said a voice close to Sukie. It sounded kind. 'Don't you worry about a thing.'

And then a hand with a tattoo of a snake on the middle finger, and that now sported glossy scarlet nails, slipped under her elbow in welcome support.

Sukie found herself being guided gently but firmly to one of the chairs in the subdued quietness of the empty bar, the owner of the blue-black tattoo deftly snatching the glass bottle of smelling salts with their free hand from an open-mouthed Mrs Bridge as they went by.

Sukie sensed rather than saw a mouthed 'thank you' directed towards the housekeeper by deep-red lips, although she heard for certain a comforting 'Let's steady the buffs, my girl, let's steady the buffs' as this was softly purred right into the shell of Sukie's ear.

They were the last words Sukie heard for quite some time.

Chapter Nineteen

When Sukie came to, she was wearing her trusted flannelette nightie and was tucked up in her own bed. She couldn't get her bearings.

She stretched out all four of her limbs to discover that she had two rubber hot-water bottles in bed with her that were wrapped in towels to make sure she didn't get burned. One bottle was at her feet, and the other nestled into her waist.

For the first time in many hours she felt toasty warm as Thing had been draped over the top of her ancient feather eiderdown too.

None of this made any sense. But feeling blissfully comfy, Sukie drifted in and out of sleep for a while, and then she could hear the sound of Pattie's approaching footsteps – she really did have a distinctive and very recognisable way of walking, Sukie thought – accompanied by the welcome chink of a china cup in a saucer. Sure enough, Pattie came into the room and put a hot drink down on Sukie's bedside table.

'Where's my rum?' came from near the door, and Sukie started as she had completely forgotten about Polly. Pattie flipped open his cage door and he jumped on to her finger, and then she put him on the back of an old wooden chair after she'd placed a sheet of newspaper under the back legs of the chair for any 'accidents', as Pattie described them, where he sat staring trans-fixed at Sukie.

Sukie realised she was really thirsty and so, ignoring Polly, she wriggled herself up the bed a foot or two as Pattie got the pillow from her own bed to prop her shoulders up a little so that she could drink her tea in comfort.

Quickly Pattie filled Sukie in on what had happened. The doctor accompanied by a nurse had arrived to Sukie's summons, and he'd declared that Sukie was suffering from exhaustion and dehydration, and that she needed to have three days without doing any sort of work at the Eddy, or voluntary service either.

Apparently he'd been very critical of Mr Bright for not noticing that Sukie had been working too-long hours, especially when Mrs Bridge told him about the loss of Wesley, and the fire-watching night after night.

Mr Bright hadn't been able to hear these criticisms though, as by then he and the doctor's nurse were in a taxi on the way to St Thomas's. Mr Bright had been signed off work too, which was understandable as he was now in the same ward at St Thomas's as Alan – in the very next bed, no less! – with a suspected severe concussion that the hospital doctors wanted to keep an eye on, as they were a little worried he might have a hairline fracture to his skull.

The filigree of blood droplets had dried in deep on the wall of the foyer, Pattie said, and had stubbornly remained there despite the best attempts of Mrs Bridge to remove them without scouring the wall, and so Pattie had volunteered to paint them over later, once the service for dinner had finished and most of the guests who were resident at the hotel had gone to bed.

In Mr Bright's absence, Pattie was going to do Sukie's shifts on reception, with Jane picking up any slack if Pattie were urgently needed elsewhere, while Chef and Housekeeping were going to juggle Mr Bright's hotel management duties alongside their own roles.

Three whole days! Bliss, thought Sukie as, with a rattle, she placed the empty teacup back in its saucer on the bedside table.

Immediately she fell asleep again, just as Pattie began to tell her about Mr Bright.

And so what Sukie missed were Pattie's final words.

'The police came and arrested the drunk – he'd been staying over at the Ritz, no less, it turned out and he is now back there. No charges are being pressed, and it's all hush-hush and very *Ritzkrieg* and the rich looking after the rich, as you'd expect—' Pattie sighed in resignation '—and so good riddance to bad rubbish, I say. It doesn't seem as if there was any reason for his behaviour. Other than being falling-down drunk, that is.'

Pattie looked down at Sukie. 'Sukie, wake up, as the choice bit is yet to come. Tracy Benn saved you from fainting, I expect you can remember that.

'But the best of it is that it wasn't yet noon. And Tracy Benn was wearing a red, floor-length, heavily-sequinned Maison Schiaparelli evening DRESS! And full make-up with a blood-red lip, and diamond earrings. The whole shebang – even nail varnish. It's lucky Mr Bright didn't snatch a glimpse, as he'd never have got over it, and he'd have fainted again if he had copped a squiz of those sequins. But Mrs Bridge is scandalised! In fact she is still speechless. Well, not really, but you know what I mean... Sukie? Sukie! Wake up, you're missing all the fun and high jinks.'

Pattie leaned down to give Sukie's shoulder nearest to her a firmish wobble, but Sukie remained dead to the world, totally oblivious as to the scandal of Tracy Benn.

'Sukie Scott, you are absolutely hopeless, do you hear me?' her friend wailed in frustration.

Pattie stalked from the room, and headed a few steps down the corridor. She trumpeted a breath of irritation through her mouth, stopped in her tracks and then turned back to the bedroom door.

'Absolutely hopeless... The best gossip in ages – better even than Julia's night of unwed passion with the terminally boring Leonard Bassett, and I didn't think anything could ever top that – and you're asleep. Asleep! Sukie Scott, you are absolutely HOPELESS!'

Sukie replied with a sleep-sunken snuffle, and Pattie knew it was time to beat a retreat, although not before she had uttered one final 'Hopeless!' and then shut the door behind her to make sure that Polly didn't escape.

Sukie slept on. She didn't notice Polly hop on to her bed and then casually use Sukie's prone body as a climbing frame. At last, happy to be on Sukie's shoulder, even though what he was standing on was mainly a huge mound of Thing, Polly carefully inspected her hair, her lips and her eyelashes.

He jumped across to take up a sentry position on Sukie's headboard until Pattie finished her shift, announcing 'Sequins!' at regular intervals, alternating with 'Mr Bright' and 'Where's the rum?'

Chapter Twenty

Sukie slept for eighteen hours straight, and felt much refreshed when she woke up mid-morning the following day. She was also ravenous, but she felt too grubby to show her face in the kitchen, so she grabbed a quick bath and hair wash. Although she allowed herself only two inches of tepid water, and she had to make do only with the tiniest sliver of Cussons Imperial Leather for both her body and hair, it felt wonderful in spite of the fact that the bathroom was icy cold due to the frosty weather outside. In fact, she felt so good that when she got back to the bedroom she even gave Polly a peanut, which he took from her in his strong claw with utmost delicacy.

Nearly all the other Eddies were going about their duties downstairs and so for the very first time Sukie didn't feel she had to hurry in her ablutions or in making herself presentable. There was only the one bath, and it had to serve more than twenty Eddies who slept on her and Pattie's floor, and there was just the one lavatory too, and so queues could build up in the mornings and the evenings, especially as the women would usually have to rinse out their smalls and their stockings at the end of the day.

Sukie dried her hair as best she could and then she wrapped it in her Liberty scarf to stop it going flyaway, and then she dressed and went down to the kitchen, with her hair still encased in her silk scarf.

'How are you feeling?' said Mrs Bridge. 'You gave us all a fright, let me tell you.'

'I'm much better, thank you very much,' said Sukie. 'More importantly, how is Mr Bright?'

'He's up and down. I telephoned St Thomas's first thing, and they are going to keep him in until they are certain what they are dealing with.'

'Well, I feel a whole lot stronger, and so I can do some work, no matter what the doctor said,' Sukie offered. 'I know how all-hands-to-the-pump it must be, and I couldn't rest up knowing that everybody else here is running around like crazy bugs.'

Chef slid a slice of toast with a perfectly fried egg on it in front of her, and put a knife and fork down beside the plate. Sukie hadn't eaten anything for close on two days, and so this simple meal looked and smelt wonderful and she tucked in greedily. It tasted even better than it looked.

'Wouldn't hear of it,' said Mrs Bridge as Sukie ate, and Chef lifted a finger to his forehead as if to reiterate to Sukie that she should take heed of Housekeeping's words.

'There's no need for you to worry about it, Miss Scott,' Mrs Bridge added, 'really there isn't, as a new girl called Gladys Blenkinsop started this morning, who we've borrowed from the Capel, and although she's been there a while right now Miss Peters is training her up to *our* standards of chambermaid. This means we won't miss Miss Yeo from the chambermaid timetable, and so it is perfectly convenient that from now on she devotes herself to the reception desk, and you take some time to yourself to get raring to go again.

'I must go upstairs now, as I need to make some telephone calls from Mr Bright's office, but we can catch up later, and in the meantime I think you should go for a walk as you need some daylight and some fresh air. I'm going to speak to the ARP co-ordinator to say I think you've done enough on the roof at night-times, at least until the warmer weather comes – Michael is going to step in to cover for you up there, until the ARP lot get themselves sorted.'

The older woman bustled off.

Sukie knew Michael would be making a big personal sacrifice by taking on her fire-watching duties, as it would mean he couldn't do his other war work. Not long after she and Pattie had arrived in London, there had been a secret midnight feast of the staff down in the kitchen when a game of Truth or Dare was played. When it was Michael's turn, he opted for truth, and confessed that he was a crack shot.

For some of his childhood he'd lived on a Highland country estate where his father was a ghillie, and had taught him to shoot. Sukie knew that his polio meant that he hadn't been able to join any of the services, which had upset him greatly. And so his contribution to the war effort was to keep the gun skills going of members of Parliament and members of the House of Lords. They regularly practised with the pistols they had each been given in case Jerry were to invade, these sessions taking place in a long subterranean room in a basement of a large 1920s office building that overlooked Blackfriars bridge. The space had once been a massive typing pool, but with the onset of war it had been converted into a shooting gallery. Michael was one of the shooting coaches, although he had said to Sukie that while he made sure to always wear the government-issued ear mufflers, he was sure the repeated loud cracks of the pistols going off was making him go deaf.

Sukie guessed that Michael hated his limp, and she suspected that as a child he'd been teased about it. Teaching important people to protect themselves meant that he could make a contribution to the war effort that any man could be proud of, even if it wasn't a contribution that was in any way on the frontline.

Oh well, Sukie told herself, every cloud has a silver lining. While Michael might not appreciate doing the fire-watching, perhaps her collapse would help save his hearing, at least a little.

Once they had the kitchen more or less to themselves, aside that is from the commis chef and the kitchen porter sorting vegetables over at the far side of the industrial ovens, Chef told Sukie that Mrs Bridge had been very worried about her, and had plodded up and down the staff stairway several times to check on her as she was sleeping.

Sukie had to swallow down a small lump in her throat at the thought of this as Mrs Bridge was quite a large woman who rarely had to venture upstairs to the staff living quarters as she had her own small bedroom tucked away next to the scullery – and there were an awful lot of steps from the basement level right up to where she and Pattie slept. Sukie knew Mrs Bridge must have been worried about her to have made her way right up to her and Pattie's bedroom and down again more than once. She guessed that Mrs Bridge had seen Polly, but presumably was still thinking over what to say about him.

After a second cup of tea, Sukie thought Mrs Bridge's idea of a walk outside was a good one as she felt she needed to stretch her legs.

She went and fetched Old Faithful, as well as her teal hat, the scarf that Evie had sent her, gloves, which had also been a gift from Evie the previous Christmas, and her handbag.

As she got ready to leave the Eddy, Sukie decided to say to Mrs Bridge that she was uncertain about cutting back on her fire-watching stints as she knew everyone had to make sacrifices for the greatest good. There was a distinct lull in bombing activity, and so Sukie couldn't pretend she was actually very busy when she was up on the roof, although of course she had to make sure that her concentration didn't falter.

Then, when she imagined actually putting on all of her night-time coats and gloves, Thing, climbing up the ladder to the roof on those harsh winter nights still to come to see where any fires might be, she couldn't prevent a small shudder. It was the start of December and already freezing at night, so reluctantly she admitted to herself that perhaps she did need a little more time to recuperate before winching herself back up to the Eddy's icy roof again.

Instead, when she put her head around the door to Mr Bright's office, Sukie said, 'Shall I take Mr Bright's spectacles to the opticians for repair?'

She was rewarded with a look of gratitude from Mrs Bridge, and a 'Yes, do, Sukie. That would be most helpful. He goes to the optician in Brushfield Street at Spitalfields, and you're to ask for Mickey. You'll know him when you see him.'

As Mr Bright was still in hospital, Sukie had risked going down the main stairs from her bedroom to reception as she wanted to see how Pattie was getting on. And Sukie was impressed to note the deft way Pattie was dealing with a woman holding a howling baby and the hand of a grumbling toddler, wanting to know if she could catch a bus from the Strand over to Marble Arch. Sukie had been proud to hear Pattie suggesting a taxi 'as then you'd have somebody to help you with the perambulator'.

Now, Pattie sounded very professional as she told a gentleman who looked ecclesiastical the way to St Paul's, and so Sukie contented herself by merely smiling at her friend as she slipped out of the foyer and on to the street.

Sukie passed the time of day with the doorman, who described Mrs Bridge's shocked face at the sight of Tracy Benn in her red silk evening dress right in the middle of the morning, a sight – both the dress and Mrs Bridge's face – that Sukie would have given her eye teeth to see. The doorman gave Sukie a mint humbug as a special treat, tapping the side his nose as he said, 'It fell off the back of a lorry.' She popped it into her mouth.

She laughed and agreed that Mrs Bridge's expression must have been a picture, and then as it was a fine crisp day she decided to walk over to Brushfield Street than to go by bus, as, after studying her London street map, it looked within walking distance, being not more than two and a half miles away, Sukie calculated quickly.

She hadn't quite made it to the end of their street though when she was halted in her tracks by a ringing, 'Ahoy, there! Hold up, Miss Scott!'

Sukie looked behind her to see, walking smartly her way, Tracy Benn, dressed today in a posh gentleman's suit complete with waistcoat and gold watch chain, and a soft pink handkerchief in the breast pocket. The brogues were black this time and the suit was a deep grape colour. And Sukie couldn't help herself thinking that this meant at least two smart suits and two decent pairs of shoes, a surfeit of riches that was just about unheard of these days.

'Oh, good morning,' said Sukie. 'I wanted to thank you very much for coming to my rescue. You were a knight in shining armour, so I hear, and therefore I'm very much in your debt!'

It felt odd to Sukie that she hadn't dare include a name in what she had just said, but 'Tracy' felt too informal, and there was still the issue over Miss, Mrs or Mister as now that she was looking at this person again she could argue both for and against either gender, and to speak the whole name as 'Tracy Benn' seemed just plain wrong although actually the person before her seemed worthy of the two names.

Sukie coloured slightly in frustration as she had been planning on buying a small thank you gift for Tracy Benn in recognition of how kindly she'd been treated. Oh bother, it would now feel too awkward to do this, and in any case she hadn't had the faintest idea of what to get.

Tracy Benn gave her a long look, and then said, 'Perhaps you can repay me right now for coming to your assistance by accompanying me for elevenses, and you can tell me about how you are feeling this morning and what all the uproar was about yesterday as I think I missed the best of the fun and games. And perhaps you can let me know what your Christian name is?'

'I'm Sukie Scott, but you must call me Sukie.'

Sukie pondered on what would Mr Bright say if he knew.

She doubted he'd be thrilled for a whole gamut of reasons, not least as he didn't approve of fraternisation between guests and Eddies.

But he was safely out of the way, lying in the hospital bed at St Thomas's, and what the eye doesn't see, the heart doesn't grieve over, Sukie reminded herself. And, in any case, he had never expressly commanded that she shouldn't spend her own private time off the premises of the Eddy with a hotel guest, if she felt so inclined...

She wrestled with her conscience, but in the end it was no contest. Duty won. Sukie knew she needed to get Mr Bright's specs repaired, and so she said as much to Tracy Benn.

'How wonderful,' came the reply. 'A trip to darkest Spitalfields first, and then somewhere much more fun afterwards. That combination sounds just my sort of morning.'

Sukie's nod of acceptance and tentative smile, as this all felt very unexpected, led to them walking side by side down to the Strand, and then a taxi right away waved to a halt beside them as if by magic, with the destination of 'Brushfield Street and then on to Claridge's' being issued in the sort of voice that brooked no argument.

As she shimmied her behind onto the seat of the cab, Sukie felt a bit over-awed and, for the very first time in her life, quite tongue-tied as the taxi chugged sedately westwards, but Tracy Benn was busy talking about this and that with the taxi driver, and so it didn't matter.

Sukie was grateful though that she had borrowed Pattie's red utility suit that morning. Pattie had wanted to wear Sukie's green one for work, but now that Sukie had Pattie's suit on, she could see it was in better nick than hers, which was a good thing now that she was on her way to Claridge's.

They had to go slowly along Brushfield Street to find the optician, and when they did, it looked a dark and poky place, and not at all the sort of business that Sukie expected Mr Bright to support. It was clearly a very poor area with lots of tenements and run-down houses. There were a plethora of pawn shops, and a sense of forlornness that enveloped everything.

While her companion waited in the taxi, Sukie went into the opticians and asked for Mickey, and was astounded to have a tiny man, a hunchback who could be no more than three foot tall, come up to her with an agility that belied how crooked his small spine was.

And when Sukie passed him the spectacles, he sprang nimbly

on to the slats of an upturned wooden box and then he studied the spectacles under a strong lamp, before looking at Sukie with a smile, as he said, 'Well, as it's for Mr Bright, they'll be ready in an hour, and there'll be no charge.'

It all seemed a bit Dickensian, a feeling heightened by the bomb destruction she could see everywhere, so much so that she imagined a gritty feel between her teeth that came from the mountainous piles of rubble, some of which had been there for such a long time that there looked to be plants growing from it.

Sukie wasn't sure what to think. She had never seen anyone like Mickey, and although she knew there were slums in London, she was shocked by how down at heel this area was, given that it wasn't much more than a couple of miles away from the Eddy. It felt like a whole different world, more run down even than the sorry state of Wesley's lodgings in Camberwell which had seemed the absolute pits to Sukie only back in the summer.

Chapter Twenty-one

If Sukie found the visit to such a poor area of London to be shocking, then it was equally matched by the next hour or two in her life. It was truly a case of the sublime to the ridiculous.

To her surprise, Sukie found she was even more shocked, although in a very different way, by Claridge's.

Upon their arrival they were whisked over to a couple of armchairs in the sitting room, and almost right away they were served with some Earl Grey tea and a small selection of fancies.

When Sukie and Pattie had first arrived to work at the Eddy they had thought it to be an extremely posh establishment. As she gazed around now at the sumptuous furnishings and the distinctive hum of upper-class chatter within Claridge's, Sukie could see that they had only felt like that about the Eddy because they hadn't known any better. Now the scales had fallen from her eyes.

Although the dear Eddy was a distinct step up from the majority of London hotels (of those that had managed to stay afloat), what the Eddy could offer was most definitely several rungs below a hotel such as the one in which Sukie was now sitting, a porcelain cup and saucer (accompanied by a real silver teaspoon) balanced in her fingers looking, she thought, for all the world as if she were Lady Muck.

Her tea was delicious, being subtle but with a depth of flavour she had never previously experienced, as was the tiny but flavour-packed Bakewell tart Tracy Benn encouraged her to choose from the tiered stand of fancies. Sukie had forgotten that food and drink could taste as interesting as this, and realised that, although compared to what a lot of people would have at home made the Eddy seem upmarket, really what they provided in terms of victuals was nothing like the sheer quality of what she had just enjoyed.

As she stroked the thick linen of her napkin, Sukie was glad that Mr Bright wasn't there to see the way she couldn't help appreciatively staring around at the small details that made a hotel like this stand out for its superior quality, as she thought he might be a trifle hurt that she was so easily impressed by another establishment.

She gazed around the sitting room, and then gasped quietly. She looked away, and then her eyes were pulled quickly again as if by a strong magnet to exactly the same spot.

For, sitting not fifteen feet away from Sukie and Tracy Benn, there was only Winnie – their leader, *Winston Churchill*, no less! – sipping an amber fluid from a heavy-looking cut-glass tumbler. She felt rude for thinking 'Winnie', as it was so familiar, but she supposed she had got a bit too used to hearing others call him that. Just a day or two previously Sukie had been reading in *The Times* about a meeting between Winston Churchill, US leader President Roosevelt, and Nationalist Chinese President Chiang Kai-shek; and now here was Winnie almost rubbing shoulders with her! He looked to be talking to a serious-looking man in a suit, who was dwarfing a ridiculous small and gold-gilded coffee cup and saucer that he had nestled in a large paw of a hand.

'That's Viscount Kemsley and he owns the *Sunday Times*,' said Tracy Benn in a matter-of-fact way, with a slight nod towards the man sitting with Winnie, as if having such important people in such close proximity was an everyday occurrence. Well, perhaps it was for Tracy Benn, but it certainly wasn't for Sukie. 'He's very important in Fleet Street. Shall I fill you in on who else is here?'

Sukie looked down to see that the second Bakewell tart had

somehow found its way on to the pretty side plate that was balanced on her knee.

'Goodness!' Sukie gasped after a heartbeat, but about Winston Churchill rather than the sweet fancy. She felt Tracy Benn would think her unsophisticated, but she couldn't help that. She simply wasn't used to seeing anyone who everybody knew, and for a few moments she had been quite dazzled. 'But no, thank you, please don't tell me who anyone else is. If you do, I might get even more awestruck, and then I'm going to feel a bigger country mouse than I do at present. That would mean that I won't be able to finish my tea or this tartlet, which would be a disaster, and most rude.'

And with that Tracy Benn laughed again, and then, rather against Sukie's expectations, the two of them fell into an easy conversation.

To her surprise, it wasn't long before Sukie heard herself describing how devastated she had felt following Wesley's death, and how, for a while, she had felt she wouldn't be able to recover from his loss. It was the first time Sukie had talked so openly and so frankly, much more so than even when Evie had visited London, or when she had been sitting on the roof that cold night with Pattie.

But Tracy Benn proved very adept at gently drawing her out of herself, and before long Sukie forgot to be at all reserved or shy, and was explaining with a searing honesty how the last few months had been so perfectly horrid that, apart from Evie's flying visit, they hardly bore thinking about.

'I knew very quickly that I loved Wesley, and he was the one for me, and I was very, very lucky he felt the same. I found his death was so senseless – he just fell to the floor quite dead and yet those nearby were only hurt. No one else died. I've been told that sort of thing happens sometimes with bombs, but it all seems so bloody unfair, excuse my French. He was so full of life, and vigour and fun, that it seems a loss to all of us somehow. I have some nice times now of course, but I miss him still every day, even though everyone tells me he wouldn't want me to feel as sad as I do,' Sukie concluded, with a sigh. Her neck felt tense and she had a fleeting headache, but her eyes were tearless.

They sat quietly for a moment or two, and then Sukie confided in a voice that was hardly even a whisper, 'There have been times when I haven't known how to go on. I sometimes feel that part of me died with him too. People say it gets better in time, but what I feel is that it gets different rather than better.'

Tracy Benn didn't offer any trite platitudes other than a 'Yes, that would have been very difficult for you' and 'it sounds as if you have been through the mill', which Sukie appreciated as there really wasn't anything else that could be said.

Sukie realised it was the first time she had properly described her feelings over the loss of Wesley, as Pattie, Evie and Mrs Bridge, although always very kind, had talked more to Sukie than she had to them. And when Sukie had been at her most distressed, they had always rushed in to offer words of comfort, as opposed to *listening*, which was probably just as well because for a long time she couldn't really articulate anything much about what she was feeling. There was something calming about Tracy Benn's stillness as she sat quietly next to Sukie that was reassuring and encouraged her to say what she really felt.

Tracy Benn had lifted an eyebrow a fraction when Sukie mentioned the colour of Wesley's skin, but then treated it as something perfectly normal, and not even worth remarking on. Sukie appreciated this, as she had always felt that the colour of Wesley's skin was the least interesting thing about him.

Tracy Benn signalled for their teapot to be refreshed.

While the waiter fussed around Sukie thought back to the last time she and Wesley had seen each other and for the first time she found herself smiling over the memory. They'd stood so blissfully near to each other for a moment that even the thinnest of cigarette papers couldn't have been slid between them. When he'd had to hurry off she remembered him turning back, catching the kiss she had blown him and performing his slick tap-dancing steps that had made her laugh. Sukie had thought at that moment how perfect life had seemed and how good it had felt to be alive.

She was suddenly pleased that their last moment together had been full of laughter and fun.

'And are you content working behind the reception desk at the Edwardes Hotel?' Tracy Benn's next question brought Sukie back to herself, but it was a Sukie who felt refreshed and more whole. She was pleased to have celebrated Wesley in some way, rather than being sad and missing her lost loved one.

Sukie had never been asked anything like this before concerning the Eddy, and she was surprised to discover that she had never considered privately this particular question.

'Um,' she said, and then stopped, pondering what exactly she did feel about her role at the Eddy. 'Well, I suppose it wasn't where a me of five years ago would have expected to be, although, when the idea came up after Christmas last year, it did seem appealing,' she said cautiously as she experimented with her opinions. 'There are many worse jobs, I know, and I've made good friends there, and of course Wesley wanted to be in London to sing, and so this was a way that we could both be in the city at the same time. But, now that you've asked the question, I don't really think I'm cut out to be a receptionist.'

'No, I think you're probably right in that assumption.'

Sukie was slightly shocked at the bluntness of the comment and the lack of pussyfooting, but she couldn't help nodding her head in agreement all the same. How refreshing to be with somebody who didn't worry about being polite.

Tracy Benn smiled again, and Sukie could see the shine of rounded gold where a back tooth should be. 'I think you're destined for much bolder things; really, I do,' said Tracy Benn.

Sukie liked the word 'bolder', she liked that somebody thought she could be bolder than she was currently, and she liked even more the idea of herself as a truly bold woman. In fact, it was a novel way of thinking about herself.

She risked the question that had been niggling her. 'May I ask what are you doing staying at the Eddy?'

But before this question could be pursued an ornate clock on the mantelpiece struck noon with a musical chime, and decisively Tracy Benn stood up, apologised for drawing their conversation to a close, and said they really must do it again soon, but time was pressing and this meant they should go.

As they put on their coats and gloves Sukie noticed several crates at the side of reception and a tall step ladder. A man in a blue overall opened the crate nearest to him, and Sukie glimpsed silver tinsel and a large gold star. Clearly the Christmas decorations were about to be put up in Claridge's, she noted. And then she thought, I wonder where the Eddy's Christmas baubles are?

A few minutes later Sukie found herself in a cab heading back to Brushfield Street, after which she would continue in the taxi to the Eddy, the whole journey already paid for and the cabbie tipped handsomely by Tracy Benn, despite Sukie's protestations as she hated the thought of anyone thinking her practically destitute.

She had sat into the back of the taxi on her own, when with a tap on the door window to tell the cabbie he could drive on, her companion had waved at Sukie, and before she could say a proper thank you, Tracy Benn had jumped into the next waiting taxi at the hotel's door and set off in quite another direction.

It was an abrupt but not rude dismissal and yet it felt somewhat odd, mainly because Sukie wasn't used to being around people who had an idea which they acted upon straight away. She thought that might be because she had grown up in a remote country area where the pace of life was sluggish, although then she remembered that both Mr Bright and Mrs Bridge tended to procrastinate a bit before they made their minds up and so she knew that not everyone who lived in London was whip-smart in their decision making.

The taxi tootled along, and the more she mulled over the hour she'd just spent in Claridge's, the more Sukie realised that despite opening up about the loss of Wesley nonetheless she'd enjoyed herself in a grown-up way that she wasn't really used to, and that actually she felt quite buoyed up. She saw too that she had been so busy answering her companion's questions that she hadn't really noticed that she had had all of her own queries about her companion very skilfully batted away.

In fact, Sukie acknowledged, she knew next to nothing more about the mysterious Tracy Benn than she had previously, which was very irksome as normally Sukie prided herself at being exceptionally good at wheedling information out of those who were reluctant to talk about themselves.

Mickey had done a wonderful job with the specs, which looked as good as new to Sukie, but he refused to take any money for his work, no matter how hard she pressed him.

Not long afterwards, the taxi turned into the street where the Eddy was, and as the doorman scurried down the steps to open the vehicle door for her with a jokey 'Milady!' as he held a white-gloved hand out for her to hold as she got out, she found herself staring up appraisingly at the portico of the hotel with new eyes.

It wasn't four hours since she had left, but as she stepped through the door and saw Pattie's face light up at the sight of her, Sukie felt like a different, reborn woman.

'You'll never guess where I've been...' she said to Pattie as she stepped across the foyer to her. And Sukie was quite right, as Pattie couldn't guess at all.

Chapter Twenty-two

That very afternoon Sukie waited until after Mrs Bridge had had her lunch, and then she said, 'Mrs Bridge, I wonder if you'd like a hand with that?'

Mrs Bridge glanced up at Sukie from the list of newly delivered ironed laundry she was ticking off. She was dwarfed by a mountainous pile of spruced and ironed pillowcases and sheets beside her that had just been sent back to the Eddy and were now piled on a clean sheet that was kept neatly washed for just this purpose of being spread over the veg prep table.

Then Mrs Bridge straightened up and said, 'I've a better idea. You go and make us both a nice cup of tea and we can have a chinwag. And why don't you make yourself a slice of toast, as you need feeding up – I've a secret pot of bramble jelly that I made back in the summer to go with it.'

'That's an impossible offer to refuse. How lovely; thank you.'

A couple of minutes later the two women sat down, and Sukie treated herself to a small teaspoon of the precious preserve to spread on her slice of toast.

'I know it's only yesterday morning that I was taken poorly, but I feel so much better, really I do, although I know I must take care not to overdo it,' she said carefully. 'I can see that Pattie is throwing herself into working on reception, and doing a wonderful job so I'm wondering if I could take on some of the donkey work that Mr Bright does to ease the burden that has been passed on to you and Chef?'

As Sukie suspected, Mrs Bridge sighed in acknowledgement that she was certainly working quite hard just at the moment. Then the housekeeper's expression altered slightly so that she was scrutinising Sukie with a keen eye.

Although she wasn't quite sure of what Mrs Bridge was thinking, Sukie continued, 'I thought it might be helpful to you to know that I feel quite well enough to continue my administration work with the ledgers and the bills, receipts and invoices, as Mr Bright taught me how to do that when I was working downstairs after Wesley's funeral. I could write out the usual cheques for the milkman and the butcher and the baker and so forth, so that Mr Bright would have them ready to sign when he is well enough to come back to work. And I could organise the postal orders too, and the paperwork for the staff wages. I wondered too whether I could also spend a bit of time on thinking up some ways we could bring some more money into the hotel. I know it's short notice as it's only three weeks away, and of course there's a war on, but I thought, for instance, we could do something special for the night before Christmas Eve that would cause a bit of a splash, and that could swell the coffers...' Sukie's words faded from her lips as she still couldn't quite interpret Mrs Bridge's expression.

They sat in silence, but it was quite a decent, amenable sort of quiet.

Then Mrs Bridge said, 'Let me have a while to think about this. I need to find out when Mr Bright is returning to us, as if he is going to be back today and then at work tomorrow it's not really worth it.'

Sukie felt it prudent not to press her case further, just at the moment, although she was pleased that she had come right out with saying what she wanted to happen.

'Of course. Right, let's get down to dealing with this laundry and then I'll put it away for you, shall I?' Sukie said encouragingly.

As she stood up and reached for the list to tick the sheets and pillowcases off, Mrs Bridge said, 'I suppose that if we were to do something for Christmas then we could see what state the Christmas decorations are in. As I say, we've not had them up since the Christmas of thirty-eight I was telling you about.'

'Well, in that case it's high time those decorations saw the light of day again!' joked Sukie, who had been intending to ask about them but was pleased to be saved the trouble. Instead she enquired again about past Christmases at the Eddy.

This sort of request was manna to Mrs Bridge, and so they had to have more tea and for quite some while the housekeeper regaled Sukie with descriptions of how lovely the festive season had been back then, and how many candles they would get through that would be placed in special little holders on the branches of a large spruce that would be in reception for the twelve days of Christmas.

'We were all very proud of how we did Christmas here, and we often said other hotels would send spies in to have a peek at what we did, although I doubt they did really,' claimed Mrs Bridge, her eyes shining at the pleasant memories. 'The whole hotel would smell of nutmeg and cinnamon from all the ginger biscuits Chef made as decorations for the tree, and if we had children staying they'd be asked down to the kitchen to ice some of the biscuits, and we'd allow them to hang them on the tree in reception. Some of the iced biscuits were right horrors, but Michael would put those a bit further up the branches when the little ones went to bed.'

'What was your favourite bit of getting the Eddy ready?' Sukie asked, her mind buzzing with ideas.

'Well, it was only a little thing, but I always used to keep decorating the main banister down into reception for myself. One year – thirty-four, I think it was – I wound gold and silver material around each and every spindle, and put big gold bows at the top of each one. It took me nearly all night it felt like, but it was ever so pretty!'

'I bet it was. Right – let's definitely make the most of Christmas this year. We can do a utility Yule, but Christmas forty-three is worthy of note, wouldn't you say?' said Sukie, and Mrs Bridge nodded agreement.

And then Sukie remembered to ask Mrs Bridge about Mickey the optician, and why he hadn't let her pay for the return of Mr Bright's specs. She was curious as he seemed to have a high regard of Mr Bright, and yet for the life of her Sukie couldn't imagine how their paths had crossed as their worlds seemed so different.

Mrs Bridge explained that back in 1940 Mickey had helped organise the system for running a huge shelter under the Fruit and Wool Exchange in Brushfield Street, when it became clear the government's idea for the underground tube stations to be used was not wholly satisfactory. It was a well-run and much-needed shelter that could house 10,000 people with a squeeze, but what made it particularly special was that, guided by Mickey, the local people had found the space and then ran it wholly by themselves.

Mickey became well known for the efficiency of the system he set up, and so Mr Bright had contacted him, asking if the Eddy could help out in any way.

'Of course they could, said Mickey, and so as the months had passed and Mr Bright organised a whip-round among the local hotels for old blankets and so forth, Mr Bright and Mickey had become firm friends. Although Mr Bright doesn't advertise the things that he's done to help Mickey, mind,' said Mrs Bridge.

Sukie listened intently until Chef spirited Mrs Bridge away to deal with two chambermaids who were fighting over whose bucket was whose. Watching Mrs Bridge bustle off, she decided that it would seem very tame if she had to go back too soon to working behind the reception desk, as she was much more interested in the ins and outs of how the whole hotel operated.

She felt she had more to offer the Eddy than simply registering new guests or preparing their departure bills for settlement. Mr Bright clearly had a bit more about him too, as on first

acquaintance with him Sukie would never have guessed that
he had altruistic leanings, as well as being naturally a kind
man. She made a promise that she must think of him more
generously – he hadn't had to help Mickey's work, and yet
he had, and Sukie was sure that a lot of ordinary people had
hugely benefited by the compassionate nature of both he and
Mickey.

Sukie stole a biscuit to share with Polly and as she went
upstairs she realised that Tracy Benn's mere use of the word
'bolder' had had an effect on her.

For she did feel bold now, Sukie acknowledged, at least in a
small way.

And although she would never wish him ill, her next thought
was that she rather hoped that Mr Bright had a bad headache
still, and so wasn't going to rush back to his office behind reception any time soon.

She remembered the laundry and so after giving Polly his
share of the biscuit and tickling him on the wing just where she
knew he liked it, she then headed to the kitchen to collect the
sheets and pillowcases to put away.

As she did so, Sukie couldn't help smiling.

She had just thought of a new plan – actually, several plans
would be more accurate, and she was still improving the plans
that Mr Bright had already sanctioned – and she wanted to put
them all into action. Now, and at this very minute!

Indeed, Sukie couldn't remember the last time she had felt
as full of energy as this. Her ideas had always been within her,
she realised, and she had just needed a bit of confidence to give
them full rein.

That, and meeting Tracy Benn, of course. Now, Sukie told
herself, if ever she began to doubt herself, she would mutter,
'And what would Tracy Benn do in this situation?'

She couldn't imagine a more satisfactory method of pushing
to the side any doubts and fears, Sukie decided, and she delighted in the possibility that imagining a successful outcome

went quite a long way actually to making the said outcome become successful.

She skipped the rest of the way downstairs to start to make a new list of things to do.

Chapter Twenty-three

Quite early the next morning Sukie learned from Pattie that Tracy Benn had extended her stay by a whole week.

'I think you're the flavour of the month,' said Pattie. 'You and Tracy Benn at Claridge's, and now a longer stay.'

'Oh, I very much doubt that,' Sukie told her. But still, Sukie thought Pattie might have a point, as she suspected that Tracy Benn might be the sort of person to pick people up casually, and then drop them rather quickly and just as casually.

Sukie had noticed that there had been an almost indistinct edge of – what was it? – something a little too pointed in the tone of Pattie's words. She considered it for a while, and then realised that although Pattie had no reason to be, she had sounded perhaps just a little bit jealous of Sukie having been taken to Claridge's by Tracy Benn.

'Pattie, do you think we ought to go to the pictures one time, when you're free and John is working?' Sukie asked. It might be a bit obvious, but Sukie thought she should make sure that in the hierarchy of friendships Pattie knew she was very valued. Pattie's ready beam and immediate 'let's plan for Monday then, before you go off the idea' told Sukie that she had done the right thing.

Still, later on Sukie ran up the stairs and slipped a note under the door to the River Suite.

It had taken more drafts than she cared to think about until she was happy with it, and even then Sukie knew it was too flowery, and she also knew that she was already determined to hold something at the Eddy that would fundraise. But she thought that flowery and vague was a better option than being rude or abrupt, and especially so in the light of her ill-thought-out comments about the dress and nail varnish of the day before as the two of them had chatted in the street. Well, she hoped this was the correct assumption, anyway, as it would be a direct appeal to pick Tracy Benn's brain for ideas as Sukie badly needed bringing up to speed on what would pass for something chipper by London standards.

Thank you so much for taking me to Claridge's. It was extremely kind of you and I do appreciate it very much. It was my very first glimpse of such a special place – and how special it was! So much so in fact that it has got me putting my thinking cap on. I'm rather inclined, inspired by our elevenses, to propose to our hotel manager that we hold a special event over the Christmas period one evening at the Edwardes, probably on the evening before Christmas Eve, but ending actually in the morning of Christmas Eve. The event (and I'm not sure what it would be quite yet, nor the form) would partly raise some money for the hotel's coffers, although the bulk of the money raised could be put towards something useful for the war effort. I am wondering therefore if you would allow me to pick your brains as to what course precisely the evening event might take, as I am certain you shall know much more about this sort of thing than I do! I have hardly been to any evening outings since arriving in town, and have helped organise just one dance previously, down in Lymbridge, and that did not go wholly to plan. It may be that I haven't left enough time to do this and it is simply a pipe dream of mine. But nothing ventured, nothing gained, as they say. Please do not worry in the slightest, however, if it isn't convenient for you that we speak, or if for even the most slightest of reasons you would prefer not to do this, as I am sure you are very busy.

With very best wishes, Sukie Scott.

Within half an hour the telephone in Mr Bright's office rang, and when Sukie picked up the receiver it was to find Tracy Benn on the line, calling down from River.

'Sukie? Thank you for your note. It would be my pleasure if you accompanied me this evening as my guest – it's a surprise, but I just know you'll be bowled over with ideas.'

'Oh my gracious, I feel so presumptuous,' stuttered Sukie, who hadn't expected a reply along these lines. She'd been thinking more that she could treat Tracy Benn to a drink in the bar of the Eddy and ask a few pertinent questions over the course of half an hour.

'Not presumptuous in the slightest,' came the silky reply. 'I think the word you are seeking is bold.'

Sukie laughed. She wished she had been bold. It was more a request borne of a desire to earn her stripes in Mr Bright's eyes. She wanted to be seen as useful and capable, and this had seemed a small step along that path if she wasn't going to remain a receptionist for ever. There really was nothing bold about it, she knew.

Quickly Tracy Benn and Sukie arranged to meet in the hotel bar at ten o'clock. Sukie thought that time sounded terribly late for them to be going out, as to her it seemed more like when she should be coming home. It was when the public houses had chucking-out, for goodness sake! Even when Sukie had had a night out with Wesley, she had always been back by ten as that was when the front door to the Eddy was locked, after which the night bell had to be rung, which all of the Eddies liked to avoid as it usually led to quite a lot of ribbing the next day about what it was that had kept them out past lock-up.

However, Sukie was assured by Tracy Benn that even at this

late hour they would still be among the first to arrive where they were going but, no matter, this would give them the pick of the plum seats.

After Sukie replaced the receiver, her brow wrinkled with the thought of what on earth was she going to wear? She had to trawl in her mind through every garment that she and Pattie had with them, and eventually she came up with an outfit she thought might just about pass muster as long as wherever she and Tracy Benn ended up wasn't too brightly lit.

Unexpected help was at hand, however, as, not longer than an hour after the telephone conversation, Pattie popped her head around the door to hand Sukie a box.

It was quite sizeable and the cardboard of the box had been covered with a marbled aquamarine paper, while 'For the attention of Sukie Scott' was written on a label in gold ink. Sukie didn't think she'd ever seen anything so ridiculously extravagant and to judge by Pattie's quizzical expression, Pattie hadn't either. Pattie stayed watching as Sukie inspected the box, and then carefully lifted its lid.

Inside it, wrapped in fold after fold of delicate pink tissue paper, was a brand-new emerald-green bias-cut satin evening dress, which Sukie lifted out with a slither of the sumptuous material.

Underneath and neatly wrapped in layers of baby-blue tissue paper was a pair of silver shoes, and in a nest of lemon-yellow paper, a small silver clutch bag. There was still more to go, as a twist of coral tissue paper was opened to reveal a soft mint-coloured set of a lace-edge camisole and a pair of matching cami-knickers. A final small package revealed a Besamé lipstick in a gold metal case, the colour dubbed 'Victory Red', some Besamé black cake mascara and brush, and a small box of Atkinsons No. 24 face powder. There was an aroma of expensive perfume surrounding everything, and so Sukie guessed the inside of the box, which was lined with garnet-coloured paper, and the tissue paper, must have been sprinkled with scent.

Sukie was, quite literally, speechless. And so was Pattie.

'I'm jealous,' said Pattie.

'*I'm* jealous of me!' said Sukie.

They stared once more at the contents of the box for a long time.

This was how rich people lived, not ordinary women from Dartmoor.

'I can't accept this,' said Sukie eventually, with an undeniable tone of regret, as she stroked the thin silk of the expensive camisole. She shook her head sadly. 'It's too much.'

Pattie asked Sukie what on earth had prompted such an extravagant gift, and when Sukie explained, Pattie – who was clearly made of sterner stuff – said, 'You ninny! Of course you can accept it. I don't think it was sent to you with the choice for you to say no. And you'd better dress up to the nines with all of this, as you'll always regret it if you don't – not least as *I* want to hear all about it tomorrow, and I'll make your life a misery if you can't fill me in on all the gen! And then I'm going to want to borrow all of this at some time, you just see if I don't!'

'I don't know what to say,' said Sukie. 'How on earth did this happen, and so quickly? And what if none of it fits? I'm speechless.'

'John says it's another world for the rich,' Pattie replied, 'and how they can work around rationing and shortages. For enough money, and a word in the right ear, then just about anything can be bought, and right then and there. It's clear that there are shops that have pre-war luxuries for those that can pay. And you're young and gorgeous, and all the silk is cut on the angle so it will drape so that it flows around you and so while it's not exactly cut to fit it will hug you as if it was. The shoes might be trickier, but they are sandals and so I expect you'll be able to squeeze your plates of meat inside them one way or another.'

'I've never worn mascara,' admitted Sukie, who was still dumbstruck, although now also niggled by a doubt as to what she might be expected to do in return for this unexpected largesse.

'Give over, you daft maid,' said Pattie. 'Putting mascara on is as easy as falling off a horse.'

Sukie didn't think that was helpful. Although she hadn't ridden since leaving Lymbridge, she was a very good horse-woman and it was many years since she had last fallen off.

Chapter Twenty-four

Sukie was working until eight o'clock that night. She was happy to stay in Mr Bright's office for such a long time, as it kept her distracted from the feeling of butterflies in her tummy. In addition she thought she might have a slow start the following morning as they were going out at such a time, which obviously necessitated an even later return, and so she could make sure she had made inroads into what needed doing the next day.

She hadn't been out at night since Wesley had died, and in fact she hadn't been out much prior to that either as Wesley worked most evenings, and so Sukie wondered if this lack of experience in what London had to offer was also contributing to her butterflies. She wondered why she had been content to stay around the Eddy so much. It was quite unlike her, she saw now, as back in Lymbridge she had always been pestering Evie to join her in the Ladies Bar at the Haywain.

When Sukie couldn't think of anything else she could do to delay herself any longer, she made her way up to her and Pattie's bedroom, which she knew would be cold as she'd had to remind Pattie only that morning that a sliver of air was needed to circulate as Polly's presence made the air in their room seem fetid. Pattie had disagreed with the fetid bit although she had compromised by opening the window a further quarter of an inch, although she had quite a lot to say about Polly not being left in a draught. Sukie thought that she spent more time looking after Polly than Pattie and she always made sure draughts were avoided, and she was slightly put out that Pattie ignored her own contribution to the parrot's welfare. Polly, on the other hand, let each of them know that it was only his due, and that they should consider themselves very honoured that he let them spoil him so.

Sukie was just thinking all of this through, tossing a grape she had brought upstairs for Polly from hand to hand, she felt a trifle guilty as she had pinched this from a bunch that had been hot-housed and sent to a guest, when Michael stopped her to say he had a surprise for her.

Five minutes later there was a tap at the bedroom door and when Sukie opened it she was delighted to see Michael with a full-length mirror propped against him. It was badly chipped at the bottom on the right-hand side, but it was a *mirror*!

'I nabbed it from room thirty-one last week, when it got damaged by that young couple from St Thomas's on their honey-moon – and only an hour later Pattie was saying the small face mirror in your room was always in bad light and she never knew what she looked like top to toe when dressing for work, or for going out, and so I made sure this one was put to one side. Nobody has mentioned it since then and so I think it's going spare – and if not, it can always be spirited back to the storeroom. You go and have your bath, and while you're gone, I'll have this up on your wall in a jiffy,' Michael said in a rush, flashing her a shy smile.

'Jiffy,' said Polly from his cage in a way that suggested he approved of having a mirror in their room too.

Sukie smiled her thanks, and thought she probably should stand Michael a stout or two come Christmas, as he really was so very obliging. She thought he had a soft spot for Pattie, as she had caught him looking at her with what looked like longing in his eyes. If that were the case, Sukie thought, Michael couldn't be enjoying having John as the hotel's maître d'. It was going into John's second week at the Eddy now, but Sukie thought that Michael would get a respite the next week as John was moving on to nights for a week or so on the river ambulance, and Mavis would be moving from the bar to become maître d' in the restaurant.

Sukie put on her housecoat and made her way to the bathroom where she immediately turned the hot tap on in the bath, making sure the window was tightly shut as she wanted to get the air steamy. Then, while the bath was filling to about four inches deep, Sukie pin-curled her hair using a touch of semi-permanent fluid now and again, and she wrapped her head in the Liberty scarf. This was a tip she remembered Pattie's sister Julia, who had a small part-time business as a hairdresser down in Lymbridge, sharing with her, as apparently it helped a hairstyle to 'hold', as long as the hair was allowed to cool down to room temperature before the pins and scarf were removed.

She quickly put some warm water in the hand-basin and shaved under her arms and then every inch of her legs, carefully rinsing the razor in the water and drying it on her towel.

Feeling more than a little guilty as there was still three days to go before her official bath night, Sukie jumped into the bath and sluiced herself off.

Once dried and back in her room with her towel around her, Sukie spied a bottle of pink nail varnish that had been placed on her pillow that Pattie had magicked up from somewhere for her, and so she painted both her fingernails and toenails. As she waited for them to dry, she screwed the top tightly back on the nail varnish bottle and put it on Pattie's bedside table so that she could return it to its owner. She opened the window a bit more than usual so that any fumes could escape, as she thought they might be nasty for Polly.

Then Sukie looked in the mirror, but her attention was diverted by the bobbing grey head of Polly, who seemed even more keen than she was to look in the mirror. Sukie sighed and then arranged the chair and the newspaper so that the parrot could sit out of harm's way, while looking in the mirror at himself.

She leaned down and opened his cage door, and then encouraged him on to a finger with a 'Go on then'. Her tone was downbeat, and Polly looked up at her as if he was going to need more encouragement than that. She tried a chirrup, and a livelier 'Go on then', and very seriously Polly stepped on to her finger.

Sukie was right. Once he was on the chair Polly looked in seventh heaven as he moved himself around on the back of the chair and stretched his wings, never taking his eyes off his reflection.

'You're getting fat, with all those nuts,' Sukie told him as he was preening just a little too obviously.

Indeed, with Mr Bright out of the way and Mrs Bridge never having mentioned the parrot, Pattie had given up on any pretence that Polly wasn't in the hotel. She had even left a small note on the noticeboard and a paper bag pinned up beneath it, saying that if, when drinks were served, a single nut could be saved each time from the peanuts the barman would sometimes dole out, there was a very hungry parrot who would appreciate the nut. She'd drawn a funny cartoon that drew heavily on the popular 'Kilroy was here' cartoon, with, instead of Kilroy, a parrot peeping over the obligatory wall. It was such a successful request that Polly was indeed getting quite round in his tummy area, and sometimes guests accosted Pattie to request that she introduce Polly around one evening.

As butterflies tumbled around her belly, Sukie found Polly squawked most inelegantly if she took up too much room looking at herself as she got ready for her night out. But, managing to lean in front of the mirror at quite a precarious angle that meant she could see some of herself while her position was the least offensive to Polly, Sukie spent five minutes staring with concentration at her face in the mirror. She decided that although she still had shadows under her eyes, generally she looked better than she had for a while.

The parrot looked on approvingly as she stepped backwards and then lightly powdered her face and then, a bit too squeamish to spit on the mascara cake as most women lucky enough to have make-up did, Sukie moistened the brush in her water glass and then placed it on the cake of mascara to pick up some of the colour. She had already practised with the clean brush for several strokes before she dared to rub it back and forth across the mascara brick. Then, with a deep breath, she brushed her lashes, and – a tip from Pattie – before the last of the mascara had dried on the brush, she ran it over her brows to tidy them. Actually it really was quite easy to put the mascara on, once she had the hang of it, Sukie decided.

'Who's a pretty boy then?' said Polly. The bird looked at Sukie and Sukie looked at the bird, and then Sukie told him she was going to take the compliment in the spirit in which it was offered, to which Polly replied, 'Rum.'

Now for the real moment of truth, she told herself, and removing her towel, she carefully put on the matching set of mint underwear. Like the dress, they had a slight bias cut and just as Pattie told her would happen, they moulded themselves perfectly around every curve of her torso. Sukie didn't think she'd ever felt anything quite so exquisite lying atop her skin.

The shoes went on next – they were very slightly on the small side, with a higher heel than Sukie had ever worn. But the leather bands across her feet were so narrow and the leather so soft that Sukie thought they would soon stretch and become comfortable.

Finally she slinked the dress over her head. It hung perfectly, looking as if made for her, and her alone, even though Sukie knew it would fit anyone like that. Daringly she decided not to wear stockings as she was sure the suspenders would cause little humps in the smooth hang of the dress and interrupt its fluidity around her figure as she walked. The shoulder straps were dainty and had the tiniest ribbon for Sukie to tie the straps of the silk and lace vest, and the dress's low cut on both its front and back exposed more skin than Sukie had ever had on display before, and she grimaced when she inspected this in the mirror.

She and Polly looked at each other, and then Polly chucked his head as if in approval, although his subsequent declaration of 'Fat' slightly spoilt the moment.

He tried again with 'Nuts', and as a reward Sukie gave him a peanut complete with shell from a screw-top jar that Pattie had placed on the window, carefully enunciating 'Nut' back at him. Polly made short work of it.

Sukie dabbed a touch of rose toilet water on each wrist and behind her ears, and finally she passed the lipstick across her lips to give them a dark red colour. Sukie had forgotten what she looked like with lipstick on, and she was struck by how dramatic the effect was.

Almost ready now, she took off the scarf and removed the hair grips. Running her hands only once through her hair, she could see that exactly as Julia had promised, an attractive burst of soft waves haloed her face.

She slipped some money, the lipstick, powder and mascara, and a clean hanky into the little silver bag, and then looked at herself once more in the mirror that Michael had put up.

It looked like a totally different Sukie peering back at her. It looked like a sleeker, better version of Sukie pirouetting this way and that, admiring the way the green material swished and swung around her legs. It looked like a Sukie who had been more well born than she; normally never one to revel in her looks, Sukie wasn't totally convinced that she either deserved or felt comfortable wearing such glamorous togs. While she loved to dress up as much as the next girl, she had never before had the luxury of such beautiful hand-stitched garments made from the most exquisite of fabrics that must have been hoarded by a bespoke dressmaker from pre-war days.

'Pretty,' piped up Polly, and although it felt strange to be so immodest, Sukie, when she looked at herself again, had to agree.

Then it was back to reality as Sukie shuffled herself into Old Faithful. She looked dejectedly at its once-vibrant maroon colour, quite faded and thin in parts after its long spell of service, and its now uneven hem and threadbare cuffs and collar. She sighed, but it was the only coat she had and, at nearly five years old, it had definitely seen better days, although she thought it had plenty of wear left in it, all the same.

The swanky effect of just a few seconds earlier was muted

by the coat's dinginess in comparison to the finery of the rest of Sukie's get-up, although hopefully not by so very much if one didn't spend too much time looking at Old Faithful. So Sukie instructed herself to hold her head up high, and not to be down-hearted as there wasn't anything she could do or any reason she should be ashamed of being a woman with a respectable job who was trying to eke out every bit of wear from her clothes.

She closed the bedroom door just as Polly was demanding another peanut, and one last plaintive 'Nut' from the parrot chased her down the corridor.

She made her way slowly and a bit clompingly down the staff stairs, feeling strange and unfamiliar with the heel height.

'Let's hope I don't have to dance,' Sukie muttered to herself as she listened to her heavy-sounding footfalls. 'I'm not exactly going to be twinkletoes.'

Chapter Twenty-five

As Sukie clattered down the uncarpeted staff back stairs, just a floor below she ran into Pattie, who was making heavy weather of climbing up the stairs, although this was understandable as it was very late if one had been up since six in the morning, as Pattie had, plus she was hefting a sizeable armful of towels. Pattie looked exhausted, with a nipped-in look around her mouth, as if she'd been on her feet for hours in shoes that pinched, so Sukie guessed that aside from covering the reception, Pattie had had to bookend this with chambermaiding.

Pattie perked up though when she saw her friend clad in her magnificent gladrags when Sukie held open Old Faithful so she could get a peep. 'Ooh! I wish Evie were here to see you. In fact, I wish I had a camera. You look ravishing, Sukie, honestly, totally tip-top, really you do. Abso-bally-lutely!'

Sukie felt a little reassured about her get-up, although she did feel bad to be going out, when all Pattie looked good for was to fall into bed.

'Thank you, dearest,' she said, as she began to button the coat. 'I'm feeling more than a bit nervous, to be honest. And of course Old Faithful is a caution these days, but I can't help that. Although naturally it does have the great advantage of not being Thing.'

'Agreed – I don't think even Tracy Benn is ready for Thing. And anyway it's what is underneath that counts,' said Pattie reassuringly. 'I wish I had a decent coat to loan you, but mine is in an even sorrier state than yours.'

Pattie quickly darted to stack the towels neatly in the linen cupboard on that floor, and then she turned around and linked arms with Sukie for moral support, and together they slowly – slowly in part because of Sukie's heels, but also because she didn't hurry unnecessarily as she didn't want to make Pattie expend any more energy than was completely necessary – and rather grandly they made their way downstairs to the hotel bar, Pattie making sure that they caught John's eye as they passed the restaurant.

He swiftly came over with a 'My, don't we scrub up well?' and he pecked Sukie on the cheek.

Sukie thought this a trifle forward, but then he turned on his heel and very gently took the arm of Mrs Brown, a long-term guest who was very elderly and a bit tottery on her pins these days, and carefully guided her towards the lift that then Sukie felt bad and as if she had been unnecessarily hard on him.

In the Eddy's bar a resplendent Tracy Benn stood with an elbow propped on the back of a chair at the bar, wearing a gun-metal-grey outfit that was exactly the same colour across the beautifully tailored silk dress (not cut on the bias) and the presumably specially dyed handbag and shoes, which had an even higher heel that Sukie's.

Clearly, everyone in the bar was transfixed by Tracy Benn, although they were all trying hard to pretend to be such people of the world that they didn't need to have a full-on goggle.

Tracy Benn looked totally aware of the situation and was playing up to it, Sukie was sure.

Sukie had never before seen black nail varnish on fingers and toes, nor such a brooding blackberry-coloured lipstick that promised all sorts of lascivious behaviour. How daring! And Tracy Benn had what looked like a short mink jacket draped casually across the shoulders, while in one hand casually dangled what seemed to be an expensive polar-white fur stole.

It could not have been a more arresting look, in Sukie's eyes at least, and she understood completely why Tracy Benn was commanding everyone's attention.

'Two Suffering Bastards please, barkeep,' Tracy Benn said in a deliberate and very clear, smoky-sounding voice considering it was angled out of the side of the darkly lipsticked mouth vaguely in the direction of the barman. All the while the pair of heavily made-up but decidedly amused eyes above the blackberry-coloured mouth were turned full-voltage on Sukie.

Conversation died a stony death among the other occupants of the bar as now everyone gave in to the inevitable, and openly stared at Sukie and her companion, waiting to see what would happen next. Considering that what counted for drama in the bar of the Eddy normally peaked at 'one olive, or two?' when a Martini cocktail was being mixed, this was entertainment of the very highest order.

The white stole was proffered to Sukie, with a husky, 'I think you might find this keeps you nice and warm tonight – I wore it to the palace on a snowy night before the war and it kept me beautifully snug. And you'll feel likewise, I'm sure, and especially so once you have that Suffering Bastard inside you too.'

Deadpan, Pattie held out her hand, although she managed a quick nudge at Sukie in the ribs over the Suffering Bastard comment as she raised her arm to take Old Faithful from her.

Silently, and taking care not to glance towards Pattie at her side as she tried not to laugh, Sukie gulped and then made a nearly inaudible peeping noise.

With slightly trembling fingers she reached towards the done-up buttons on her coat front – and why on earth she had fastened them as she knew she was going to stop by the bar before she went out into the cold, she would never know, Sukie berated herself, as now she was making herself look ridiculous by not being able easily to shrug off Old Faithful – and then, after only the briefest of further struggles with the buttons as she'd come over all finger and thumbs, she squirmed at last out of her tatty outer garment and shook it vaguely in the direction of Pattie, hoping that Tracy Benn didn't notice how the coat's once-silky innards were now more holes than lining.

With an agreeable 'Have a lovely time', Pattie took Sukie's coat and then made herself scarce, although Sukie doubted her old friend would have strayed too far away while she and Tracy Benn were still in the Eddy's bar, as she wouldn't have wanted to miss the fun.

Sure enough, several seconds later, Sukie thought she heard a stifled gulp of laughter in Pattie's characteristic way from the corridor outside, with the lower timbre of John's answering chuckle, and Tracy Benn's eyes amplified from amused to provocatively twinkling.

Well, good, Sukie supposed, as at least one of them was positively enjoying themselves then.

With great care Sukie placed the thickly furred stole across her shoulders, the ivory silk of its lining causing a shiver of cold as it slid chill over her flesh. Sukie took care that neither the stole nor its plush lining came anywhere near her own dark red lipstick.

Then, remembering at the tinkle of ice cubes in the glass as their drinks were being prepared that she'd not yet actually even had a sniff yet of the Suffering Bastard, only just a little bit foolishly Sukie wriggled off the stole, and placed it carefully on a nearby chair.

She didn't dare glance over to look properly towards the small staff doorway at the side of the room. She was painfully aware that John and Mrs Bridge were now each craning their heads and happily jostling each other as to who could get the better view of Sukie and Tracy Benn through the door's small window. Still, a small happiness flared in Sukie's chest as she knew that John must have settled in well as an honorary Eddie in just a few short days.

All the same, Sukie hoped very much that they hadn't heard that latest comment about the cocktail as she thought she might never live it down. In fact, she'd wanted to laugh too as it was so ribald, but she hadn't dared.

The drinks were placed on the bar in front of them.

'*Gesondheid*,' said Tracy Benn, raising the glass to Sukie.

'Bottoms up,' Sukie replied before she could stop herself, and for a moment she froze with her own glass suspended at the perfect halfway point between the bar and her mouth.

She didn't know which was the more embarrassing: the prompt titter that erupted instantly from the barman that he swiftly bit back, or Tracy Benn announcing to the bar at large in a very clear voice, '*Precisely*. I can see that we *are* going to have fun!' as the hand with the snake tattoo was slipped for a moment around Sukie's waist, followed by, 'My, you look wonderful.'

Sukie took a sizeable sip of her Suffering Bastard. She thought she might be going to be in great need of its fortification.

The gin-based cocktail was stronger than anything Sukie had ever tasted, and definitely had a lot of pep about it. She had to admit to herself that it beat her usual port and lemon into a cocked hat.

Sukie couldn't think of anything to say and, perturbingly, Tracy Benn seemed happy just to keep smiling at her.

To fill the growing silence, the barman stepped in manfully to tell them that these cocktails were the very height of fashion. They had been invented at a hotel in Cairo just before El Alamein the previous year, he said, when Rommel was closing in on the city and good liquor was scarce – and were back then, allegedly, a cure for British servicemen suffering hideous hangovers through imbibing duff locally brewed booze.

Sukie thought the cocktail was so strong that it probably defeated the purpose of easing a hangover. Then it turned out Tracy Benn had visited that very hotel apparently, only several years before the outbreak of war. Of course Tracy Benn would have, Sukie told herself.

Their exit from the bar of the Eddy a few minutes later prompted a bevy of calls of the 'don't do anything that I wouldn't do' variety that were encouragingly voiced in their direction by the other patrons of the bar as Sukie and Tracy

Benn made their out to the hotel foyer. Sukie noted, however, that these patrons waited until the two of them were more or less through the door before risking a heckle, just to be sure that if either of them took offence it would be hard for them to come back in complaining, as they wouldn't know who had said what.

Once they were on their way, sitting side by side in the back seat of a taxi, a rather relieved Sukie couldn't decide whether the flush to her cheeks was due to the alcohol she'd just enjoyed, or the warmth of the luxurious white stole she was nestled into.

Or was it because she couldn't forget the look on the faces of all the other Eddies as she had stood in the bar as if she were a guest, most of whom seemed to find urgent business either in the foyer or the bar that they simply had to attend to At That Very Moment, and who stared narrow-eyed at Sukie in a way that left her in no doubt that she would be up for a grilling tomorrow about whatever it was that she was about to get up to.

At least Mr Bright was being kept in hospital for a little longer; thank heaven for small mercies, Sukie told herself. The mere thought of what his expression would have been just then if he had seen her simply didn't bear thinking about.

In fact, Sukie admitted to herself, he would have been so taken aback that he would surely have had a further conniption, pulled apart by the shock of Tracy Benn's outrageousness and him not wanting to make a scene near an affluent guest.

Chapter Twenty-six

The taxi pulled up outside the Ritz. Sukie had never been to the Ritz, and she felt a dazzle of excitement at the prospect. This was quickly doused somewhat, however, as Tracy Benn promptly led Sukie around the corner to a much less splendid entrance at the side.

A smartly dressed doorman opened a door for them, and they went down some steps that led to an underground restaurant that as far as Sukie could see had a clientele comprised nearly wholly of servicemen, with very few women around.

Sukie glanced around for a welcoming maître d' whom she expected would come to assist them, but then when she looked over again at Tracy Benn, it was to see her companion already waiting for Sukie at the far side of the restaurant, standing beside an unobtrusive door, and so Sukie made her way across the floor to that door.

They had to press a bell, and wait for somebody to open it for them. Tracy Benn stood in front of the peephole, and nudged Sukie close to her and told her to look at the peephole too. Presumably they passed muster, as the door opened silently on well-oiled hinges, and they stepped into a dark and silent vestibule.

Once they had passed through not one but two sets of heavy, inky blue velvet curtains that looked to Sukie as if they were padded, they finally reached where they were going.

It was a spectacular and jaw-dropping nightclub, with people dressed to the right and to the left in expensive colourful clothing that belied the frugality of clothes rationing and the dowdiness of the way most people had to dress these days. The affluent and the powerful really did live in a very different manner, Sukie thought.

Her senses were assaulted by the sudden riot of noise and colour, and Sukie's next thought was that for such a country maid as she, it was a little like descending into Hades.

She breathed in deeply, smelling the intermingling of tobacco and cigar smoke with expensive perfume (for the ladies) and cologne (for the gentlemen), followed by an after-whiff of alcohol and perspiration. If the Eddies, suitably scandalised over her and Tracy Benn in the bar of the Eddy, were here, there would have been no telling how they would have reacted when faced with all of this.

Sukie's second thought was that this might be the wartime equivalent of what the speakeasies were like during Prohibition in the United States twenty years earlier, as there was a sense of secrecy and hidden riches about the whole experience. Aside from the jazzy music, there was a loud hum of laughing and chattering, and so Sukie understood the need for the thick drapery at the entrance to the nightclub as this would mean that the noise didn't travel through to the diners in the restaurant.

She had quite a practical bent and so she peered upwards, and then at the wall dividing the nightclub from the restaurant, and from what she spied, she would have bet her weekly wage that a false ceiling and false wall had been installed, again for noise reasons, she suspected.

Sukie began to watch more closely what was happening around her, and then her eyes felt as if they were on stalks, as what she noticed now wasn't like anywhere she had ever imagined before.

But before she could consider more deeply the vista in front of her, a man came up to them. He was very clearly a man as he had a flat and hairy chest very obviously on display, a chest so hairy in fact that it was almost a pelt that had flourished itself into distinct whorls and twists. Just for a second Sukie wondered what it might be like to push her fingers through it. But the most extraordinary thing about him was that he was dressed as a woman, with a lot of glittering paste jewellery that matched his shiny silver dress, which was even more daringly cut that Sukie's. He smiled and said, 'Good evening, and welcome to the Pink Sink, dearies.'

Sukie was particularly impressed with his rose evening gloves, onto which a huge number of rings and bracelets had been placed.

'Hello, Raymond,' said Tracy Benn, and then Raymond pecked Tracy Benn right on the lips, an act that took place mere inches from Sukie's own face.

It wasn't a lingering kiss as immediately Raymond turned on his gold heel, accompanied by the sing-song sound of the bracelets softly clicking and clacking against each other as he (or should it be 'she', Sukie wondered) escorted them both to a table, whereupon he indicated that a waiter should trot over to serve them.

Sukie couldn't help but compare Raymond to both Alan and John, as maître d's at the Eddy, and she smiled to herself at how traditional, how *safe*, dear Alan and John were in their black dinner jackets and shiny patent shoes in comparison to this peacock vision who was now sashaying provocatively away from them in his high strappy heels as he headed back towards the door.

Not much later, Sukie felt she should give herself a little credit for how calmly she stared around with an affected casualness. It took a bit of effort, but she thought she just about pulled it off.

What she saw ranged from Pattie's vernacular of 'lavender' (well, what Sukie assumed that Pattie meant by it, anyway, although she wasn't one hundred per cent certain), and then across every persuasion and nuance of human behaviour, from the very mannish to the most feminine, and all manner of individuals in between, with many people dressed very extraordinarily.

She realised that although Tracy Benn stood out when somewhere staid and traditional such as the Eddy, here at the Pink Sink it was a quite different matter, as there were plenty of people who were posing and prancing about – yes, prancing was the only word for what some of them were doing, Sukie felt – in a much more eye-catching manner.

At first it all seemed very extreme, but then very quickly not so much so, especially as Sukie began to notice then some quite ordinary-looking people dotted around too, who all looked pretty relaxed, as well as some of the uniformed types that had been enjoying their supper in the room next door, who now looked much more up for fun as they lolled in their chairs with a shirt button or two undone and with their legs slung over the occasional armrest or empty seat. They certainly weren't on parade or making sure they were sitting up smartly. Goodness! What would their leaders have to say? Then the penny dropped – some of those in uniform who she was looking at would *be* the leaders.

Furthermore nobody seemed to be batting an eye at how anybody was dressed, nor how they behaved, nor how they sat or sashayed. Sukie realised she had been dazzled by the bravado of the 'Raymond' types, and she instructed herself that she 'mustn't judge a book by its cover'.

There was a lively, happy-go-lucky atmosphere, and although she had only been in the place for a short while, it seemed to Sukie as if the pervasive mood of the nightclub was that the country wasn't at war. Immediately, she remembered the shock when several of the young men that she and Sukie had grown up with had been killed in action or were declared missing, and she thought that those conflicting feelings – the feeling that every moment must be made to count, and the horror of fatalities – were what made wartime so confusing. One minute you could feel so buoyant, and the next so cast down, just like a puppet in somebody else's drama. And either mood would turn out to be very disorientating.

It was a nice, carefree feeling, though, here in the Pink Sink, and Sukie decided to enjoy it. In fact the mood of it took her back to the joyous summer when she'd turned eighteen, which was the last time she could remember feeling anything that approximated the impression she was getting from all around her.

'Chin-chin,' said Tracy Benn, and Sukie looked down to see a gold-rimmed champagne saucer before her, and that the three-quarters-full champagne bottle itself had been dunked in a silver bucket of iced water, that now had droplets of condensation quickly collecting on the outside.

The bubbles in her glass were tiny, and Sukie remembered Mr Smith once telling her that the very best champagne had the most minuscule bubbles. Taking his wise words into account, this looked to be among the very best champagne there was.

'Chin-chin,' said Sukie in reply, and they touched their glasses together carefully, making a soft, ringing ting. Sukie had only had champagne twice before, and the bubbles in her first sip made her eyes water.

Tracy Benn took a sip and then another, and then she put her glass down so that she could speak to Sukie without distraction.

'If you are going to organise your Christmas event at the Edwards, I thought the Pink Sink might be an eye-opener for you—'

Not half, thought Sukie, taking a large gulp of her champagne, as she was watching two men openly hug each other. This clasp wasn't in the way, say, that rugger teammates might put their arms around each other in celebration after scoring a try. Instead these men clutched at each other like lovers, with one loudly calling the other duckie – and then Sukie reminded herself: cover/book and book/cover, and with a force of effort she turned her concentration back to Tracy Benn.

'—and give you lots of ideas. Everyone here is very different to everyone else who is here, and yet everyone is having fun. A little shine and sparkle goes a long way in helping people enjoy themselves, and actually I think a lot of this is being done on quite a slim budget.'

Under Tracy Benn's guidance, Sukie stared about anew, this time paying attention to the smaller details. She noticed that if the music was louder than normal, and there were some eye-catching distractions, and lots of drink, any grubbiness on the carpet or scrapes on the wall faded into the background. The lighting added to this, with the beams being directed upwards, while the flamboyant waiters made sure they served with a flourish, they again kept the patrons' eyes quite carefully directed. Sukie could learn from all of this, she decided.

She tried not to be distracted by seeing some new arrivals, complete in fancy dress on what looked to be a theme of sybaritic satyrs, centaurs and other Greek gods.

'Yes, everyone certainly seems to be enjoying themselves. Does the Ritz know that this is below? It seems a... um... slightly... um... *challenging* set of folks here, I would have thought, when compared to what the Ritz must be used to.'

'Hmmn. I think you'd be surprised, Sukie, at what goes on behind closed doors in a place like the Ritz, and maybe even the Edwardes too. But yes, the Ritz does know, of course, not least as I dare say it owns this cellar. I wanted to give you a peep into another world. I was thinking that you could invent a new world for *your* guests, and then they'd enjoy whatever it might be that you'd create for them much more than just an ordinary tame old-fashioned Christmas party. I'm not suggesting anything quite like this, of course, as even I don't think the Edwardes is quite the place for *that*. But I am hoping you find something here tonight to be inspired by. I always find that I come away with more than I arrived with. Ideas, I mean, of course.'

Sukie took another sip of her champagne. Her new confidante certainly had a provocative way with words.

And then she remembered that the drunk who had floored Mr Bright so abruptly had been staying at the Ritz, and so she was sure that Tracy Benn was correct that the wealthy got up to all sorts on the floors above, the more unsavoury of which would be smoothed over by the hotel, if so needed, Sukie supposed.

Tracy Benn pointed out this and that to Sukie, and told her

to pay close attention to the lighting and how the waiters ran around, and the staff behind the bar; the paper streamers hanging from the ceiling, the gold-painted papier-mâché stars and moons that slowly spun suspended high above their heads, and so on.

Sukie noticed off her own bat small, out-of-the-way curtained-off nooks with comfy seating, and the way the more traditional nightclub tables were arranged all higgledy-piggledy, and Sukie realised the effect of this was to instil a friendly informality in the crowd. The music was jazz, but apparently the type of music patrons shimmied to changed most nights. The more Sukie looked about her, the more she started to notice the details of how the Pink Sink operated. By comparison, Tracy Benn herself, who had seemed so wildly exotic back in the Eddy, now looked perfectly ordinary to Sukie.

A second bottle of champagne was ordered, and fortified by Dutch courage, at last Sukie took the plunge.

'May I ask about you?' she said very cautiously. 'I've never met anyone like you before, and so you seem very mysterious to someone such as me.'

'Well, I expect you've been wondering if I'm a man or a woman,' said Tracy Benn bluntly, 'as most people do. And you'll have noticed – of course, as you're a smart cookie – that I do like to tease. I usually never say either way unless directly asked, which surprisingly few people dare to do as usually I like to give them what I call is "the look of No", so top marks to you for asking anyway.'

Tracy Benn raised the champagne saucer towards Sukie, who smiled back. She didn't think she'd ever been shot 'the look of No'.

'I won't put you on the spot by asking what you think—' thank heavens for small mercies, thought Sukie, as she still couldn't decide whether Tracy Benn was male or female, as she seemed most convincing in both roles '—but I was born a woman. However, I am a woman who has, even as a child, always looked mannish, or more accurately, boyish back then, much more so than I ever did girlish or womanly. I quickly discovered that quite often I liked pretending to be a boy, and then later a man, to the point that at times in my life I've lived wholly as a man, although admittedly not in this country.

'This is because it's been my opinion that men have, quite often, more interesting lives than women. Naturally, nothing compares to the sense of – and I can't think of a better word to say exactly what I mean – *power* that wearing a shirt and tie, and a handmade men's suit, and sturdy leather lace-ups, imbues on the wearer. A fine homburg and tightly belted trench coat really can see one through an awful lot, I find.

'My father made lots of money as an industrialist, and my grandfather left me enough also that I am independently wealthy, and so I have always been able to please myself. I've had plenty of lovers of both male and female persuasion, and a short marriage even. To a man, it goes without saying. But these days I find I'm not so interested in satisfying my actual carnal desires so much as I am in spending time just in contemplation of the mere idea of them.'

Sukie kept very quiet. She had never considered that a woman – or a man, for that matter – might be quite happy to have a lover of either sex, and then choose to go back again the other way, and perhaps back again. She thought she might have to ponder on this further, but that now probably wasn't the time.

As they drank more champagne, Tracy Benn opened up, drawing a picture of growing up in a world of too much money, vacuous acquaintances, and a family who had used a succession of nannies, governesses and tutors to bring her up.

It wasn't long before Sukie started to feel a bit sorry for her. She sounded restless and rootless, and as if she was constantly searching for something, or someone, with which to fill her time. It didn't sound as if Tracy Benn, who had been an only child, had a close relationship with either of her parents.

'Have you considered working with your father?'

'We don't get on terribly well, and in any case his factories in this country have now been turned over to the war effort. And now I find I don't know how to do anything useful, and because of the way I look and behave I find too that people aren't falling over themselves to give me useful things to do,' said Tracy Benn.

'That seems a shame,' said Sukie, 'as I am sure you have a lot to offer. And I, for one, am very impressed that you were able to provide me with a whole outfit while never coming near me with a tape measure. May I ask a very impertinent question? Why have you gone out of your way to be so nice to me?'

Tracy Benn told Sukie that she had seen something of herself in her, in that Sukie was bright and intelligent. 'When I was your age, I wish somebody had told me that it's fine to try, and to fail, and I suppose that was what got me talking to you. I don't think we regret the things we do as much as the things we don't do, and I wish I'd realised that sooner, as well as the fact that it's fine sometimes if people don't like you, and I thought that maybe I could tell you that. I spent years trying to make my father care for me, and he never has – and now that I know he never will, I feel happier about that as I don't have to try hard all the time to please him.'

The comment about regretting what one hadn't done struck a chord with Sukie, and she stared at her drink. She had mulled long and hard already on her regrets that she and Wesley had never consummated their relationship.

'Right,' said Tracy Benn firmly, and Sukie looked up at her. 'That's enough about me for tonight, although I must add that you were very easy to sort out an outfit for as I knew a dress shop with a wonderful choice of things for a young woman like you, and so all it took was a single telephone call. And now I'm going to rustle up a nice young man to trot you around the dance floor, before we jump into our carriage home.'

This Tracy Benn duly did, although in fact it was a succession of young men who whisked Sukie this way and that across the dance floor.

Now and again Sukie would catch sight of herself in one of the large wall mirrors as a partner shimmied her past, and she could hardly recognise herself in her posh green silk dress and her glamorous red lipstick.

It felt heady and quite dreamlike, and as if she'd stepped into somebody else's life just for an hour or two.

The best dancer was, without doubt, a rather handsome man in army uniform, who told Sukie his name was Simon. The red-lined crown uniform sign on his neatly buttoned jacket meant, Sukie knew, that he was a major, and that he must be active on duty in the UK as no uniform signs like this were allowed on uniforms in active service abroad.

They danced three times on the trot, and as they paused for breath after their third dance she noticed Simon risk undoing a top button of his shirt under his tie. Sukie thought for an instant that he looked as if he might be about to offer her a drink, but then she caught Tracy Benn's eye, and she thought she had left her on her own for too long, and so she explained politely that she really must return to her table.

Simon took this in good heart and escorted Sukie back to her table, before rejoining his party of fellow officers who were seated at a large table at the other side of the nightclub.

Tracy Benn raised an eyebrow impressively in an unspoken query as to whether Sukie had found the young major attractive, and when Sukie shook her head, she leaned forward and whispered a jokey 'Liar, methinks!' right into Sukie's ear.

Sukie distracted Tracy Benn by pointing out that there was someone in a white shirt and bow tie, and old-fashioned tails, who was standing behind her, clearly wondering if she wanted to dance.

As she watched her friend move across the dance floor, Sukie wondered what she had felt like when she was in Simon's arms. He hadn't ignited anything comparable to the heart-leaping thrill she had found when dancing with Wesley, and he had kept the conversation very formal. But he had been quite fun neverthe-less, and he had made Sukie laugh, which was the first time any man had managed to do this for quite some time. She knew she would never feel for another man how Wesley had made her feel, but maybe that was a good thing, she wondered for the first time. If she were to meet somebody else, it would all be very different. And then, with a start, Sukie realised that this was the first time that she had allowed herself to think of the possibility that one day, a long time in the future, she might come to care for somebody again.

It was all very lively and jolly, and Sukie found she was sorry when it was time to go home, but Tracy Benn pointed out it was past three o'clock in the morning and that Sukie would be very tired the next day if they didn't call it a night. She had a party to plan for, after all, and that wasn't going to organise itself. And she had only a fortnight and a bit to get it all organised.

Sukie gulped when Tracy Benn pointed out the short time – it would be a real rush, that's if she could get it off the ground.

Still, Sukie was a little sad her night out was coming to an end. She nodded that it was indeed time to go, and made sure she caught Simon's eye on the way out to mouth a thank you at him for dancing with her so nicely. It was the polite thing to do, she told herself as she followed Tracy Benn into the cold night air of Piccadilly.

Polly was still perched on the back of the chair when Sukie crept bare-footed, holding her silver shoes, into her and Pattie's room. For an interloper parrot, he looked very much at home, and never showed any interest in the crack of air at the top of the window or their open bedroom door as potential means of escape, but then, thought Sukie, she wouldn't either if someone like Pattie was going to feed peanuts more or less on demand. Polly definitely knew which side his bread was buttered. Sukie offered a peanut, just in case he was peckish.

Pattie didn't stir or break the rhythm of her snuffly snores as Sukie undressed and carefully hung the expensive clothes Tracy Benn had given her in their cupboard.

She was just settling herself in bed when Polly flapped from the chair back across to her bed head. Sukie closed her eyes and tried to ignore him.

'Suffering bastard,' he announced in a rather good approximation of Tracy Benn's voice.

And Sukie chuckled to herself as she knew Pattie had a good ear for mimicry and that she would have taken great pains to teach him that just to make Sukie laugh, even though Pattie had had a long day at work and she had been very, very tired.

Chapter Twenty-seven

The next morning Sukie made sure she didn't get up too late as she didn't want to set tongues wagging about her night out any more than they probably were. Dressed and pouring herself a cup of tea in the kitchen, she overheard Mrs Bridge on the telephone agreeing to see Mr Bright in hospital.

Politely handing Mrs Bridge a cup of tea, Sukie asked her if she had any news on Mr Bright and Alan.

The housekeeper explained Mr Bright needed to be kept in for another few days and that she was going to visit; she planned to drop in on Alan while she was there. Looking over the rim of her cup at Sukie, Mrs Bridge suggested that she could join her if she fancied it, and Sukie felt rather flattered that she had been singled out from all the other Eddies to accompany her on such an important trip.

While Mrs Bridge issued Pattie with a rather long list of instructions for what to do in her absence (Pattie later said to Sukie that just about every eventuality had been covered, up to and very probably including the end of the world), Sukie prepared two baskets.

Into each she placed some clean pyjamas and leather slippers, a dressing gown and some hankies, a flannel and a hand towel. The Eddy always had spares of pyjamas and slippers in case guests had lost their luggage en route to the hotel, and Sukie thought both Alan and Mr Bridges could do with some clean clothes after such a long time in the hospital, especially as they had gone in with no toiletries, as each seemed likely to be there only a short time when admitted. Michael had taken a few bits and bobs over previously, but it was over a week later and so Sukie thought that both patients might be running low on what they needed.

Sukie raided the supplies cupboard, which again was kept for the convenience of guests. Concierge Stephen had the key to the cupboard, and Sukie had to wheedle him to part with it for a few minutes. Her haul included two of each of the following: razors with new blades inside, sticks of Levers Easy shaving soap, hand mirrors (monogramed with Edwardes Hotel on the back), small bars of hand soap, toothbrushes and some Colgate toothpowder, tortoiseshell combs, small notebooks and a pencil each.

Then Sukie added two copies of the previous day's *London Evening Standard*, hoping that Mr Bright and Alan wouldn't be too distracted by warnings of a rumoured new night-time bombing offensive that was about to be unleashed and that would put London under the cosh once more.

She even remembered a pair of clean shoe-bags for Mr Bright and Alan to put these possessions in, in case the hospital beds were free-standing with no bedside cabinet to hand; these simple calico shoe-bags with a drawstring were ordinarily left in each bedroom at the Eddy, so that guests could put their shoes in them to leave in the corridor overnight so that they would be whisked away and cleaned. Sukie had only been inside The Grange before, and as that was an auxiliary hospital converted from a large house, she didn't know what a purpose-built hospital such as St Thomas's offered to its patients.

Chef wrapped some biscuits he'd cooked specially in grease-proof paper, and Michael added a pack of cards for Alan in case he was feeling up to it. Sukie chose a selection of Agatha Christie novels from the hotel library, reminding herself to ask Alan if he wanted her to put a bet on a race or a football match for him, as she knew he was partial to an occasional flutter on the gee-gees. Sukie even remembered a couple of laundry bags so that she and Mrs Bridge could bring back the clothes and nightwear that would need a wash.

Sukie had a nagging feeling the she had left something out, and it was nearly five minutes before she remembered what it was. Mr Bright's spectacles, of course! She ran to fetch them from the top drawer in his office, where she had placed them after returning from Claridge's, and now she carefully wrapped them in another clean hanky. To her eyes it looked most definitely as if Mickey had done a splendid job as they shone as if brand new, and unless you knew how mangled the metal frame had been, it was impossible to guess.

Predictably, before they left for the hospital, Sukie found she had amassed quite an audience of fellow Eddies before her in the kitchen as she gave a final check to the contents of each basket.

She thought it best to get the ritual taking-apart-of-the-night-before out of the way.

'I was taken to a very posh nightclub, thank you all for your interest. It's called the Pink Sink and it is underneath the Ritz, although you enter by a side door. Tracy Benn behaved very properly throughout the evening, as did I, and although we didn't have any more cocktails after we left here, we shared some champagne. I had a very nice time, thank you, and we were back here at the Eddy not too long after midnight,' Sukie announced loudly and in such a way as to discourage further queries, hoping that she had headed off all the usual questions.

She buttoned up Old Faithful as she spoke and put on her scarf, favourite teal hat and gloves to fuel further the impression that she had Somewhere Else To Be.

She'd decided that a heavily edited version of the truth was much more sensible than going into too much detail.

She also felt the Eddies didn't need to know quite the extent of her griping headache on waking up, nor that she had been parched with thirst, or that actually she still felt a bit heavy-headed (tiresomely, her achy brow was still hanging around, despite having taken a couple of aspirins, and two hours later, another two) as well as an unfamiliar almost shivery feeling that left her most shaky on her pins. A Suffering Bastard and the champagne might have been a lot of fun the night before; much less so this morning, Sukie discovered.

'Not too long after midnight, my foot, as I woke up at two and your bed hadn't been disturbed,' hissed Pattie as she and Sukie watched the Eddies disperse and go back to work after Sukie had told them to 'shoo'. Their audible mutters of disappointment and, oddly, the occasion chirp of amusement could be clearly heard over the apparent tameness of Sukie's night, especially after such a promising start. 'And you might like to know before you see Mr Bright that your coat is buttoned squint.'

'Suffering Bastard,' Sukie hissed back. She looked down and gave a little groan of exasperation. She had, as Pattie had said, buttoned her coat 'one-over', so that it didn't sit square because the ill-matched buttons to their proper holes, and certainly didn't align with the efficient impression she hoped she'd left the fellow Eddies with.

'Suffering?' said Pattie.

Clever, thought Sukie, as she could take that either way.

'Bastard!' she retorted, and then quickly had to grimace a silent apology to Pattie as normally she was never that coarse. Mrs Bridge was now putting her (much smarter than Old Faithful) coat on at the other side of the kitchen, and so Sukie didn't have time to voice her apology. Sukie blamed the alcohol of the previous evening for her unexpected response.

Sukie needn't have worried as Pattie was still sniggering when she sat down on reception a minute or so later.

The two women set off, chatting happily about the Christmas decorations that Sukie would go through later, and whether they might be able to rustle up some Christmas trees from somewhere. Sukie realised that these days she looked forward to her chats with Mrs Bridge, and she sensed that the older woman liked talking to her too, which was nice.

At the hospital it was easier for them to pop in to see Alan first as they were told that Mr Bright, who'd been moved to a small side ward, was having a chat with his doctor.

Alan's bed was halfway down a long ward, and Sukie saw what Michael had meant when he had told them about the poor health of many of the other patients, as there were a lot of sighs and groans.

But although he was white-faced and very tired, Alan didn't look as bad as Sukie had feared, given how ill he had been when he was admitted. His speech wasn't great, and the muscles on one side of his face were very much at odds with the muscles on the other side, which gave the impression that part of Alan's face was slowly melting and slipping down. But his eyes looked alert and without too much difficulty he was able to let them know that he was feeling better, although he still had difficulty in walking and sometimes in remembering the right words to things he used every day.

Sukie asked him if he was able to read, and he nodded that he was. He cheered up no end once she said that, if he looked at the form while she and Mrs Bridge saw Mr Bright, then she would put a shilling bet on his top choice, any winnings to be divided equally. Before his stroke, Alan had been delighted to discover that Sukie knew almost as much about racing as he, and was just as willing to have a flutter.

Sukie actually knew a fair bit about racing as pre-war she had ridden out point-to-pointers for a local trainer who had been quite close to Lymbridge, and she had always loved going to the races at Newton Abbot, until racing had been suspended there at the outbreak of war. Now the racing sport was a bit erratic, as some racecourses in other parts of the country had started to have races again, while others had had to build temporary courses elsewhere if their facilities had been turned into an airfield, as quite a lot had. Sukie knew that Newton Abbot was being used for the troops to practise manoeuvres, and so she felt slightly – but only slightly – out of touch with the current form books.

For a couple of minutes she and Alan exchanged views on various runners and riders (it was more Sukie chatting, and Alan listening and then nodding or shaking his head to indicate whether he agreed with her or not). But as she and Mrs Bridge went to find Mr Bright, who'd been moved into a side ward, Alan managed to give Sukie a thumbs up in appreciation of her horsey knowledge and then he began studying the afternoon's race cards, his brow crinkled in concentration.

'You've done him the power of good, Sukie, well done,' said Mrs Bridge, and Sukie felt a small flush of pleasure at being able to make somebody's day better by doing so little.

Although Alan's improving health was reassuring, the same couldn't be said, however, for Mr Bright, and Sukie's mood immediately darkened on meeting him.

In fact both Mrs Bridge and Sukie were more worried about Mr Bright when they saw him than they cared to let on to each other.

He looked shrunken and washed out as he lay in the bed, his pigeon chest not seeming very pigeon-like at all now, and his lips a strange purplish-blue. His blinking was ponderous, and he could only turn his head and bloodshot eyes towards them very slowly.

It was hard to imagine him strutting around the Eddy in his distinctive manner just a week or two previously, or his inquisitive look out of the little window high in his office door.

His chin was whiskery and he was wearing a nightshirt that looked as if it had once been somebody else's. Sukie's heart went out to him. Mr Bright was such a *particular* sort of person that she was sure he would hate her and Mrs Bridge seeing him brought so low.

At first Sukie couldn't make out exactly what it was about him that looked at odds. And then she remembered that it was the first time that she was looking at him properly without his spectacles on. She could see deep two indentations, one on either side of his nose, where they ordinarily sat.

'Mr Bright, I have something for you,' she said, and she passed Mr Bright his recently repaired spectacles. 'Mickey sends you his best, of course. He was very busy, but he put you right to the top of the queue, and he wouldn't take a penny.'

Sukie was rather embarrassed to see Mr Bright's eyes well with tears as he put the glasses on, pulling the covered wire bits carefully behind each ear, and then he said, 'He's a good man, a very good man.'

Fortunately Sukie was holding the hanky in which the specs had been wrapped, and so she passed that to him so that he could have a quick mop-up, and tried to smile in a sympathetic way that she hoped he'd understand meant that she knew all of this must be very loathsome for him.

He told Sukie and Mrs Bridge that he had a terrible headache still, and that they thought he might have had a bleed on the brain. He'd been moved to the side room so that the nurses could keep a better check on him.

Then, in a small voice, Mr Bright confessed that he didn't think he'd been coming back to work for a while, as he didn't seem able to stay awake for very long.

Sukie felt unsure of what to say, but Mrs Bridge rallied, and she began speaking of life at the Eddy, and how much they needed him to get better as she and Chef were very busy without him, while reassuring him that they were all pulling together to manage in his absence, and so he wasn't to come back to work until he was well and truly up to snuff.

'And young Miss Scott here has got everything spick and span in the office for when you come back,' Mrs Bridge said, and she explained all the things Sukie had been doing, and how many covers they had had in for evening service in the restaurant the night before following a small advertisement in the *Evening Standard* that Sukie had talked the paper into giving them. 'And Miss Yeo has manfully stepped up to the plate too, by keeping her chambermaid duties going at the same time as spending some of the day on reception.'

When Mrs Bridge had to pause for breath, which took quite

a long time as she was a very skilled talker, Sukie stepped in to say that she was doing everything he had taught her already, and there didn't seem to be any area that was falling down. And the moment she thought she needed to get guidance from him, she would make very sure to come back and ask him what the procedure was, and what he would advise.

'Very good, Miss Scott, very good,' said Mr Bright. He looked towards Mrs Bridge and asked, 'It looks like everything is in hand then?'

Mrs Bridge replied that she thought it was, and that Sukie was being very helpful.

Encouraged, Sukie took the plunge, making sure very quickly to mention the money side of things. 'I have had an idea for a Christmas party to increase profits as regards the Eddy's accounts. And now that I've met Mickey, perhaps a proportion of the profits of the party could also be directed towards the good works he is doing in Spitalfields.'

Mr Bright looked very tired now, and he nodded feebly, although his 'Good' was so weak that Sukie had to crane to hear it. Mrs Bridge and Sukie caught each other's eye – it was time for them to leave. He closed his eyes and seemed to nod off instantly.

They put on their coats, and Sukie made sure Mr Bright had a drink of water nearby, as well as the items they had brought him, while Mrs Bridge went to have a word with a nurse.

'Ready now?' said Mrs Bridge said to Sukie when she returned a couple of minutes later.

'Miss Scott,' Mr Bright suddenly rallied with a manful effort, and called to them both just before Sukie walked out of the door to go and get Alan's tip for the bet she was going to place on his behalf. 'That party sounds a good thing, so I think you should go ahead. Mickey would be pleased to have a little money for the shelter, and you could also ask that poor mother of your former fiancé if there is a good cause in Bristol that a sum could be put towards in his memory.'

Sukie felt very touched. 'What a nice thing to say, Mr Bright, and how thoughtful of you. I'll get right on to it. We'll try very hard to throw a party that would be as good as if you were organising it.'

'And, Mrs Bridge,' said Mr Bright, 'if you want to promote Miss Yeo to Chief Receptionist in my absence, and Miss Scott to Junior Under Manager, with the appropriate badges, of course, with maybe the word "acting" in brackets for both Miss Yeo and Miss Scott, and recruit another chambermaid to relieve Miss Yeo, then that is perfectly acceptable to me. When I return to work we might have to rejig, but for now that looks to be the most sensible option. Assuming that is satisfactory with you, Miss Scott?'

It was satisfactory. Very satisfactory indeed, Sukie assured him.

And on the way back to the Eddy, Mrs Bridge treated Sukie to cup of tea in a tea shop in celebration of her (temporary) promotion.

Chapter Twenty-eight

By quite early that same afternoon Sukie and Pattie were already proudly wearing their new name badges, having been applauded by the Eddies and Chef in the kitchen. This was after they pinned the badges to their chests, and then were anointed in public confirmation of new roles by Chef. He presided over the proceedings with a playful pomp and ceremony, requesting that they knelt before him in turn on Mrs Bridge's footstool, whereupon softly he touched each of their shoulders with his favourite spatula, saying then 'Arise Lady Sukie of the Manager's Office' and 'Arise Lady Pattie of the Eddy Reception', exactly as Mrs Bridge claimed the king himself did when he knighted his loyal subjects.

Pattie was thrilled to have a complete break from chamber-maiding, and she kept saying thank you to Sukie, although Sukie had to insist repeatedly that she hadn't done anything to write home about, and that instead it was a combination of Mrs Bridge and Mr Bright whom Pattie should be thanking.

On the quiet Sukie had made up another badge with 'Lord Pattie (*acting*)' carefully inscribed upon it, and while Pattie was showing her proper badge off and generally larking about down in the kitchen with the other Eddies, Sukie nipped upstairs and attached the joke badge to Pattie's pillow for her to find later.

'Rum?' enquired Polly.

'No rum,' said Sukie firmly. 'Lord Pattie. Lord Pattie. Lord Pattie. Lord Pattie. LORD PATTIE.'

She hoped she'd schooled Polly enough in what he had to do when Pattie next went into their room.

Mrs Bridge told Michael where she thought the Eddy's Christmas decorations might be lurking, which was in a crawl space under the back staff stairs. But no, although he clambered gingerly right inside the cramped cupboard as a whole array of broken standard lamps and doddery staff dining chairs had to be pulled over and then passed by him out to a waiting Sukie to make enough room for him to have a good old poke around, there was no sign of what he and Sukie were looking for.

These Christmas decorations had last been put up in the Eddy five years ago now and a lot had happened since then, and so when Sukie and Michael returned empty-handed to the kitchen Mrs Bridge then announced that if they weren't there, then she really had no idea where they would be.

Sukie was determined to find them though, convinced that they would still be closeted away somewhere. The Eddy was the sort of place where it was rare that anything was thrown away, to judge by the stacks of old menus, the oldest being from a summer shindig in 1929 where rather a lot of dishes covered in aspic had been served – Sukie shuddered at the very idea, as she thought aspic revolting – and worn-through or cigar-burnt table cloths that Michael unearthed as he scavenged about in the various dusty tea chests.

Michael still had an hour or two to kill until he was next on duty and he seemed quite happy to investigate further, not least, thought Sukie, as he took the opportunity to ask her all sorts of things about Pattie, while managing to make sly digs at John at every opportunity. Sukie tried not to encourage him too much, although she did find it amusing.

An irregularly shaped box bedroom at the end of a dark corridor where overspill items of guest-room furniture had been placed proved equally as unyielding as far as the decorations were concerned, as did a small attic space that hadn't yet been given over to staff bedrooms.

What Michael and Sukie did come across in the small attic, however, was a sizeable collection of mirrors, that had been propped upright against three of the four walls. The mirrors ranged in size from the modest to the mightily stupendous, but what they all had in common was damage to their gilt and plaster frames. Presumably they had been collected there for repair but nobody had ever got around to it.

Sukie almost clapped when she saw the mirrors as, damaged or not, they were perfect for what she wanted.

Michael also unearthed a large and ornate bird cage, dating from decades earlier to judge by the huge amount of dust in which it was swathed. Michael said he would disinfect it and then give a lick and a promise to the paintwork, as it was much roomier than Polly's current home.

Sukie said if he got a move on with this, then perhaps Polly could be moved down while Mr Bright was still in hospital to either the foyer or to near the window in the hotel bar (as long as he was in the no smoking part of the bar), as guests might find the parrot amusing, and being stuck in their bedroom must be very dull for him. But before Michael did anything with the cleaning of the cage, she would check and see if parrots were allergic to disinfectant, as she didn't want to be responsible for, quite literally, knocking Polly off his perch.

Sukie was just about to concede defeat on the decorations front and accept that the Eddy had probably borrowed the decorations from the Capel, after all, when she remembered the little office on the kitchen level where Mr Bright had put her to work right after Wesley had died. She remembered that one day she had noticed, while idly staring off into the distance, an almost hidden wooden hatch at the back of the room.

And sure enough, once he'd crouched down and leaned through in a rather perilous manner – leaving Sukie with a comical sight of his up-ended bony behind weaving about – and accompanied by a selection of appropriate swear words, Michael was, with some difficulty, able to haul out five or six large tea chests, each stuffed to the gills with baubles and tinsel. Eureka!

She looked inside the small card boxes stacked inside the tea chests that the coloured glass dainties were carefully packed into, each box having internal dividers so that the decorations were all individually housed and wrapped in a twist of newspaper; suddenly an idea of the party she would organise began to come to her.

Sukie bribed the new chambermaid Gladys with the promise of a port and lemon at the end of the week, and asked her carefully to wash every single bauble, and to very gently shake and then brush out all the dust from the tinsel.

In a couple of tea chests were what looked to be eighty or ninety large red bows, and so Sukie asked Mrs Bridge the best way of perking those up. Mrs Bridge thought steaming might work, and then she said, 'Leave them with me, Miss Scott, and I'll see what I can do.'

Sukie retreated to the quiet of Mr Bright's office and began to make a list of all the things she needed to do, beginning with a telephone call to London Zoo to find out whether disinfectant could be used on the bird cage that was now sitting in the alleyway behind the hotel.

An hour later she was still deep into making her list, and jumped when Pattie came in unexpectedly, carrying a very welcome cup of tea for her.

At the top of the list was 'MAKE THIS THE BEST PARTY THE EDDY HAS EVER SEEN', followed by 'MAKE A HUGE AMOUNT OF MONEY FOR THE EDDY'.

Pattie read those two lines, and quipped, 'Easy-peasy then,' quickly dodging out of the way of the screwed-up ball of scrap paper that Sukie had scribbled all over and crossed out, and then lobbed at her friend. Pattie closed the door behind her, and Sukie turned back to her list, all forty-seven points of it so far. She dreaded to think about the Eddy's future if they couldn't work out ways of bolstering their income. A lot of people's homes (both Eddies and guests) and livelihoods (Eddies) were at stake, Sukie believed. It was a sobering thought.

Sukie had to ask herself for several minutes 'What would Tracy Benn do' before her nerves at the enormity of what would happen if it all went wrong dissipated, and she could concentrate once more on putting a proper To Do list together.

Chapter Twenty-nine

An insistent hum, then an ominous silence, followed by a dull thump.

Sukie stirred and turned over in bed. It was almost as if she had been dreaming but as she stared around the room she didn't feel the same as just after she had dreamt. Something had happened, she felt sure. She put on the bedside light and looked at Polly, who stared back at her with his feathers on the top of his head fanned upwards as if in agreement. She looked at the alarm clock, which read four forty-nine.

There was a screeching, sliding noise from outside. It was very loud. Polly squawked in fear and jumped on to Sukie's headboard on her bed, and she reached up to give him a comforting stroke as she swung her feet to the floor. He was so tame now, and housetrained as to where he did his business on a fold of newspaper, and so these days Polly had the run of their room, although quite often they found him happily sitting in his cage.

And with that, there was a serious of hideous groans as wood timbers broke, and slates and window glass slid to the ground, followed by shouts from people in the street outside.

Pattie stumbled out of bed and, clearly very groggy, grabbed on to Sukie for balance.

The noise, which Sukie had thought almost deafening before, more than doubled in intensity, and Sukie felt her wariness at the unfamiliar happening give way to a surge of adrenalin.

'I don't know what's going on,' she almost shouted, 'but I think we need to get out.'

Her voice panicked Polly, who began flapping around the room, and he screeched unhappily.

'Pattie, stand still while I get him,' Sukie said. There was a burst of running feet from the corridor outside and this sent Polly to Sukie's finger, his eyes wild and almost opaque in fear. She put him in his cage, which she hoped he would think of as a place of safety, and she flung his tartan blanket and her eiderdown over the top in the vain hope he would settle down and go to sleep.

Sukie and Pattie pulled on their clothes any old how, and shoved their feet into their shoes and their arms into coats.

They collided as they both tried to run through the door at the same time, and then Pattie said, 'Should we take Polly?' to which Sukie replied, 'I think he might be better here, at least until we know what has happened. It's too cold for him outside.'

There was an even louder clatter of falling masonry, and the friends raced down the stairs to see what had happened, and what they could do to help.

Outside, the Capel hotel, just along the street, had taken a hit from a bomb.

Stephen and Michael, both in coats over their pyjamas, each had an armful of slippers that guests had left at the Eddy over the years, and were handing them out to bare-footed guests who were staggering out of the Capel. 'It'll be a buzz bomb, you mark my words,' said Michael.

Sukie thought he was probably right.

And even though the bomb hadn't exploded, as far as she could tell, the way it came down onto the roof of the hotel must have been angled in such way that a catastrophic amount of damage was done all the same.

Nearly all the Eddies were in the street trying to do what they could to help, although Sukie had noted that Jane and Gladys had stayed behind in the Eddy to shuffle anxious guests down to the huge cellar and anterooms on the floor beneath the kitchen for safety, as this was the bomb shelter for both guests and staff.

Sukie could see that a huge section of the Capel's roof had sheared off and crashed down noisily into the street below, annihilating their staff accommodation. The air-raid sirens hadn't sounded, and so the staff and guests from the Capel must be very shocked and agitated.

She looked up, and even in the denseness of blackout on a moonless night, it was clear that the whole roof had gone. And the fact that there hadn't been an explosion told Sukie that the building was incredibly dangerous – there was an unexploded bomb somewhere on, in or near the building, and until that had been made safe the area was, quite literally, a minefield.

Chef, Stephen and Michael organised the Capel's guests and staff to stand well back from the hotel just in case more of the roof came down, and Jane came out with more slippers and shoes as the street had so much broken glass and shards of roof slate on it that every time Sukie or Pattie moved they could hear a crunching sound from beneath their feet. They helped put the guests into groups, and Sukie suggested to the Capel's doorman that if he got either his hotel manager Mr Sykes or, failing that, a receptionist to run back inside to get the registration book, and the ledger where the room allocation would be, then a roll call could be made of staff and guests.

She felt bad suggesting that somebody go back into a possibly dangerous building, but she knew that everyone needed to be accounted for. Sukie would have nipped in herself but she didn't know where the books would be. She'd impressed on the doorman, who was the only member of the Capel's staff she recognised, that time was of the essence as once the police arrived they almost definitely would close off the building.

And then a couple of bobbies did run into the street to take control, keeping people back and so forth, shouting that everyone from the Capel must remain in the street so they could be accounted for. Sukie raced back to the Eddy with a clutch of Eddies whom she ordered quite bossily to collect blankets, coats and yet more shoes and slippers for the Capel's guests. Many had had to dash out of the building in terror without even a dressing gown over their nightclothes, and were now standing with chattering teeth and bare feet on broken glass on an already icy road as the weather had turned very wintry.

Sukie stayed in Mr Bright's office as she quickly totted up the unoccupied rooms at the Eddy. Once she had done that, she asked Mrs Bridge to see which Eddies didn't mind topping and tailing in the staff beds, in order that emergency accommodation could be offered to a few of the staff from the Capel if they could bear the idea of slumming it alongside the Eddies on the staff floors.

Sukie then telephoned around local hotels for vacancies. Once she had a list of who could take who, and what the facilities were if a person only had the clothes he or she stood up in, she ran back to the Capel with a notebook and pen. She found that it seemed nothing was being done along these lines by the staff who belonged to the hotel, so Sukie began making lists of names, and then shifting people into groups ready to move them to new accommodation.

Two hours later, it was full daylight and the guests had by now all been dispatched by Sukie to new rooms, either at the Eddy or other hotels nearby, and most of the Capel's staff had been sorted too. Sukie had a master list of where everybody was, and their home addresses and contact numbers, and the room numbers of where they had been staying at the Capel.

Sukie kept expecting somebody from the Capel to tell her to stop interfering or that they had it all in hand. But nobody did, which she thought very shabby, and so she kept on doing what she was doing, helped by Michael who had nipped down on the Strand to hail early-morning taxis and send them up to the Eddy to collect the people who needed to be taken elsewhere.

Tracy Benn organised getting the taxis filled, and made sure everyone knew where they were going, and had business cards with the Eddy's number on it, and she'd scribbled Miss Sukie Scott on each card so that there would be a contact for them to speak to.

The whole procedure proved to be quite a test of the taxi

drivers' skill as it did take a bit of nifty driving backwards and forwards as the taxi drivers manoeuvred their cabs to turn around in the road once they had their fares on board, as the police wouldn't let anybody drive past the Capel as it was too dangerous.

But it was obvious that it was an emergency, and so not a single taxi driver complained, and they all took the rides for free.

Just when Pattie was about to go back to the Eddy to take her place behind reception, relieving Mrs Bridge, who had stepped in to cover for a couple of hours while Pattie ran about getting things for the Capel's guests, there came distressing news.

A young waitress called Irene, with whom Pattie had become friendly, occasionally going to the flicks together or window shopping in the West End, had been found dead in a stairwell at the Capel.

It seemed that poor Irene was the only serious casualty, and Pattie was distraught when she heard what had happened.

They were still in the street outside when the news came through, and Sukie saw Pattie's horrified expression. The colour washed instantly from her face and she began to shake, and Sukie thought Pattie was suffering from shock, the effects of which were very likely exacerbated by being tired and cold.

'Pattie, love, I think you need to go back to the Eddy and have a cup of sweet tea. Tell Mrs Bridge that I've sent you, and then go upstairs and check on Polly, and have a quick lie-down. I'll cover for you on reception and take over there from Mrs Bridge, and I'll come and get you after you have had a nap. You've had a big shock, I know, so don't try to be a heroine any longer,' said Sukie.

Pattie couldn't even raise the smallest smile of thanks, and so she just turned and plodded her way back to the Eddy. Sukie thought that at only twenty years of age, Pattie had seen a bit too much of what the war had to offer, and she hoped she would be able to have a little sleep.

Sukie sighed. The timing of this bomb was a total nuisance as she wanted to get on with her Christmas party preparations as time was most pressing on that. But obviously what had happened at the Capel meant that was the biggest concern, and so she didn't begrudge spending time trying to help in any way she could as she saw that they all needed to pull together in such an emergency.

She rubbed her back, which felt a bit achy, and turned to go back to the Eddy.

But then she saw the Capel's manager, Mr Sykes, was giving an interview to someone who looked to be a journalist to judge by the reporter's notebook, and so Sukie stopped to listen. The journalist had just arrived at the scene, accompanied by a photographer who quickly got to work, obviously keen to take dramatic pictures before the bomb was diffused and the clean-up began.

Mr Sykes said, rather pompously, 'It is a tragedy that a historic hotel such as the Capel has been so badly damaged. We believe the bomb is a V-1, and that it is still on the top floor of the hotel. We are almost certain that it has not exploded and therefore we are waiting for the specialists to come and make it safe, after which we will be able to evaluate the full extent of the damage to the building, and work out when we can reopen. It is a miracle we have only lost one life, that of a waitress.'

That was his statement in its entirety, and he refused to answer any of the journalist's questions.

Sukie felt disappointed in him. She didn't think it very fair to Irene that her death had been described as 'a miracle', and nor did she think it quite right that Irene's full name and age and place of birth had not been given.

In Sukie's eyes it seemed terribly disrespectful to the poor young woman, and she thought that if Mr Bright didn't come back to work very soon, and she herself had to be a spokesman for the Eddy if – God forbid! – there was a similar situation there and the press needed a statement, then she must learn by Mr Sykes's comments, and do it differently. After all, Irene would have a family somewhere, who would miss her very much, and for her employer to describe her simply as an unnamed 'waitress' just didn't feel good enough.

Then Sukie peered more intently at Mr Sykes. She felt a little guilty at that point as he looked very shaken, and Sukie could see his trouser legs vibrating, and so she knew that although he was trying very hard to keep the proverbial stiff upper lip, really he was very upset. It must have been horrible seeing his hotel descend into such chaos.

Sukie glanced upwards as she turned around again to begin her working day at the Eddy, and through a bit of wall that had come down immediately under where the roof of the Capel had once been supported, she noticed something most interesting. It looked to her to be some artificial Christmas trees poking through the gap in the masonry with the express intention of pointing themselves out to her.

There was a rumble, and a ripping noise that culminated in a crash that was loud, but not as deafening as when the bomb had hit, as some more of the masonry that was right under the hotel's roof tumbled down into the street, although this did shatter several more windows at the Capel.

The crowd gasped, and moved even further back.

Well, the Capel wouldn't be needing those Christmas trees now, Sukie reasoned as it was impossible that they would be ready to reopen for the festive season. And, for a while at least, those window boxes wouldn't be required either. They would, however, make the Eddy look very Christmassy.

She waited for a few minutes, and then she walked up to Mr Sykes. She should have done this earlier, she realised.

'Good morning, Mr Sykes. May I introduce myself? I am Sukie Scott, the acting under-manager at the Eddy, I mean the Edwardes, while our hotel manager Mr Bright is on a short stay in hospital. Please do come with me and have a cup of tea and something to eat at the Edwardes as our guest, as *you* need to keep your strength up, don't you think, as you are going to need to be on the top of your form over the next day or two, with so much to do.'

Mr Sykes nodded meekly in agreement; his feet, however, seemed to be rooted to the spot in shock.

'What a dreadful thing to happen to the Capel; you must feel very bad,' Sukie continued in the soothing voice she used for ruffled guests. 'Of course we want to do everything to help that we possibly can. I will let the policemen know where you are.'

She indicated to the nearest bobby where she was taking Mr Sykes. Then she softly slipped a hand under the hotel manager's elbow, and encouraged him to walk with her. Without a word, he did as she wanted, obedient as a small boy, although Sukie thought she heard him whisper, 'My sister in Deptford will be worried, I must go to her,' and so she said she would help him make the arrangements.

Then Sukie said, 'My friend Pattie, the receptionist at the Eddy, was terribly fond of Irene, and her loss is almost over-whelming news, so please accept our condolences. We have put eleven of your guests in rooms at the Eddy, and I have a list here of where we have found your other guests temporary accommodation.' Sukie gave Mr Sykes a moment to take this in, but only a moment. He looked as if he was thinking of something else, rather like Mr Bright had after the drunk from the Ritz had floored him so spectacularly in the Eddy's recep-tion, and Sukie wondered if Mr Sykes might have a concussion. 'Meanwhile there is something I'd like to discuss. I know the timing might seem opportunistic, but I wonder if we can come to an arrangement regarding those artificial Christmas trees and the window...'

Mr Sykes nodded vaguely, and Sukie helped him to a couch in the Eddy's reception. She indicated to Mrs Bridge that she thought he needed to go to hospital.

Still, before he was put in the next taxi Sukie asked for what she really wanted, getting another nod. While she felt compas-sion for what Mr Sykes must be going through personally, it wasn't to the extent that she was going to forget the Christmas trees or the window boxes, as the Capel didn't need them just at the minute but the Eddy most certainly could put them to use.

She knew she might feel bad about being so tactless later, but Sukie decided to worry about that, as and when.

Chapter Thirty

It was unfortunate that the morning that the buzz bomb dropped on the Capel was also the day that Operation Gravy Train began in earnest.

The previous year's profits from the black-market selling-on of turkeys for *breeding* and not *eating* had proved so successful that Chef had not been able to resist temptation again this Christmas. The Eddies had the previous year jokingly called it Operation Gravy and it had ended up involving just about everyone, other than Mr Bright, who had remained totally oblivious to the one hundred turkeys that were being ferried around the building at various times.

When Pattie heard that the one hundred turkeys of last year would be doubled to two hundred for this Christmas, she said it sounded as if it would be Operation Gravy Train.

Sukie thought that an amusing comment, and so did the other Eddies when Sukie repeated it to them, crediting Pattie for being funny, much as she would have liked to claim the joke as her own.

Careful plans had been drawn up, and every contingency possible taken into account for Operation Gravy Train. Every contingency except one, that is: an unexploded bomb on a hotel roof nearby, which meant police were swarming all over the street on the very day that all two hundred turkeys were making their way from the turkey farm in Norfolk by van to the Eddy.

Chef was beside himself, as he knew that the Norfolk turkey breeder would want to drop the turkeys off and then vamoose as quickly as possible. It was going to tempt fate if they tried to bring two hundred turkeys into the hotel, some probably weighing as much as sixteen pounds, right under the noses of the coppers outside.

It was Pattie who came up with the solution. Clearly her hour's lie-down had proved beneficial as she looked much restored, and as if the distraction of working out a way to bring the turkeys in was a welcome respite from thinking about Irene's death.

'Michael can head off the delivery van and direct it to a nearby side street,' Pattie said. 'Some of you Eddies can wheel those giant wicker baskets we use for the dirty linen down the back alley and to the van to get the birds.' She paused. 'The prettiest Eddies – you know who you are! – can divert the attention of the bobbies with tea and sandwiches, and a bit of chat, making sure the bobbies have their backs to the Eddy. I think I'm going to be *very* complimentary about their uniforms, strong arms and so on.'

And so a plan of action was agreed without any trouble, and Sukie understood fully why Pattie was so successful at getting men interested in her.

Rather against the odds, Pattie's hastily put together plan worked like clockwork, and none of the bobbies noticed the Eddies pushing the giant wicker baskets across the road at the end on the way to the van.

Of course Pattie was the ringleader of the Eddies who took trays over to the bobbies, and she made sure she had a slick of Sukie's new lipstick on, and she had rolled her favourite red skirt several times as the waistband to show at least two inches more leg than she usually would. The bobbies were transfixed.

In fact the plan worked so smoothly that afterwards, despite what had happened just down the road to the Capel and the sad death of Irene, once the turkeys were piled in the alleyway, and covered by newspaper and topped with two tarpaulins, a mood of happy buoyancy suddenly permeated the Eddy.

While what they were doing with the turkeys meant they were technically breaking the law, somehow it felt more like a playful bending of the official rules rather than an out-and-out heinous deed. Everyone had had to put up with so much scrimping and saving for so many years, and had struggled with eking out their meagre rations, that Sukie could see the appeal the other Eddies found at the thought of getting a share of the Operation Gravy Train windfall. It meant too that these turkey treats could spread a little welcome festive cheer among Londoners who would otherwise have a much less appealing meal to celebrate their own Christmases. Even so, Sukie didn't want to get involved herself.

Tracy Benn came to see Sukie, and clearly knew precisely what was afoot to judge by her comments along the lines of 'fowl day', 'mustn't get in a flap', 'feathering our nests' and 'let's hope nobody will be up before the beak'.

Sukie found it a comical exchange, but when she was on her own again, the more she thought about the turkeys, the more she realised she felt more than a bit peculiar about the whole thing.

She was very relieved too that Mr Bright wasn't in the Eddy, as she didn't think she would have been able to maintain a poker face in front of him. It was totally illegal, after all, and possibly would be an offence deemed to be treason, if the police discovered it, as it was contravening food distribution. Treason, at its most serious level of judicial penalty, carried the death sentence, Sukie remembered with a shudder. And what she found particularly distressing was the thought that some people elsewhere might find they got less than their entitlement of their already meagre ration of meat through this damned Operation Gravy Train.

Increasingly, Sukie felt very uncomfortable. What had seemed so amusing as an anecdote of the previous Christmas when shared over a late-night cocoa in the kitchen seemed anything but amusing now, she thought.

Also, she found herself to be more than a bit surprised that Pattie had allowed herself to be so instrumental in the plan for getting the turkeys from van to hotel, and so she wondered briefly whether this was a sign of John's increasing influence on her, or just Pattie growing into a woman who was a little bit less scrupulous than Sukie. She thought both Evie and Susan would have a lot to say about Pattie's involvement, if they knew, not that she, Sukie, planned on saying anything, but... And this feeling of misgiving intensified when she overheard Mrs Bridge say in a humorous, mock-serious voice to Chef as they dealt with the final stragglers of the turkeys, 'We need to keep an eye on our Miss Yeo, as it seems she's a bit of a minx, with all the makings of a criminal mastermind.'

Sukie thought she ought to pick a good time to have a word with Pattie, and suggest that she didn't make a habit of stepping outside the law. Sukie would use herself as an example: she was, and always would be, thoroughly law-abiding, no matter what the temptation.

Sukie was sitting on reception as she thought about how she should broach the issue with Pattie, as she listened to Mrs Bridge and Chef finesse the plans for turkey distribution as they sat in Mr Bright's office with the door ajar, when her thoughts were interrupted by a new guest checking in.

As luck would have it, he turned out to be a journalist who had made a reservation the previous evening, although Sukie hadn't known his occupation when she had made the telephone booking.

It wasn't the journalist that Mr Sykes had given a comment to, but a younger man who obviously thought Sukie was attractive enough that he should show off a little, presumably of the opinion that Sukie would be impressed if he boasted for long enough about the story he was researching. Sukie let his monologue at her continue for quite a long time as she worked out how to deal with it.

'Oh yes, Mr Franklin, how lovely to have you with us. You are in room four-o-three. And how interesting you are working on a story on all the different things that are, scandalously, being sold on the black market. Yes, the readers of your newspaper will want you to uncover some perpetrators if you can as it will be a very exciting scoop for you, won't it?' Sukie then – well, this the only word for it – bellowed, in the hope that Mrs Bridge and Chef heard, and could understand the gravity of the situation.

What Sukie wanted them to know was that, without warning, they now had a journalist in the hotel who would be *very* interested in the darn turkeys that were in the Eddy illegally, every single one of them.

Meanwhile the journalist had to take quite a step back, clearly thinking Sukie was deaf, or daft. Or, quite possibly, both.

As Mr Franklin grabbed his room key and then scuttled quickly across the foyer – his cardboard suitcase and his type-writer case hampering him somewhat as they banged awkwardly against his legs as he hurried away in search of the lift – he clearly did not want to stay around Sukie any longer in case she shouted at him again.

As she watched him hop from foot to foot until the lift arrived, Sukie had to face the fact that now she was herself implicated in Operation Gravy Train by helping to cover it up, which really hadn't been her intention, seeing as how wholeheartedly she didn't approve.

She realised then with a bit of a clunk how patronising she had been over the whole affair and how judgemental of Pattie, as really it was quite easy to step over the line of acceptability. Well, her own interaction with Mr Franklin had shown her this, and thus put her firmly in her place, Sukie thought, and then she ruefully acknowledged privately that, in the more general sense, life had a way of doing this and taking one down a peg or two when necessary. She decided she would try harder not to be full of pride or the belief that she was always in the right.

Damn and blast, she grumbled, thinking of the turkeys again.

And then Sukie promised that to make sure she wasn't a hypo-crite, she wouldn't eat any of the turkey Chef would cook on Christmas Day, even though that would be from a legally bought bird.

Chapter Thirty-one

Over the next few days, Sukie found she barely had a moment to herself, she was so completely run off her feet.

Firstly, she had to get Nellie's Christmas present off to Evie. Although it was a bit advanced for the baby girl just yet, Sukie's gift was a brand-new wooden jigsaw picturing a lamb and some daffodils that was designed for very young children. A guest had left it in the hotel when Sukie had first arrived at the Eddy, and it had never been claimed. Sukie retrieved the jigsaw from lost property, making sure she put five shillings in the honesty box.

Back in the hot days of summer, Mr Bright had spent a long time one afternoon describing to Sukie the tradition that the Eddy's manager would attend the morning service at the local church, when he would put the year's takings from the honesty box in the collection salver at the end of the church service. Sukie had realised she would most probably be representing the Eddy this year at the service, although Mrs Bridge had already joked that she'd go with Sukie to church in order 'to keep her on the straight and narrow'.

Later the same day as she sent Nellie's present down to Devon, Tracy Benn announced to Sukie that she had decided to stay at the Eddy for the foreseeable future, and so this meant that Sukie offered her the preferential rate for long-term residents, and then had to draw up the special letter of agreement to define the terms of the arrangement. It was the first time she had been in charge of preparing the documents, and so she took very special care to make sure that everything was correct. It took her quite a long time, but she didn't mind.

'How nice you are going to be with us longer,' said Sukie as Tracy Benn signed two copies, and then Sukie countersigned. 'You make us duller folk shine a little more by being near you.' It sounded trite, but Sukie believe this to be true. Certainly, it was in her own case, and Tracy Benn smiled back and said she wouldn't miss Sukie's fundraising Christmas knees-up for the world.

Sukie was especially well disposed towards Tracy Benn at the moment. For, only the day before, she'd received a thank you note sent to the Eddy by a grateful taxi driver, asking if the person with the tattoo on their hand could be thanked for the kind gesture.

Sukie had no idea what this meant, but she had contacted the taxi driver that morning to discover that Tracy Benn had taken the driver's number in each and every taxi, and then personally sent £5 in postal orders for every single man, dropped off at the taxi depots, to thank them for what they had done in the aftermath of the bomb at the Capel, when not a single driver had so much as mentioned that any fare should be offered as they ferried the shocked Capel guests, many with cut feet and goose-pimpled arms, to other hotels.

Sukie thought that Evie and Tracy Benn were very different women. And yet there was something about each of them that seemed to make Sukie respond to them. It was a nice feeling to think that she had made a good friend in London, and especially one who displayed, quite bravely, such a lot of character.

It had to be said though that Sukie couldn't help but wonder too, if Wesley had lived, whether she would have been quite so taken by such a strong personality. She would never know now, Sukie told herself, and so it was probably best not to think on it further. Instead she should just acknowledge she was lucky to have met somebody who encouraged her to be more confident.

Tracy Benn could never replace Evie in her affections, Sukie knew, but she thought she had room enough in her heart for both of them. And Pattie as well, as her right-hand woman. And Polly too, obviously.

In terms of getting everything ready for the party, Sukie discovered that she more or less had to make it all up as she went along as to how the party should unfold. She wished there was a rule book, or a list of handy tips, but there wasn't and so she simply had to get on with it.

Luckily, she remembered Evie organising an afternoon of summer revels in Lymbridge quite a while back, and then Evie partly putting together a New Year's dance, although Sukie had had to step into Evie's shoes to finish off getting things ready for the dance as Evie had been struck down with influenza. Now, Sukie freely stole from the happy memories of both those occasions, even if the stealing turned out to be more along the lines of the 'let's not do that' variety.

Sukie had decided to borrow a naval term to name the Christmas party.

It was: 'Crew to Dance and Skylark'.

This was Sukie's way of paying tribute to Wesley, as it reminded her of the last time she had seen him, as he had used this popular naval saying in his final words to her. She knew he would have loved such a party as she was planning.

Sukie also thought that the phrase 'Crew to Dance and Skylark' had something joyous about it, and therefore it seemed very appropriate for what she was trying to organise.

The war had dragged on mercilessly for far too long, and Sukie felt wholeheartedly that everyone deserved a bit of dancing and skylarking so that, for an hour or two, they could put aside the gloom of constant rationing, difficulties of travelling around, the horrible destruction they saw every day in London, and worries about loved ones who were elsewhere.

Sukie's thoughts drifted to 1939 and the first few months of the war, when everyone claimed it would be over come *that* Christmas.

How on earth did they get to the end of 1943, with still no sense of an immediate resolution in sight? It hardly bore thinking about, but the longer the war lasted, the prouder everyone seemed to be of discovering a fortitude and resilience deep within them that they didn't know they had.

Sukie felt her generation had had to grow up very quickly, but that at least she and Evie and their friends had had their childhood. For children born just before or during the war, they would have some very bleak memories to look back on, and Sukie's heart went out to them.

One morning Sukie went to a small printer's behind Fleet Street to price having some posters made that would advertise the event, as well as some artwork so that they could run a small advertisement in the *London Evening Standard*. There was an elderly person at the printer's who was very experienced in all things to do with lay-out, and he told her that there would be lots to work with from 'Crew to Dance and Skylark' so that the poster could marry a sense of Christmas with people dancing and larking around, and he could even bring in some of the themes of the fancy dress competition too.

Sukie had decided it would be prudent not to ask those who would attend the dance for a set fee for attending; she wasn't *that* confident of her organisational abilities. Much wiser, she thought, to give the attendees the chance to make donations on the night of what they felt to be an appropriate amount.

She canvassed Chef and Mrs Bridge's opinion, and then decided that the lion's share of the proceeds from the donations (assuming there were any, of course) should probably go to 'Mickey's shelter', which was now well known across London, and had proved the model for other similarly run publicly organised bomb shelters across the whole country.

After consultation with Wesley's mother, Sukie had decided that a much smaller amount should be spent in Wesley's memory.

For a modest sum, concierge Stephen had a friend who even these days could provide the Eddy with a modestly priced but nicely made wooden park seat that would be placed high on a hill in Clifton, where there was a lovely scenic view and where Wesley had enjoyed letting off steam as a boy. The seat would be dedicated to Wesley in a small brass plaque, and local people would be invited to sit there peacefully as they remembered their own lost loved ones.

As far as the music for the party was concerned, Wesley's band members who had been on stage with him on the day he died told Sukie that although they would have to leave the Eddy at midnight on the dot, they could do a nine to eleven-thirty set for Sukie, and they wouldn't charge for this, seeing as it was to be in Wesley's memory. They would set up earlier in the day with their second-best instruments, and just scoot off to their paid-for concert afterwards, as long as Sukie didn't mind them not picking up their belongings until the next day.

Sukie was a little disappointed that they couldn't stay playing until later, but they assured her that if the drinks had been flowing, by the time they left nobody would mind if the entertainment switched at that point to records.

They suggested the upright piano in the hotel bar could be moved downstairs, as she might find it came in useful, and Sukie felt that to be a very good idea. Michael and Stephen found themselves much less convinced when she made them haul it down the four flights of stairs to where Sukie wanted it, but she turned a deaf ear to their moans and groans.

However, before she confirmed anything with anyone, Sukie returned to the hospital to pay a visit to Mr Bright. She wanted to make sure he hadn't had a change of heart.

He hadn't, and so she explained that she didn't want to charge an admission fee for people who came, as she believed that if she waited until everyone had a couple of drinks and a dance or two by the time that she went around with a hat asking for donations, they would make more money that way.

Mr Bright, still reeling from the news about the Capel's un-exploded bomb and the death of a member of their staff, looked rather shocked at hearing the extent of Sukie's ambitious plans, although she was pleased to see him looking a bit brighter than he had when she and Mrs Bridge had visited.

Sukie was quick to reassure Mr Bright that although the dona-tions jar would be kept separate for the good causes, nonetheless the Eddy would make lots of money through a paid bar as they could do a slight mark-up on their ordinary prices.

But, she added, every person at the party should be given their first drink free, and as much lemonade or tea or coffee as they could manage would also be free, as would a simple spread of sandwiches, pork pie slices and Woolton pie.

She would ask the papers to send photographers, and she hoped the resulting publicity would be positive.

The party would be in the lower basement, currently the Eddy's bomb shelter, meaning it would keep everyone safe as houses should anything terrible happen. When Sukie had first thought of the basement area as a place where everyone could really let their hair down, it had been primarily for reasons of noise and not wanting to disturb any guests who weren't interested in attending the party. But then she thought it was a prudent place to hold it anyway, as the papers were full of rumours still as to a looming bombing campaign by Jerry, and so it would save a lot of dashing about on the night if the air-raid sirens were to sound.

And Sukie wasn't blind to the fact that although it was a large space in its entirety, and there was a perfect area for dan-cing, there were lots of private areas that could be themed so that there could be a quiet area, and a more formal area, and some secluded areas. She remembered from her evening at the Pink Sink, how eagerly people had disappeared into the dark-ened spaces, and although she didn't expect quite such louche behaviour from the revellers at the Eddy, she was sure many of them might like to spend a little time during the evening away from the hubbub of the larger areas.

She didn't go into this though when she described her plans to Mr Bright, merely assuring him that she had lots of ideas of how the downstairs area could be made to seem inviting.

She went into a little more detail when she told him that there would be photo opportunities galore, as there would be a fancy dress competition on the theme 'The Twelve Days of Christmas', as well as a tombola, lucky dip and a turkey that would be raffled off. Sukie felt a rush of hotness as she mentioned 'turkey', thinking if only Mr Bright knew what had been going on behind his back as regards Operation Gravy Train.

Still, it was obvious that Mr Bright wasn't aware of anything to do with illegally sold turkeys as his expression didn't alter one iota.

And meanwhile back at the Eddy, to everyone's relief, neither had Mr Franklin, the journalist doing a story on the black market, twigged that anything was going on right beneath his nose. This was something of a small miracle as a couple of times one Eddie or another would be lugging a tea-towel-wrapped bird upstairs to a guest bedroom for the guest who'd bought it to give away or to sell on to family or friends when Mr Franklin would walk by, and so another Eddie would have to leap into the breach to distract the journalist.

Although she was relieved that he hadn't got wind of Operation Gravy Train, Sukie thought Mr Franklin probably wasn't a very good journalist, as she was very sure that if she'd been in his position, she would have cottoned on very quickly there was a thumpingly good story unfurling right before her. She hoped that he would find a good story to report on, just not one that had anything to do with turkeys.

'And we have a new long-term guest called Tracy Benn, who has offered to be master of ceremonies for the evening,' Sukie told Mr Bright, thinking it would complicate matters if she tried to explain that really 'mistress of ceremonies' would be more appropriate. 'And as a thank you for our trade over the year, the butcher has offered to make us as many sausages as we need, and so I thought we could serve sausage sandwiches at two-thirty, with everyone out of the door by four o'clock on Christmas Eve morning. For a while I wondered if we should have the party on Christmas Eve, but then I thought that might not sit well with guests who wanted to go to midnight mass, or who wanted to go to church early on Christmas Day.'

Sukie thought she had managed to gloss over quite well the reason that the butcher had been so generous with the sausages was because Chef had let him have twelve turkeys at a vastly reduced rate.

'It promises to be exhausting,' said Mr Bright with a sigh, 'but it sounds as if you youngsters will all have the opportunity to paint the town red.'

'Well, I hope we'll have some older people there too, and that they will also have a lot of fun as well.'

Sukie had to laugh when Mr Bright then said that she'd better make sure their supplies of wax ear plugs they kept in the supplies cupboard were replenished in quantity before the party in that case, as if the older people were anything like him, they'd be needed... Sukie didn't think the older people at the party could be like Mr Bright, as she was pretty certain the mould had been broken when they made him.

Before she returned to the Eddy, Sukie popped in to say hello to Alan, who looked more or less the same as on her last visit, although his speech seemed a little more certain, and he was definitely most alert when it came to him saying that Sukie was mistaken if she thought the Derby was going to go back to Epsom from its wartime home of Newmarket the next year. Sukie liked to throw out provocative comments just to see how well he was. She'd forgotten to bring his winnings from his previous bet, which had romped home at twelve to one, but she made a joke of writing him an IOU for the six shillings and sixpence she owed him. She suggested a quick game of gin rummy with the cards Michael had sent Alan on his last visit, and was pleased that Alan was pretty on the ball as they played.

Now that she had Mr Bright's metaphorical rubber stamp on her plans, Sukie felt able to spend the rest of that day confirming the booking with the band. She ordered the posters at the printer's and paid for the advertisement to be placed in the *London Evening Standard*. She ticked many other items off her list too, including the sausage delivery, buying extra beverages (both alcoholic and plenty of lemonade), sorting out some extra ear plugs (in case Mr Bright had a point), giving Chef a budget for sandwiches both during the evening (these would be reconstituted egg, with lashings of salt and pepper), and after midnight (including a mammoth supply of Colman's mustard to perk up the sausage sandwiches).

Chapter Thirty-two

Over the next couple of days, Sukie spent a long time with Michael, who was proving himself increasingly useful as the Eddy's resident handyman as well as bellboy, down in the lower basement as they decided where all the mirrors would go. They also debated on what useful furniture could be moved down to that level from elsewhere in the hotel and the technicalities of putting up the Christmas decorations.

Once Sukie had it clearly in her mind how the lower basement should look, she nipped outside with a tray of tea and over to the couple of bobbies who were still, although it was days later, on duty outside the Capel to prevent any pilfering as there was a real problem now in London of people taking what wasn't theirs from damaged buildings.

This was to ask if they could rustle up a group of themselves and a few other young policemen who in their free time would be happy to slap a new coat of paint on the cellar walls and on the walls of the stairway up to the kitchen level (Sukie wanted dark grey, or dark green for this).

Sukie pointed out the party was a fundraiser for charity, and that anyone who helped get the rooms ready would be able to come to the party, where all their drinks would be provided for free, and she would provide a case of stout for the mess room of all the policemen who helped, but only after she had said their hard work was up to scratch.

The first snowy flakes of the winter were falling as she stood chatting with the men, and they all agreed that the smoky air from the coal fires locally and the brief flurry of snow made it seem very Christmassy, despite a lessening of the pre-war traditions of carol singers on street corners and people nailing Christmas wreaths to their front doors.

Tracy Benn consulted Sukie on prizes for the fancy dress. And once the bomb at the Capel had been diffused, and the building declared reasonably safe, Tracy Benn rustled up a couple of strong lads that she knew from the Pink Sink to help move the window boxes and securely fasten them in front of the Eddy's windows, and lug the Christmas trees down the road to the Eddy too.

Each day flew by in what felt like minutes, rather than hours, and it wasn't long before there was only a week to go until the party, and Sukie realised she was really enjoying herself.

In fact Sukie had always loved Christmas time, as it seemed such a celebratory, happy time. Up until now she had always spent it with the Yeos, and while she knew it would be a very different sort of Christmas for herself and Pattie now they were in London, she became determined to make it one of the best Christmases the Eddy had ever seen. The Eddy's meagre funds might mean they didn't have two pennies to rub together, but she wasn't going to let this get in the way of some top-notch dancing and partying.

Sukie had a flash of memory back to when she had danced with Simon at the Pink Sink; he had been wonderful at whisking her over the floor, and the time in his arms had simply flown. Sukie wanted that sensation to be one that every reveller and dancer would feel at her 'Crew to Dance and Skylark' party.

Of course it wasn't the first time she had thought of Simon since Tracy Benn had taken her to the Pink Sink, but it was the first time she remembered quite so vividly the sensation of him leading her so adroitly and twirling her across the dance floor without that thought ending abruptly and being replaced by a much sadder one of it going to be her first Christmas without Wesley.

Pattie was happy too, as things seemed to be going well between her and John. Sukie didn't see much of them together when they went out on their dates, but she noticed how he would always seek out Pattie for a word or two when it was quiet in the Eddy's restaurant once the main rush of patrons needing to be escorted to their tables had subsided. And several times when Sukie went to the kitchen for her night-time cocoa she thought she heard Pattie giggle from behind the closed door to the scullery, and an answering, deeper laugh from John at whatever she had said to him.

Sukie was pleased as well that Pattie was so obviously thrilled with the resurrected bird cage when Michael presented it to her. He had spent a long time secretly working on sorting it out, getting cold and shivery out in the alleyway behind the Eddy as he poured kettle after kettle of boiling water over it so that it was as clean as a whistle, and then putting it in an airing cupboard to dry thoroughly.

Pattie threw her arms around Michael and kissed him on the cheek when he gave it to her, saying, 'Polly will love this – he can come down to reception, at least until Mr Bright gets back, as I expect he gets so bored upstairs, and he'll find lots to look at. Thank you, Michael – what a wonderful thing for you to do.'

Pattie oversaw Michael's careful positioning of the bird cage, which he placed on a writing table that had been found in the attic and that he had lugged down to the Eddy's foyer. To make way for this, the aspidistra was moved from beside the grand-father clock in reception to a spot in the bar where it could denote the shift from the smoking area to a non-smoking areas.

Polly was duly installed in the cage in the foyer with much pomp and ceremony by Pattie, where he did his stuff entertaining the guests, very quickly being able to replicate the chimes of the grandfather clock in reception so accurately that soon nobody knew what time of day it was unless they actually looked at the clock. He could also mimic perfectly Pattie's Good Morning or Good Afternoon, with which she would greet new guests, causing a great deal of hilarity to the normally routine process of checking in guests, as he would call it to them from behind their backs as they were waiting for their room keys.

His calls for rum and shouts of Lord Pattie caused hoots of laughter too. Polly looked delighted at all the attention – like Pattie and Sukie, he was evidently having a whale of a time, and all the more so when Chef found a little red and white Santa Claus hat, which he placed over the handle to the cage. It looked ridiculous, but undoubtedly fun and festive, and it made Sukie smile every morning when she saw Polly try to work out a way that he could pull the hat into the cage. Sukie had tried to remove the offending bootee Pattie had knitted for Nellie and which was still in his cage, but Polly absolutely wouldn't let her have it. And then when she had him sitting on top of a turned-off lamp in Mr Bright's office for an hour or two after breakfast, and she could have nipped over to snatch the bootee from the cage, she found that she couldn't bring herself to do it as he loved it so much.

If Polly was being very good of an afternoon, sometimes Pattie would lift him from the cage and place him at the side of the reception desk on a tiny perch Michael made for him.

There the parrot sat in a very serious fashion as he surveyed his fiefdom, looking for all the world like a small grey king, with Pattie his loyal subject. Which was pretty accurate really, Pattie acknowledged, when Sukie said what a comical pair they were to look at.

Four days before the party, at the end of a long working day, Sukie spent a few minutes relaxing in Mr Bright's office as she had just made sure that all the books and the ledgers were thoroughly up to date. Even though she much preferred throwing herself into the party preparations, she knew that all the normal day-to-day running of the Eddy needed to be kept on top of, especially now that Mrs Bridge and Chef seemed content to let her get on with the hotel's administration.

Sukie's reverie was disturbed by John tapping on the office

door, asking if Sukie could accompany him as he had something to show her.

He led her into the dining room, and there she had a pleasant surprise.

It was only Mr Smith, who was dining with several dark-suited men who looked to Sukie very much as if they were War Office bigwigs, as indeed she knew Mr Smith was himself.

Sukie had long suspected that Mr Smith had managed to persuade Mr Bright to keep mum about Evie's surprise visit by promising that he would have a meal with friends at the hotel, or something similar. She knew too that they must have had dealings previously, as Mr Smith had recommended both herself and Pattie to Mr Bright's employ nearly a year ago now. Mr Smith had helped Evie in the past, after the Ministry of War had sent him from London to stay at Pemberley, the guest house where Evie was lodging at the time, and he had quickly made himself a much-loved member of the tight-knit Lymbridge community.

What a nice man Mr Smith was; Sukie had always thought so, and this just convinced her further.

His party had already eaten their meal, to judge by the coffee cups now sitting in front of them.

'Mr Smith!' Sukie cried. 'How very lovely to see you here. I didn't know you'd made a reservation with us, but it is wonderful to see you.'

He introduced Sukie to his friends, and then he said, 'I'll let you into a secret, Sukie.' Mr Smith dropped his voice to a whisper. 'I used a pretend name when I made the booking for our supper. I thought if you knew I was coming, you might have made a to-do about it, and I didn't want that.'

She laughed as of course she would have insisted on making a fuss if she knew he was coming.

Mr Smith grinned back at Sukie, evidently rather pleased with his skills of subterfuge, and then he and Sukie fell to talking about the goings-on in Lymbridge, and about Evie and the baby, in which Sukie was especially interested. She grilled him on what they were all going to be doing for Christmas in Lymbridge, and she asked especially about Susan and Robert Yeo.

'I think it promises to be a quieter Christmas for them than usual,' said Mr Smith, after he had answered all her questions, 'but it will be Nellie's first, and so she will be the centre of attention.'

Sukie smiled – this was a lovely thought. She had a stab of homesickness for Evie and Nellie, and Lymbridge and Bluebells, and having a sing-song around the piano in the Haywain.

But then Pattie came over with some brandy balloons and a bottle of the hard stuff, and as she and Pattie caught each other's eye, Sukie thought that while it wouldn't be the same having a London Yule, there might be very nice things about it here, all the same.

Mr Smith asked Sukie and Pattie to join his table, and John too, but Sukie declined as she didn't want to keep them hanging about at the hotel if they really wanted to get home. The rumours about an intended renewed aerial offensive soon to strike still abounded, and although Sukie hadn't noticed a decline in covers each evening in the dining room, she thought it prudent not to try to detain anyone, just in case the rumours turned out to be true. Pattie and John thought differently though, and pulled up some chairs, after John had gone to get a further two brandy balloons for them both.

What Mr Smith didn't know, however, was that Sukie had made the secret sign to John that the bill for Mr Smith's table was to be on the house, and John had nodded back to show that he had received and understood the message Sukie had signalled.

Sukie thought it wouldn't hurt their reputation if some high-ups at the War Office had a nice meal at the Eddy, as that would, very likely, make them eager to return. And the fact that she could say a small thank you to Mr Smith for bringing Evie to see her when she had *so* needed her was simply the cherry on top of the cake.

Chapter Thirty-three

On the day of the party, which was the day before Christmas Eve, everyone was up bright and early, working hard on the party preparations.

Mr Bright's radiogram had been moved into the kitchen, and the BBC was broadcasting quite a lot of festive choral music.

Pattie was full of energy, and so was Sukie. Every time Sukie saw an Eddie, they seemed to have a merry smile on their face, and this mood of cheerfulness and vigour seemed to spread to the guests, who proved without exception good-natured and very pleasant to deal with. All the Eddies remarked on this, and Mrs Bridge told them to enjoy it as come the bleak, short days of the New Year, the guests would be back to their normal, sometimes demanding, selves.

Pattie and Sukie braved the blustery weather to make a lovely visit to Covent Garden market.

Dawn hadn't yet broken, but the fruit and veg market had been trading for what felt like hours. The traders wheeled their wooden flat-bedded wheelbarrows of produce this way and that, keeping up a lively banter between them. There was lots of shouting and whistling, and the sounds of shunts and bumps as crates of potatoes and sprouts were hefted about. There were crates of onions, and leeks, and greens. And in the first large box of carrots they saw that someone had put up a makeshift sign that read 'Don't let Rudolph go hungry this Christmas!'

The customers, who were greengrocers or hoteliers or restaurateurs, were almost as gabby as the traders, and there was a lot of noisy bargaining going on, with the traders trying to keep the prices high, and the purchasers attempting to whittle them down.

Sukie thought that the lively hubbub going on around them probably hadn't changed very much in the 300 years the fruit and vegetable market had been trading. She breathed in deeply, enjoying the earthy smells that reminded her of Lymbridge.

'What a din,' said Pattie, who was not so impressed. 'It would give me a headache to work here. And look how dirty everyone's hands are.'

'It is full of bustle, but I suppose one would get used to it very quickly,' agreed Sukie. 'And I think it's good dirt from soil, and not the dirty grime that we're more used to in London.'

Pattie and Sukie were on the hunt for one thing: mistletoe.

At first they thought there wasn't any as they couldn't see anybody selling it, and so they spent a little while discussing whether they could make something that approximated mistletoe.

Then a trader who called himself Big Rob sent them to Old Tom who sent them to Young Tom, each one of them promising they would bet their bottom dollar that while they didn't have any, there definitely was mistletoe to be had in the market. Somewhere.

'We're going to be sent to Old Nick next,' Pattie joked with Sukie, who told her to 'give over'.

But sure enough, it was indeed Old Nick they were told to find, and Pattie and Sukie had to clutch at each other in amusement.

They were pointed to the far side of the market, and there in the back of a decrepit and rusty van sat Old Nick, who was pretty ancient but who was sporting a red scarf wrapped around his pudgy neck that along with his white hair and mutton chop sideburns gave more than a hint of Santa Claus about him. Sukie went to say something along these lines, then thought it rude and shut her mouth – but Old Nick had caught the merriment in her eye and so obliged anyway with a cheerful 'Ho! Ho! Ho!'

Fortunately Old Nick proved to have bunches and bunches of mistletoe. He refused to take any money, saying if two such lovely lasses took a Christmas toddy with him, it would be payment enough.

They shared a toddy, and then a second as they had a lot of toasting to do, once they had started on raising their tin mugs to Sir Winston Churchill, and King George, and the Princesses Elizabeth and Margaret. It was only when they were halfway through toasting each of the reindeer in Rudolph's troupe that Sukie thought they had better stop with the toasting, fun as it was.

Grasping ridiculous amounts of mistletoe and having thanked Old Nick for his generosity with a quick Christmas peck on his whiskery cheek under a spare sprig, Sukie and Pattie agreed they felt quite tipsy as they made their way back to the Eddy.

It wasn't yet nine o'clock in the morning, but they had a real spring in their step, and their cheeks were rosy as they had been clapped out of the market by a bevy of good-natured traders who had jested, as they applauded, whether they might also be in line for a Christmas kiss, seeing as Sukie and Pattie had the necessary mistletoe.

It had all been going too well.

The hours passed, and suddenly Sukie was struck by a dreadful case of the collywobbles, which Mrs Bridge tried, and failed, to soothe with a large schooner of Harvey's Bristol Cream, which only gave Sukie an unpleasantly throbbing head. She hadn't mentioned the couple of toddies she'd already had, as she thought Mrs Bridge might have thought her wanton. But there was a mischievous glint in the housekeeper's eyes, and so Sukie wondered if she had guessed anyway.

As she rubbed her temples to no avail, Sukie was shocked that her happy mood had so suddenly taken such a backwards step. Her mood continued to plummet, and she couldn't get rid of her headache, and soon she was thoroughly regretting she had ever had the idea of putting on a party.

As is nearly always the case with these things, the preparations had all been very rushed towards the end, and during the afternoon Sukie's list of completed things to tick off never seemed to lessen, no matter how many were done, with the result that she felt exhausted to be point of shakiness and horribly under pressure. She hid in Mr Bright's office for a while, desperate for a bit of piece and quiet, and wrote out a new To Do list.

At five o'clock, Pattie rang Sukie from downstairs, asking if she could pop down to the party area to help her with something.

It was the right thing for Pattie to do, for when Sukie went to the lower basement to find Pattie, she could only stop and stare at how it had been transformed. It looked marvellous, she had to admit, and despite her relentless march of personal misgivings for the night ahead, everything did look most inviting and very Christmassy.

The tiled floor was sparkling clean, and all the bomb-shelter camp beds that were normally scattered about had been carefully stacked and locked away in a small anteroom. All the Eddy's paraffin heaters were warming the air – they would be turned off and removed at seven o'clock.

The mirrors hanging on the newly painted dark walls lent a magical feeling to the space, helped by the reflections that shone off the mirrors from a host of judiciously placed lamps. Each mirror had springs of holly and ivy tucked behind the top of the frame. The glass decorations had been suspended by threads tacked to the ceiling, and they too sparkled in the lamplight and winked charmingly in the mirrors as they turned slowly in the currents of the rising warm air.

The Eddies had made swathes of paper chains during their breaks that were now festooned everywhere, while there was a huge pile of paper hats for partygoers to wear that the Eddies had folded from rolls of red crepe paper that had been left over from some pre-war party. Some long strips of wallpaper lining paper that had been just sitting doing nothing in the attic had been carefully cut into long strips and then painted and left to dry wrapped around milk bottles. Suspended from the ceiling, they now hung down in seductive coils. 'Snow' has been made from wisps of cotton wool, and on the basement's shelves there were armfuls of fir cones and holly branches that had been collected on foraging expeditions by Pattie and John to Hampstead Heath northwards, and Peckham Rye to the south. Wallpaper lining paper had been painted green, and made into decorations, and yet more paper hats.

Here and there dotted around were washed coal sacks filled with pretend presents overspilling the top, as if some busy elf had been called away. Sukie knew the present sacks were to distract the partygoers' eyes from the basement's ventilation system, but she did like the way they added to the atmosphere.

Mrs Bridge's Mavis had sweet-talked a beau with a yen for painting into illustrating each of the twelve days of Christmas onto large pieces of paper, and Sukie had stuck these on a single wall near the dance floor in a harum-scarum manner as a talking point. And on the oldest and most battered tables hauled down from the attic, Sukie had got Michael to glue the colourful fronts of all the old Christmas cards sent to the Eddy pre-war, which she had found in the bottom drawer of Mr Bright's filing cabinet. The glue held the illustrations well on the tables, so much so that Sukie was very proud of how this had turned out, as it made the clapped-out furniture look fresh and very festive.

Changing the room from a bland bomb shelter into a Christmas feast for the eyes hadn't been easy, and it had required a lot of imagination on Sukie's part. But, my! How successfully it had been pulled off.

The cellar now looked like a proper-sized version of Santa's grotto, helped by signs like 'This way for Rudolph the Red-Nosed Reindeer's favourite tipple' and an arrow pointing towards where the drinks would be served, 'Dasher says you can sit here' pointing to a seating area, 'Donner and Cupid's favourite party snacks', 'The only Blitz(en) we like!', and – Sukie's favourite – 'Can you out-hoof Dancer and Prancer?' on a wall to another side of the dancing area.

Mrs Bridge had retrieved from under her bed a collection of party horns that would unfurl when blown into, some of which had a gaily coloured feather stuck to the end, and a huge collection of balloons. Apparently the Eddy had been going to host a society wedding the weekend after war was declared, and the celebration had had to be cancelled when the groom was conscripted before the wedding had taken place. Mrs Bridge had saved the horns and balloons, thinking they would come in useful one day.

Sukie was very pleased she had. They lent a cheeky air of frivolity that she liked.

A stage had been built, and the band had set their instruments up already. Behind, and above the piano that had been set against the wall, in large silver letters (courtesy of the printer) was glued to the wall in a cheerful curve the words 'CREW TO DANCE AND SKYLARK', with some musical notes playfully positioned both above and below the words.

Two bars for serving drinks had had been constructed, and John was currently overseeing their stocking. Boxes and boxes of glasses had been placed behind the bars, mostly borrowed from the Capel.

In fact, Sukie had to admit, it turned out to be very useful that they had the extra staff from the Capel to hand, as this meant she had been able to organise a quite complicated rota so that all the Eddies (the Capel staff had been told that while they were under the roof of the Eddy, they were most definitely honorary Eddies) could have some time to enjoy themselves at the party, and some time on duty.

On a large chart, she had allocated everyone places where they needed to be, from welcoming people as they arrived, to working in either the proper hotel bar upstairs or the two bars downstairs. She planned to have as many staff strategically spread around the hotel as possible to ensure that partygoers from outside the hotel didn't have the run of the upstairs floors, as Sukie knew those guest rooms needed to remain secured. Mr Bright's office should remain locked too, complete with the registrations book from reception inside, as they couldn't run the risk of giving trade secrets away to any stray hotel competitors if they so cared to visit.

Every guest at the Eddy had been given a bright orange ribbon to wear on a wrist so that the Eddies knew who should be allowed through their cordon. And all the Eddies were wearing similarly a clearly displayed bottle-green ribbon, so that the Eddy's guests and the partygoers from outside knew exactly who was attached to the hotel.

As a treat, Sukie had said the Eddies could dress up for the evening and not wear their Edwardes uniforms, which had caused great excitement. Aside from the fact that she wanted the Eddies to relax and enjoy themselves, she hadn't wanted the event to look too carefully policed in any pictures the press photographer might take.

There were various photographs displayed of the turkey next to a box of matches so people could see the scale of the bird for the raffle. Chef would bring the bird down when the raffle was drawn, and there would be a bottle of whisky as a prize for the nearest guess to its weight. It was one of only four turkeys left.

Operation Gravy Train had run like clockwork, and everyone would get a handsome bonus come Christmas morning, but Sukie had told Chef and Mrs Bridge that she thought it was the last time the Eddy should be used for any illegal activity like this. They had had a good run over the last two Christmases, Sukie pointed out, but it would be foolhardy to imagine that this luck could hold over a third year.

'I feel awkward about it, truth to tell,' admitted Sukie. 'The rationing is horrible, I know, and of course nobody has any spare pennies these days, but I think all the same the rules are meant to be followed. I know nobody got hurt, and this is a loophole that is widely being plundered, but I still don't think it sits well. I know some people will be getting turkey dinners who might not have had them, but I do so hate the thought of perhaps some other people going short on their rations due to a turkey shortage.'

Chef and Mrs Bridge had the grace to look contrite, and without Sukie needing to say anything else, they nodded their agreement that this is where all the turkey shenanigans stopped. They had winged it this year, they knew, but they really didn't want to go through it all again as it was very risky.

On the wall opposite, where the images of the turkey were displayed, hung a selection of photographs that had been taken of the various rooms in Mickey's shelter.

And at the bottom of the stairs there was Wesley's publicity photograph, with his name, birth and death dates neatly written on a card tucked into the left-hand lower corner of the frame. Wesley looked very handsome. A smaller photograph beside it was of the small brass plaque, already engraved, that would be screwed to the bench. Mrs Bridge had given Sukie a brass plant holder and one of the bobbies from the Capel had arranged for it to be made into the plaque. It had been delivered to the Eddy three days earlier, and had spent the time since then safe under Sukie's pillow, where she would hold it in her hand as she went to sleep. She knew she would feel a wrench when the plaque was sent off to Bristol.

On a happier note, the artificial Christmas trees Sukie had spied at the Capel had proved to be a great success. They were large and verdant-looking, and had obviously been very expensive when they were new.

Sukie made sure they were placed in strategic spots, so that now two flanked the hotel's entrance on the street, with one in the bar, another in the foyer, and the remaining three in the lower basement. They were all decorated with the big red bows, which Mrs Bridge had been able to do wonders with during their steamy rejuvenation, and so the decorated trees lent a real air of festivity to the proceedings.

Bunches of fresh mistletoe had been hung in strategic places, suspended by green and red ribbons that Tracy Benn had supplied and then showed Sukie how to run a scissor blade down the length of dangling ribbon so that it coiled fancily, and Sukie thought how pretty the pearl-like berries on the green foliage looked against the vibrant colours of the silk ribbons. She hoped these bunches would see a lot of kissing underneath them.

Sukie checked around the last of the tables and chairs that were being brought down from the restaurant. The restaurant had closed for the night and its double doors shut, with the hotel guests provided with complimentary suppers on trays in their rooms. The corridor to the restaurant had been turned into a makeshift cloakroom for coats.

To his great displeasure, Polly's cage had been moved to the empty restaurant, where it had been placed near the furthest window. Sukie was worried that the perfume the ladies would be wearing and the wafting cigarette smoke would be overpowering for him if he remained in the foyer with so many people walking past him.

Polly was livid though, and so they'd had to cover a lot of his cage with a couple of eiderdowns, as his turn of phrase had turned too fruity for public consumption.

Sukie wandered here and there, checking everything that she could think of. It all looked as it should do, she thought, standing in the middle of the small dance floor. It looked wonderful, and actually much better than she had imagined it would.

But Sukie felt depressed. She wished she could match the sparkle of the scene before her and the happy anticipation of the Eddies with her own mood, but no matter how she tried to gee herself up, she felt numb and sad.

She didn't know why she felt so blue. She had expected to feel, at this point, a sense of satisfaction at the very least, but instead all she had was a series of disagreeable lurches in the pit of her stomach, a dry throat and cold hands.

A dressed-up and heavily perfumed Mrs Bridge came up to Sukie, and gave her a brief hug, saying, 'Well done, Miss Scott.

Everything looks top-hole, and very professional. I'll hold the fort while you nip upstairs and get yourself ready – you look like the wreck of the Hesperus, if you don't mind me saying, and I'm sure that isn't the impression you want to give.'

Sukie looked at herself in one of the mirrors. Mrs Bridge was right – she was obviously very much in need of a wash and brush-up. Her hair had gone fluffy and wild, and she had a smear of dirt right across her nose.

'I've bought six bottles of champagne at my own expense, and so all the Eddies know to meet in the hotel bar at seven,' added Mrs Bridge. 'We'll all have a snifter to get in the mood. The guests at the Eddy have been told the bar is closed to them until seven-thirty, although of course we can serve them beverages in their rooms.'

Sukie felt her headache worsen, and so, as she began the long trudge up to her and Pattie's room, she raided the first-aid box in the kitchen for a couple of aspirins. She glanced at the clock and saw she needed to get a move on as the party revellers could arrive at any time from seven-thirty onwards.

By the time Sukie reached her room, Pattie had already got herself ready and disappeared back downstairs.

Sukie had the quickest of quick baths and dolled herself up in the same clothes she had worn to the Pink Sink. To her chagrin, she noticed the white fur stole still hanging in the cupboard. She had totally forgotten to return it to Tracy Benn, who had been too polite to point this out to her, which was embarrassing and very rude of her. Her oversight seemed to match her downcast mood.

She slapped some make-up on, and did what she could with her hair, which wasn't really playing ball as it remained frizzy and untamed, but by now she didn't really care one way or another.

Sukie's headache pounded and she sat on her bed for a minute. Hosting a party was the very last thing in the world that she felt like doing right now.

Her pillow looked increasingly tempting, but with a huge

force of will she turned her head away, and then made herself stand up and trudge downstairs, plastering on her face what she hoped was a smile.

The other Eddies didn't share her mood. The hum of happy voices drifted out of the hotel bar sounding excited, and, as she stood in the hall, Sukie heard the pop of a champagne cork.

She couldn't face seeing her fellow Eddies just yet, and so she let herself into the darkened restaurant, and went to stand by Polly's cage.

When she lifted the eiderdown, he looked dispirited too, managing only a desultory 'Rum?', followed by the faintest sound of a popping cork.

'I know how you feel, Polly,' Sukie told him gloomily, sticking a finger through the bars of his cage and tickling his head. Gently he took her finger in his claw, and they spent a little while looking at each other in quiet contemplation.

Then she heard Pattie say from outside the restaurant, 'I'll nip up and get her,' and Sukie knew it was time to join the Eddies and put on a bit of a show. So she gently extracted her finger from Polly's foot, and slid the eiderdown back down across the cage with a soft 'night, night'.

In the bar, Sukie had no sooner had a champagne saucer placed in her hand when all the lights went out, to a mixture of groans and cheers. Across the room in the darkness Sukie could see the orange light of several people mid-draw on their cigarettes.

She was close to the window and so lifted the heavy blackout curtain to peer outside to find the whole street black as pitch. It must be a power failure locally and Sukie congratulated herself on having planned for this ahead of time.

'Torches and storm lanterns while we get the generators going,' she shouted.

What she hadn't expected five minutes later though was Michael and Chef coming across by the light of a torch to have a word in Sukie's ear, as they had found that neither of the Eddy's two emergency electricity generators would start.

Meanwhile the band had arrived and Sukie could hear them lumbering about in the foyer in the dark.

With a 'John, will you sort the band please?', suddenly Sukie felt woozy and she put a hand to her brow. Dammit, she hadn't thought to get an electrician on-site for the evening, she berated herself, as it had never occurred to her that both generators could fail at the same time. How lax and incredibly stupid of her.

Sukie felt an overwhelming stab of dread. She knew that while they had enough light with the hurricane lanterns and the torches for the illumination needed for a normal air raid, these lights weren't in any way going to be suitable for a party.

She wasn't usually a quitter, but suddenly the failure of these two generators became the straw that broke the camel's back, and she felt the muscles in her neck tighten and her lower lip quiver as tears threatened.

They were going to have to cancel the whole party, decided Sukie; there was nothing else for it. She had tried her best to get a pleasant event organised, one that would unite all the Eddies into a new mood of them helping transform the fortunes of the Eddy as they headed towards 1944.

But, Sukie decided, she'd been deluded and on a fool's errand. She looked stupid, the Eddy had been made to look stupid, and the Eddies were stupid for allowing her to think that maybe she could make a difference. Deluded was the only word that could describe her.

And then she felt a quick wave of relief wash over her at the possibility that they didn't have to go ahead with the party. At least they hadn't taken money from people that they would have to refund. And she could go to bed to sleep off her headache.

Then Sukie felt her eyes fill with tears of frustration, completely subsuming the brief sense of relief. She felt furious, although quite spent in the physical sense. All that hard work and for nothing! The fickle finger of fate reducing her and the party to such a state of nothingness. The party *should* go ahead, but she didn't see how it could. Sukie could have gnashed her teeth in temper, except she couldn't risk a dental bill.

She stood there in the dark, wracked with indecision and quietly seething as she swore softly to herself.

She realised that she didn't know what it was that she wanted to happen – the party to go ahead, or the party to be abandoned – and neither had she a clue of what to say or do in either scenario.

She felt exhausted, and as if she might howl with anxiety. Earlier, for the first time since Wesley's death, Sukie had removed her engagement from the gold chain around her neck when she was getting ready, although she had carefully knotted the delicate strap of her silk chemise around it, positioning the ring directly over her heart. She couldn't bear, just yet, to not have it to hand, but Sukie had decided that it was at last time for her to stop wearing it in open view with her evening clothes.

She knew Wesley would have agreed it was time for her to do this, and she didn't feel she was besmirching his memory. And now as she touched it through the silk of her evening dress she felt fortified, almost as if Wesley were whispering in her ear: 'Take heart, Sukie, take heart. You have done the best you can, and it will all be all right.'

She felt a rush of love for him, but it wasn't quite the same feeling she'd had when Wesley was alive. Calmed, she closed her eyes and listened in the dark to the chatter of the Eddies around her, silently thanking Wesley for understanding.

'Where's the toolbox, Michael?' came Pattie's voice from somewhere near the door to the bar. 'I've had a tinker with a couple of generators in the past. And I had a boyfriend a long time ago who gave me a secret concoction of a rust-preventer and de-greaser that works wonders, so much so that I brought it to the Eddy with me – I'll nip upstairs and fetch it.'

Dear Pattie, thought Sukie. She was good with her hands, and while Sukie didn't for a second think there was a realistic chance of the generators springing back into life, she did appreciate Pattie's gung-ho attitude.

It was a very long twenty minutes before the electricity rumbled again, and a grubby and dishevelled Pattie and Michael came upstairs to what was quite literally a standing ovation, complete with catcalls and stamping feet, and loud applause.

Luckily the band had been able to sing a capella to keep everybody entertained, as both Eddy residents and the early birds for the party were now all squeezing into the bar.

Everyone seemed almost deliriously happy.

Everyone, that is, except for Sukie. Her headache was all-consuming, and for about the hundredth time over the last hour she wished heartily the evening was over, and that all she had to look forward to was a mug of weak cocoa.

Chapter Thirty-four

Despite the jolliness of those in the bar, Sukie's evening didn't take a quick upturn.

For the next hour and a bit there was hardly anybody at the party other than the Eddies. The guests at the hotel were few and far between, it seemed, while it turned out that there were only a very few outsiders who'd arrived on the dot of seven-thirty.

When she saw the twenty or so outer garments gently swaying on their coat hangers in the corridor, Sukie felt foolish that she had allocated such a huge amount of space for a cloakroom. What a relief that Mr Bright wasn't there to see her failure.

Tracy Benn found her sitting on her own in a corner of the bar, the famous red Schiaparelli dress looking perfect for the occasion as she walked over to Sukie. 'There you are. Stop hiding yourself away. You need to come downstairs and help us get into the party spirit.'

'I can't. It's a disaster. There wasn't enough time to organise a proper event, and I feel dreadful that all the Eddies have worked so hard to make the evening a success, and for absolutely nothing. I thought that some of the police would come at least, and I put a poster up in the staff room at the hospital, and with the mobile canteen people, hoping that they'd come too, but I suppose everyone is working. Our guests probably have much better things to do at other hotels. Whatever was I thinking?

We're not going to make any money, and Mr Bright will be livid.' Sukie rested her forehead on an upturned hand.

Tracy Benn laughed at Sukie's gloomy words. 'Rubbish!'

'Go away!' was all that Sukie could think of to say. She was beyond caring that this was a very rude way to speak to a guest.

John called across from his spot behind the bar, and said it would all be fine, he was sure, and as it was obviously going to be the sort of do that got going later, why didn't Sukie take the advantage of a thirty-minute nap as she looked done in?

'Topping idea,' said Tracy Benn, and more or less marched Sukie all the way up to the staff floor, saying that she would come back and get her later. Pattie was just leaving their bedroom, having had a wash and repaired her hair and make-up from the grime of the generators.

As Sukie pulled off her dress, she heard Pattie say to Tracy Benn as she shut the door that she wasn't to worry as Pattie was very happy to run upstairs and get Sukie.

On their beside tables, Pattie and Sukie had each piled presents, letters and cards from Lymbridge – they had agreed that they weren't going to open them until Christmas morning. Sukie reached for Evie's present, and she found too a letter from Susan. It was comforting just to hold them, and after a minute or two she felt better as she went to replace them on the bedside table. But as she did so, she noticed a few words Evie had penned on the outside of the brown paper package that she hadn't noticed earlier: 'For Sukie Scott, the very best Eddie, and the most wonderful friend anyone could have, with love.'

Trust Evie to find a way to bolster Sukie's spirits from all those miles away!

Sukie had a quick cry as everyone was being so kind and understanding, and then she fell into a deep sleep.

Pattie shook her awake as promised. Sukie sat up groggily, and decided she felt better.

'What time is it?' she joked.

'Just gone ten.'

'I'm hoping you mean ten in the morning, and then I don't have to get up.'

'You great lummox. Stir your stumps! The proper electricity is back on, by the way.'

Sukie had slept for well over an hour, she realised.

Her eyes were hideously puffy, and even though she reapplied her mascara, and Pattie tried to calm her hair by running a drop or two of semi-permanent lotion through, Sukie knew she didn't look her best. Still, there wasn't anything that could be done about it now, and so Sukie decided she wouldn't dwell on it further.

Good idea, Pattie's look seemed to say, although what her mouth said was, 'For goodness sake, get a move on, Sukie Scott, as we really shall have missed everything.'

They made their way downstairs using the staff staircase. Everywhere seemed deserted, a bit like the *Marie Celeste*.

But as they approached the dimly lit half-landing where the 'staff room' was, on the seats of the battered old sofa a couple were entwined and so intent on each other that they seemed oblivious to anything else. A satiny evening dress had been slid up to show rather a lot of thigh.

Sukie went 'A-hem' quite loudly, which she thought the polite thing to do.

The couple sprang apart and Sukie was momentarily deafened by Pattie squealing far too close to her ear.

The person in the shiny dress looked more than a little shocked.

But the person who'd been more or less underneath the person in the shiny dress was John, and he was hastily tucking his shirt back into his trousers. He looked more horrified at being discovered by Pattie and herself than contrite at what he'd been caught doing, Sukie couldn't help but notice.

Without a word, Pattie darted forward and punched him in the face as hard as she could, as she loomed over him sitting still on the tatty old cushions of the ancient couch.

'Ow!' the satin dress wearer went in sympathy.

Pattie didn't say anything. It was quite clear she was not best pleased, and now the message had been delivered she didn't really need to say anything further.

Sukie winced at the power of the punch, and thought it prudent not to say anything either.

John stood up and slunk downstairs, pulling the person in a shiny dress after him.

Pattie stood square, staring furiously after his retreating back.

'Well, I'll be blowed!' said a shocked Sukie, although whether she was more disturbed by John's cavalier attitude considering the staff room was never exactly private, or at her friend's rapid dispensing of punishment, she couldn't tell.

Pattie didn't seem to have heard her.

They stood looking at the empty staircase John and his friend had just escaped down.

Sukie was more shocked than she cared to let Pattie know that they had discovered John behaving so blatantly, but probably not as surprised as she should have been, she realised. She had always felt him to be something of a dark horse, very amenable on the surface but somehow a bit Machiavellian underneath. But still, she thought, it was a very shabby way for him to behave when he and Pattie were more or less promised to each other.

Pattie slowly turned her head in Sukie's direction.

'I'm just about to give him hell,' she said evilly.

Looking at the vindictive cast to Pattie's eyes, for an instant Sukie felt almost sorry for John. And then she said practically and with a hint of a smile, 'Maybe you could do that out of sight and earshot of the guests?'

Chapter Thirty-five

In the lower basement, it was a very different sight that greeted Sukie to when she was last there.

Pattie immediately left Sukie and made a beeline to have it out with John, who was obviously going to have a first-class shiner on his left eye. There was no sign of the person he'd kissed, who wasn't seen again that night.

Sukie heard raised voices momentarily and then John tried with only questionable success to usher Pattie into a quiet corner to avoid them becoming a spectacle, although Sukie thought Pattie had managed to say very quickly in the earshot of at least a couple of Eddies what he'd been up to and what she thought of that, before she let herself be led somewhere quieter. And what Pattie thought of John's behaviour right at this minute wasn't much, clearly.

Sukie was amused to see that Michael looked to be well aware of what John had been up to, and so he was hovering with the expressed intention of comforting Pattie, once she had had it out with John. Sukie didn't rate Michael's chances, sadly, as although he was very nice as a person, she doubted he had quite the looks to turn Pattie's head, and so Sukie hoped Pattie would let him down gently.

Leaving them all to it, the very first person Sukie saw was Viscount Kemsley, who had a photographer standing on one side as they pointed at one person or another, presumably deciding who to photograph, while on the Viscount's other side was a tipsy-looking woman.

Sukie nodded a demure good evening, and walked by without stopping.

When she felt she was sufficiently past them, she halted and looked carefully all around her.

It was a wonderful sight before her.

The basement was packed with people who were laughing and loudly chattering, and it was clear the paper hats and horns were a great success. The band were going great guns, and many people were dancing. Sukie smiled as Mrs Bridge and Chef foxtrotted past as they showed the young Eddies how to do it.

The nurses, policemen and mobile canteen people had by now turned out in force, just as Sukie had hoped they would. The Eddy's guests were there en masse too, as were lots and lots of people from outside, including many service people in uniform. Some revellers were in fancy dress, and Sukie found it impressive what people had been able to do with the 'Twelve Days of Christmas' theme.

She guessed the temporary cloakroom would be almost full now.

Best of all, Tracy Benn had clearly rustled up a large contingent of gaudily dressed and gently sozzled patrons of the Pink Sink who were definitely helping the party go with a swing.

They were wonderfully colourful and outrageous, and although some of the other more conservative attendees were giving these carefree characters second and third looks, Sukie thought that en masse they brought an enviable liveliness to the party. She sniffed and decided she could almost smell a palpable feeling of bonhomie radiating throughout the room.

Sukie closed her eyes for an instant and lifted a hand to her forehead, as if to check she wasn't dreaming.

But she wasn't. She smiled and sloughed off the last remnants of the anxiety and exhaustion of just a few hours earlier.

What was before her was beyond her wildest dreams, and the sense of relief she felt was almost overwhelming.

Tracy Benn spied Sukie and waved at her before she walked to the front of the stage and quieted the band, and then clapped her hands authoritatively for attention, and the crowd fell silent.

'Ladies and gentlemen,' Tracy Benn said in a clear and authoritative voice, 'in a moment I'm going to request that you *all* please take your partners to the dance floor, as we are going to J – I – V – E.... Jive! I'm going to teach those that don't know the steps by calling out what you have to do, and so we will have a dummy run. And I want you all to throw your hearts and souls into it as, after a practice, it simply has to be the most special jive ever.

'This is because this particular jive shall be in the memory of a man called Wesley, who was very special to our own Sukie Scott, who has put on this wonderful evening for us all tonight. Thank you, Sukie, and thank you, Wesley, for making our very admired Sukie so happy.'

There was cheering and applause, and Sukie felt very blessed to be surrounded by the people at the Eddy she had come to know and love, and she felt very happy that Wesley had been acknowledged so publicly. A while back she had felt wretched she couldn't spend Christmas with Evie and her new daughter, and the other Yeos, but now as she gazed around, she saw that the alternative was just as special.

'Wesley loved to sing,' Tracy Benn went on, 'in fact he was singing with this very band standing behind me at the precise moment he died – and Wesley loved to jive. But he was killed before he could take Sukie out for the dance he promised her on his last day alive, which was only this summer just gone. I never met Wesley I'm sad to say, but I know Sukie, and she is very dear to us all at the Edwardes, both colleagues and guests, and so as a thank you to her, and to Wesley, please jive and strut for all you are worth, and show Wesley, who will be Up There somewhere, I'm sure, how very much we all appreciate the sacrifice young men like him are making on our behalf. For poor Wesley would still, like many others, be alive today if we weren't fighting for freedom and what we believe in.'

The crowd went wild, and shouted as one when Tracy Benn commanded them, 'Wesley, hip hip hooray!'

The band started up, and Tracy Benn began to call out the steps for a practice. And when it was the jive proper, all those on the dance floor threw themselves into their best jive ever.

Sukie had been totally unprepared for what she had just heard, and she stood there, her mouth not quite shut. Pattie came up and slid her arm around Sukie's waist, giving her a squeeze, and Sukie put her arm around Pattie's waist. They stood, heads angled together, as they watched the dance unfurl before them, standing side by side, united in true understanding and friendship.

As the jive neared its end, Sukie told Pattie she'd be back soon.

She felt overwhelmed, as if the dazzling colours and myriad sounds of the party were going to make her faint.

Sukie went upstairs to their bedroom, intending to get her coat to spend five minutes outside, but even though there were spells of moonlight, snow was now falling quite heavily and so it felt too cold to do this. Back downstairs, she stared through the glass of the entrance door to the Eddy with the thick velvet blackout curtain closed behind her, and watched the snow come down for a while. It looked very Christmassy, and extremely pretty, especially as Sukie could see both of the large Christmas trees with their red bows standing proud of either side of the entrance to the hotel.

She turned and wandered into the hotel bar, which was very quiet with hardly anybody there. John was behind the bar, looking exactly like a man would do when he'd just been mightily torn off a strip or two by a very affronted woman. One eye was quite swollen.

'I'm not going to say a thing,' Sukie told him. John looked a little relieved at this. Sukie paused to let John know that she actually could say quite a lot on the matter of his fumble on the staff room couch, but that she was holding back. He didn't say anything, she then said, 'A double brandy please, though, and you'd better have one as well.'

John poured them both very large drinks, and he nodded to Sukie, indicating she should look behind her.

There, in the no smoking section, were only sitting Mr Bright, Alan and the very recognisable form of Mickey. They were sharing a bottle of whisky, and they all wore red crepe paper hats and were in their shirt sleeves. They were laughing, and looked very chummy, and the sight of them looking so comfy and jolly warmed the cockles of Sukie's heart.

Sukie wasn't particularly surprised to see Mickey, as he'd been invited, Sukie very much wanting him to be on hand because of the party being in honour of his shelter. But she absolutely hadn't expected Mr Bright or Alan to be there. She looked at John questioningly.

'Mrs Bridge and Chef sorted it with the hospital that they both could come back today, as I think St Thomas's was trying to get patients signed off before Christmas, if they can. I went out at five-thirty and collected Mr Bright and Alan, in part as a surprise for you as we thought you'd be tickled if they were at the party. And so when Pattie called you downstairs, we hid them in Mrs Bridge's bedroom until you went up to change. Mr Bright is going to be back in his bedroom later, and we're putting Alan in that small attic room where you found the mirrors,' explained John.

Picking up her brandy, Sukie went across to say hello, and to remind Alan that she still owed him his winnings. Alan told her to put it in the donations kitty, and so Sukie thanked him, thinking that she must remember to do that in the morning.

It looked as if the three men had made quite a respectable inroad to the bottle whisky, and then Sukie heard the exclamation, 'Tracy Benn's friend!'

Sukie jumped at this fourth voice, and turned to her left to discover that sitting hidden behind the aspidistra but very much part of the group was Raymond, the curling pelt of his chest hair peeping around the décolletage of his evening dress with just as much insouciance as it had the last time Sukie had seen him.

The four men couldn't stop laughing, even Mr Bright (who seemed totally oblivious to the fact that even by Pink Sink standards, Raymond was dressed very provocatively).

Sukie found that spending a few minutes with Mr Bright and his partners in crime really cheered her, to the point that when she stood up to leave them she took on their dare of chugging back the rest of her brandy in one huge gulp.

She was left spluttering and gasping, and she saw John raise the eyebrow that wasn't swollen, as if to say 'Really?'

She bowed in acknowledgement of the applause from Mr Bright and his chums, and turned to go.

'Can you keep an eye on them? And go with them when they want to go to bed, just in case they need a hand?' Sukie asked John as she passed him on her way out of the bar. She thought it wouldn't hurt John to have something altruistic to do. 'Don't mention Polly though, as I'll deal with that tomorrow with Mr Bright,' she added as an afterthought, as this might be quite a long conversation.

'Right-o,' John said, his voice rueful as he agreed to make sure they didn't come to any harm, considering they might well still be woozy after their stay in hospital. 'It's not as though I've anything else to look forward to tonight, I don't suppose. You'd better hurry if you don't want to miss Chef and the turkey raffle, and the judging of the fancy dress.' His tone had slipped from rueful to downright morose.

Sukie leaned over and patted his arm. 'Give her a bit of time, John. She might just get over it. Pattie's good at not holding a grudge, you know.'

Sukie thought Pattie needed to make her own mind up over what she felt about John's indiscretion, although she also believed that the Eddy was too small for anyone to openly bear a grudge. And while Alan was back with them, somehow Sukie doubted he was going to be able to return to being a maître d' any time soon, and so if John was going to be sticking around, there mustn't be any awkwardness that the guests could pick up on, Sukie decided, and she resolved to make this clear to Pattie, and to John, if he stayed. John was able-bodied and might well be a hard dog for Pattie to keep in the porch, Sukie could see. On the other hand, everyone knew there would be a shortage of men once the war ended and so who could blame Pattie if she decided ultimately that a healthy and obviously lusty man such as John was a prudent choice. And this was quite aside from the 'better the dog you know than the dog you don't' aspect to how it would be once the war ended, if soldiers returned with shellshock as they had from the Great War. Perhaps John would decide to leave the Eddy in order to concentrate on his river ambulancing, but whatever happened, Sukie thought he and Pattie should work out what they wanted to do without the benefit of her opinions one way or another.

John rubbed his chin and then gingerly touched his eye. 'That Pattie's got heck of a punch for a small maid, that's for certain.'

'Best remember that from now on then,' Sukie advised, the twinkle in her eye belying the solemn tone of her words.

Chapter Thirty-six

Downstairs in the basement the party was moving to the very-jolly-but-verging-on-raucous stage, and the Eddies manning the downstairs bars looked to be very busy.

The party revellers seemed to be enjoying themselves and to judge by the large glass jar Sukie had borrowed from the local sweetshop, it looked as if people had donated handsomely to the good causes as there was lots of money inside. Sukie caught Tracy Benn's eye and gave her the thumbs up, which was answered by a corresponding thumbs up back.

Sukie knew this money was for Wesley's bench and Mickey's shelter, and she felt very pleased.

She wondered then how much money the Eddy would take through its profit on the bar take.

Then she stared around, and laughed to herself. Lots and lots of cash would be swelling those coffers tomorrow, Sukie could see, to judge by the huge amount of alcohol that had been and was being consumed.

She felt vindicated in her belief that the party could be a fundraiser for the hotel, even without making people pay for their tickets.

A thought about Christmas 1944 flashed in front of her – and Sukie decided that if she were still at the Eddy then, this evening would look like a dolly's tea party compared to *that* Christmas party. Boy, would she go to town on the organisation! And she would set a proper target for the amount of money to be raised, which she hadn't dared to do this year.

Sukie had clearly quite forgotten her pre-party nerves of just a few hours previously.

She watched the various prizes being handed out for the fancy dress, and Mr Franklin looking quizzically and wrinkle-browed with confusion at the Eddies who roared with laughter and cheered and clapped when Chef held the turkey aloft and asked Tracy Benn to draw the winning ticket for the raffle.

Then Tracy Benn told the guests there was a pile of song sheets, after which the Eddies amassed in front of the stage to lead the room in singing five Christmas carols, and Jane took a seat at the piano. Sukie joined her fellow Eddies, even though she was just about tone deaf; it felt very special and she was proud to stand alongside them.

Sukie felt something being slipped into her hand. It was a fold of pink tissue paper, and the person pressing it on her was the impossibly glamorous Mavis, who leaned over and whispered to Sukie, 'Merry Christmas, dear – it's a small thank you for being so nice to Mother, and for putting on all of this for the rest of us.'

'Oh, you really didn't need...'

'I know,' said Mavis, with a smile. 'It's from both of us. Let me help you with it.' It was a small, delicate gold chain bracelet, beautiful in its simplicity.

Once the dancing started again – this time to records, as the band had had to leave – Sukie headed over to where Tracy Benn was standing and thanked her for her total triumph as mistress of ceremonies. Then Sukie thanked her for her lovely words about Wesley.

'Dance with me?' said Tracy Benn a trifle coquettishly.

And although Sukie had never danced with a woman before, at least not in the way she was about to, she decided she would enjoy the experience, no matter what anybody thought.

A couple of minutes later, there was a tap on Tracy Benn's

shoulder and Sukie turned her head to look straight into the eyes of Simon, the major with whom she had trotted around the dance floor so pleasantly during that night at the Pink Sink. She hadn't seen Simon arrive, and her heart gave a little flip that told her she was pleased to see him.

'Miss Scott?' he asked, holding a hand out to her.

Sukie glanced at Tracy Benn to see if she would be making a faux pas if she changed partners. The answering smile suggested not.

'Major,' said Sukie politely, as she moved seamlessly forward into his arms. She fitted them perfectly; it was as if they had been made for her.

'Simon, please.'

'Sukie.'

'So you are the brains behind this, I hear?'

'Well, I'm the guilty party, if that's what you mean...' For almost the first time in her life Sukie found herself flirting, and she was just a little shocked to find how much she enjoyed the experience.

Time flew by, and then suddenly a few more lights were turned on and Chef was announcing the arrival of the sausage sandwiches, and saying that the Edwardes hoped that everybody had enjoyed the 'Crew to Dance and Skylark' party and had found it the perfect aperitif to get them in the spirit for Christmas Day, which was – he looked at his watch – tomorrow!

Goodness, how time had flown. With a shiver of joy, Sukie realised that she and Simon must have been dancing together for well over an hour. She realised too that they were in a not particularly brightly lit part of the room.

And then she noticed that they were standing directly beneath the biggest, and to Sukie's eyes, prettiest bunch of mistletoe, as it had the perfect balance of green foliage to white berries.

Sukie felt herself teetering on the cusp of a new era.

She looked at Simon, and she saw him spy the mistletoe. She smiled, but then a happy memory of kissing Wesley under the mistletoe at the Haywain the year before intruded. Instead of feeling bad, she instead had a feeling of acceptance, and regret that she could never do that again.

Sukie looked at Simon. She did, maybe, just a little, want to kiss him, but she could tell that for her it still felt just a little too soon to do this, too near to the loss of Wesley for her to enjoy it. And there was something about Simon that made Sukie think that if ever he and she did kiss, she wanted to enjoy it very much indeed.

Her smile stiffened slightly, and Simon realised the moment had passed.

Instead he hugged her tight to him and kissed her chastely on her forehead, murmuring, 'Let me escort you over to your friends. Thank you, Sukie, for making my night so special, and Merry Christmas. And I hope there'll be a third time lucky when I won't need to deliver you back to your pals after you and me dancing together.'

Sukie smiled again at him, a proper smile this time, but she didn't comment on the third time lucky bit.

And so Simon whirled and twirled her across the floor until she was right in the centre of all the Eddies who were laughing and dancing in a group in front of the stage, flanked by the nurses and the policemen, and rather a lot of the Pink Sink clientele, few of whom had left the Eddy to go on there.

Sukie looked around her at the dear faces of the Eddies, and she laughed, as, right now, at this very minute, this felt like *exactly* where she belonged.

Simon lifted her up as if she was as light as a feather, and gently plonked her down so that she was standing on the lip of the stage. She reached out a hand for Pattie, who was hefted up to stand beside her by Michael. And then Sukie extended a hand in Mrs Bridge's direction. The housekeeper was picked up by Simon and wobbled up and onto the stage, although with a quite a lot less finesse than when he had placed Sukie there, although he managed it anyway without making it look as if the housekeeper had been almost too heavy for him.

'I would just like to thank all of my friends—' Sukie held up Pattie's hand in one of hers '—and the wonderful Eddies of whom I've become so fond.' She hoisted one of Mrs Bridge's hands high, catching sight of a glint of gold chain on her wrist as she did so, causing her heart to give a happy leap. 'And of course everybody else who is here tonight. On behalf of the Edwardes hotel, I say Merry Christmas to one and all, with a special vote of thanks to our wonderful mistress of ceremonies, Tracy Benn.' Sukie paused so that the crowd could clap their thanks for the mistress of ceremonies.

Sukie's face grew more serious, and then she said, 'I thought I had lost my family earlier in the year, and I felt as if my world had ended. But I look around me at you all, and now I see I have found a wonderful, wonderful new family, full of love and laughter and nice thoughts, and it's a family that's made of everyone I work with at the Eddy, and so I want to say a very special thank you, from the bottom of my heart.'

Sukie's final words were drowned out by claps and cheers, and it wasn't only the Eddies who were making a racket. But Jane, and Michael, and Mavis, and Gladys and concierge Stephen, and Chef, and all the other Eddies did certainly look to be making the majority of the noise, Sukie thought.

She made a special effort to catch Tracy Benn's eye, and mouthed a 'thank you' at her. Tracy Benn saluted her, and then went back to draping herself around a young and rather surprised-looking GI.

Sukie was determined not to be defeated in finishing what she wanted to say. 'Now, let's have a rousing sing-along of "The Twelve Days of Christmas" and then we can do "Rudolph the Red-Nosed Reindeer". We'll close with "We'll Meet Again", "Auld Lang Syne" and "God Save the King". And anyone who doesn't sing gets to do the washing-up! And as you leave, any coppers you might have left will be gratefully received in the donations jar. Thank you! Now count us in, Jane, over there on the piano...'

And with that, the Eddy's roof was pretty nearly raised as

everyone belted out a medley of Christmas songs for all they were worth, as Jane bashed out an accompaniment on the piano and those who weren't singing made good use of standing beneath the mistletoe, while Sukie stood there on stage, embraced on all sides by the tender warmth and the support and love that she had found with her new family of Eddies.

Upstairs meanwhile in the unnatural quiet of the rest of the hotel, a slightly squiffy Mr Bright was tottering his way along the corridor on the reception floor towards his room, having decided at last that it was time to call it a night. He'd insisted that Michael help Alan to his room half an hour earlier, and just now Mr Bright had refused John's offer of an arm to help him get to where he needed to be (although he was rather regretting that now, as he didn't feel quite as steady on his pins as he'd expected).

Out of the blue, he heard a faint but nonetheless quite distinct: 'Where's the rum? Mr Bright.'

The Eddy's manager stopped and peered around him in all directions. There was nobody in sight. He closed his eyes and blinked very obviously, and then he looked again both in front of him and behind him. He was still quite alone in the corridor. He even looked up to the ceiling, but there was no answer there.

'Where's the rum, Mr Bright?'

There it was again. He *had* heard it!

But this made no sense to Mr Bright as he could see that he was quite alone as he stood in the corridor beside the pulled-to doors of the darkened restaurant. He peered inside the restaurant to see if an Eddie was joshing him, but no, it was quite devoid of all human life. However, Mr Bright thought that he might have heard a slight rustle and, worried about mice, as he closed the door he told himself that he must remember to have a word with Sukie in the morning.

Miss Scott had proved herself very capable, and Mr Bright knew the party had been a roaring success and raised a lot of money for the Eddy, not least as Mrs Bridge had found him to tell him so. And so Mr Bright thought he could rely on Sukie to make sure that Stephen or Michael dealt with any intruding rodents appropriately.

'Where's the rum, Mr Bright?'

There it was, a third time!

Mr Bright felt confused as he was certain that he hadn't had enough whisky to cause such a hallucination.

He wondered cautiously if there was a ghost. As far as he knew there had never been the sighting of anything remotely ghostly in the Eddy, let alone one that spoke, and so he really hoped he hadn't woken a spectre.

'The rum is in the bar,' Mr Bright said firmly after a moment's further indecision, and with that he hurried to his room and resolutely locked the door behind him in a 'best to be on the safe side' sort of way.

There was a beat or two of silence, punctuated by the tick of the grandfather clock in reception, and then came a happy sound of a piglet snorting and rooting through mud for acorns that drifted out from under an eiderdown from deep within the restaurant.

It sounded very much like Sukie laughing.

Acknowledgements

A massive thank you to all the team at Orion, with a special mention for the fabulously talented Victoria Oundjian. And, of course, not forgetting my agent, the force of nature that is Cathryn Summerhayes.